Companion to the Count

The Seductive Sleuths
Book 1

Melissa Kendall

Dragonblade Publishing, Inc. is an imprint of Kathryn Le Veque Novels, Inc.
P.O. Box 23
Moreno Valley, CA 92556
ceo@dragonbladepublishing.com

Produced in the United States of America

First Edition August 2024
Print Edition

ARE YOU SIGNED UP FOR DRAGONBLADE'S BLOG?

You'll get the latest news and information on exclusive giveaways, exclusive excerpts, coming releases, sales, free books, cover reveals and more.

Check out our complete list of authors, too!

No spam, no junk. That's a promise!

Sign Up Here

www.dragonbladepublishing.com

Dearest Reader;

Thank you for your support of a small press. At Dragonblade Publishing, we strive to bring you the highest quality Historical Romance from some of the best authors in the business. Without your support, there is no 'us', so we sincerely hope you adore these stories and find some new favorite authors along the way.

Happy Reading!

CEO, Dragonblade Publishing

Chapter One

England, 1800

SAFFRON SUMMERSBY'S BREATH formed a cloud of mist as she searched the murky night for a spray of peacock feathers or a flash of pale yellow.

A perfectly manicured lawn stretched out in front of her, bisected by a white, stone path. To her right, twin onyx lions guarded the entrance to a hedge maze. To her left, the path wound around a circular structure with a domed top.

A cool wind brushed across the terrace, bringing with it the mixed perfume of flowering plants. She rubbed her gloved hands over the exposed skin of her upper arms. Had she known she would be chasing her foolish younger sister around in near-freezing temperatures, she would have worn a shawl over her brown, wool gown.

The last time she had seen Angelica, the Duke of Canterbury had collected her for the dance he'd claimed, a quadrille. The thought of her sister wrapped in the elderly duke's arms made her insides squirm, but they were running out of options.

She pried her chilled fingers from the balustrade and returned to the cloying warmth of the ballroom, where couples twirled and stomped to the tune of a simple country dance, illuminated by candles set in low-hanging chandeliers. Paintings covered the walls, from brash depictions of horses stampeding to war to gentle landscapes in hues of green and brown.

Each lady wore a unique color, their hair decorated with bobbing feathers or sparkling gems. All the colors blurred together in Saffron's vision, like she was spinning in circles, and it made her nauseated. Sweat dripped down her back, but she forced herself to keep moving.

She managed three steps into the refreshment room, the last notes of the orchestra still hanging in the air, before the Dowager Duchess of St. Clair caught her.

"Oh, Miss Summersby," the woman said. She fluttered her fan, causing locks of silver hair to float away from her face. "I did not know you would be in attendance. How kind of Lord and Lady Jarvis to invite your family, despite your... unfortunate circumstances."

Saffron forced a pretty smile. She could not respond to the taunt without giving the society matrons another reason to shun her. She dipped into a curtsey. "Your Grace."

The dowager clicked her tongue. "Come, let me look at you. I have not seen you for ages. We're discussing the newest production of *The Brides of Garryowen* at the Adelphi."

Against her wishes, she joined the entourage surrounding the duchess. To do otherwise would have been rude. She would have to hope the woman would tire of her company quickly. "I have not seen it, Your Grace."

"Why, you must. It is a splendid time." The dowager helped herself to a fruit tart from her serving plate. She had crammed her ample bosom into a crimson gown of jacquard-woven silk, the neckline pulled so low that half the gentlemen surrounding her had trouble keeping their gaze on her face.

Saffron envied the duchess and her independence. As a titled woman of wealth and power, she was above reproach. She could ride a white stallion around the park in a Grecian toga and still receive invitations for every major event of the Season.

"I might lend you my private box," the dowager added, brushing crumbs from her bosom. "You could watch it with your aunt, and that darling sister of yours."

Her sister would love that. Angelica hid her disappointment well, but the sadness in her eyes every time they had to sell another piece of their mother's precious jewelry made Saffron feel like a monster. Soon they would have nothing of their mother but a handful of faded portraits and the one item Saffron refused to part with, her mother's diamond broach.

At least they hadn't yet sold the books. When that day came, they would both cry.

"It would be an honor." She bowed her head.

"Where is your sister, my dear?" Rouged lips curved into a devious smile. "I have not seen her since dinner."

A cold needle of fear pierced her heart and she used the first lie that came to her mind. "She is suffering a megrim. She has not been feeling quite herself lately."

The dowager made a humming sound. "Yes, the two of you are quite the pair. One strange, the other flighty. I pity your aunt."

Saffron's cheeks burned. As the eldest, it was her responsibility to guide her sister through the shark-infested waters of society. Unfortunately, keeping Angelica out of trouble was like trying to cage the wind.

This would never have happened if Basil were still alive.

Everything had changed after her brother's death. With no male heirs, the Crown had awarded the baronet title to a distant cousin, who cared not one whit for his estranged family. The funds that had once seemed endless had rapidly dried up. They had scrimped and saved every penny, but the small pension her widowed aunt, Rosemary, had received from her first husband couldn't support them. Then the newly widowed Duke of Canterbury had arrived in town like a white knight and immediately set his sights on Angelica. His wealth meant a lack of dowry was of no consequence, but he had insisted upon an old-fashioned, lengthy courtship. That would not have been a problem, except that they had missed the last payment on their townhouse, and the two prior payments had been short. It would not be long before the bank ran out of patience.

We will make it, Saffron thought. *If I must become a governess, we'll make it.*

But first she had to prevent her sister from ruining herself.

She clenched her jaw and, with a prayer for luck, took a half-step back as a young man laden with drinks passed behind her. The sound of tearing cloth split the air, sending her sprawling. Two glasses of lemonade shattered against the marble floor. Servants descended upon the broken glass, ushering them away.

The young man stared at Saffron in horror. "Dreadfully sorry." His ears turned a bright red, the same shade as his curly hair. He dabbed at a wet spot on his brown wool jacket. "I did not see you."

"Enough of that." The dowager waved her empty plate in the air. "The deed is done. Off with you. Accompany Miss Summersby to the retiring room."

With that dismissal, Saffron took the boy's arm. He stammered apologies as they cut their way around the carnage. Fans snapped open as they passed, but not quick enough to obscure grinning faces. The whispers and tittering laughter made her fingers curl.

Society loved drama. Especially when it was at her expense. It felt as if the whispers and giggles were only ever directed at her, even when Angelica and Rosemary were present.

When they were out of sight of the dowager, she patted her chaperone's arm and murmured her thanks, then gathered her bulky skirts and dashed through a gap in the crowd and into a hallway. Her slippers caught on a bunch in the thin carpeting and sent her sprawling to her knees. After struggling to her feet, she discovered that the delicate French lace on her collar had torn.

A small bit of damage that she could fix in an hour sitting by the fire with her sewing kit, but it was enough to send her spiraling.

She pressed her fists over her eyes. She could not have a fit. Not yet. When she was safe in her bed, then despair could overtake her. But not yet.

She adjusted her collar to hide the damage and continued down the hallway, pausing at each closed door to listen before peeking inside. The first two she checked were silent and empty, but when she stopped at the third, she heard a faint crackle of fire.

Preparing for the worst, she pushed open the door to see Angelica curled up on a horsehair sofa near the fireplace, a book resting open on her chest, her eyes closed in slumber. Her golden curls shone in the firelight and her yellow-and-cream gown spilled over the chair and onto the floor. She had inherited their mother's beauty. Saffron's dark hair and stubborn chin were gifts from their father.

Saffron gripped the doorframe and took a deep, calming breath, letting the familiar smells of the library envelop her. Varnished wood, old books, and the sweet, ashy undertone of cigar smoke. Then she charged forward and swiped the book from her sister's arms. When she turned it over, she huffed.

Wuthering Heights.

Angelica's eyes fluttered open, and her lips curved in a sleepy smile. "Is it time to go home?"

"It's time to return to the ballroom." She waggled the book. "You won't find your Heathcliff hiding in here, sister."

Angelica straightened her dress and stood. "I apologize. My toes could not take another pounding."

The reprimand on Saffron's tongue flitted away when she saw the tears glittering in her sister's eyes.

"Was it something the duke said?" she asked softly. If the man had insulted Angelica or done anything else even slightly inappropriate, she would confront him and demand he leave Angelica alone. All she needed was an excuse.

"No." Angelica grabbed the book and crushed it to her chest.

Saffron sighed. So much for her opportunity. "Then what is the matter?"

Angelica's lower lip trembled. "I've read every book in our library three times. Lady Jarvis won't notice one book missing, would she? The dust on the shelves is an inch thick."

Greif clotted in Saffron's throat. Her sister had resorted to theft.

"I-I'll buy you a new one," she lied. She would have said anything to wipe the desperation off her sister's face.

Angelica opened her mouth, then frowned and tilted her head. "Do you hear that?"

It was the sound of approaching footsteps, followed by bubbly laughter. Saffron grabbed her sister's arm and dragged her behind a bookshelf. The copy of *Wuthering Heights* thumped to the ground in front of the fireplace.

"Who is it?" Angelica whispered.

She shushed her sister and peered through the cracks in the books. The door creaked open, and Lady Jarvis stumbled inside, her arms wrapped around the neck of a man who was not her husband. The sounds coming from the pair made her want to slap her hands over Angelica's ears. They had to get away before their gossiping host caught them spying on the amorous encounter.

She searched the room for alternative exits and caught the outline of a door halfway hidden behind a drape. She tugged her sister's fingers to get her attention, then whispered, "Follow me."

They carefully maneuvered between the bookshelves, serenaded by Lady Jarvis's increasingly loud moans, then slipped through the door. "Hello," a male voice said, making Saffron jump.

A man sat in a chair in the corner of the antechamber, holding a cigar in one hand. He wore dark, form-fitting trousers and a frock coat of the same color, unbuttoned, and parted on either side to reveal a black, satin shirt beneath. His wavy, blond hair was unfashionably long and untied, so it rested on his shoulders like the mane of a great lion.

Heat flushed through her body when she realized the man wasn't alone. A woman in a blood-red evening gown crouched before him, the inky-black fall of her hair obscuring her face. As Saffron stared, frozen in shock and horror, the woman rose to her feet and pulled her hair back to reveal bright-green eyes and full, pouty lips. She had the kind of painful beauty one imagined when reading Homer's description of Helen of Troy.

"Thank you for the entertaining interlude, darling," the woman said. She pressed a kiss to the man's cheek, eliciting a squeak from Angelica, then stepped back into the darkness and vanished. There was a creak of a door opening and then thudding shut.

"Who was that?" Angelica whispered.

The words broke the spell that had frozen Saffron in place, and she jerked her head in the direction the woman had gone. "I don't know, but we should follow her."

Then the man laughed, startling them both.

"The Misses Summersby, isn't it?" The man took a long draw of his cigar, tilted his head back, then blew a trail of smoke. "Leopold Mayweather, at your service."

She clenched her teeth on a gasp. She'd heard his name before, whispered by ill-natured women who congregated near the wallflowers to whisper stories about dangerous men. Viscount Briarwood, Leopold "Leo" Mayweather, was one of the worst, a confirmed rake and despoiler of innocents. Rumors held he had ruined a dozen debutantes and survived twice that many duels with angry fathers and brothers.

"Sister, who is that man?" Angelica whispered. "He looks like a devil."

Saffron hoped he hadn't heard that.

He chuckled. "A devil, is it? And you have stumbled into my lair." He gestured to an oil painting on the wall depicting a group of naked women feasting on the slaughtered remains of a goat, their hands and faces covered in blood.

Fear pulsed through Saffron like a living thing. With every second they remained alone with the man, the risk of ruin increased. She knew she should follow the woman out whatever exit she had taken, but her legs refused to move.

Lord Briarwood was dangerous, but he didn't elicit in her the scattered, nervy sensations she was used to feeling around strange men. He looked like a lion and had the reputation of a scoundrel, but something in his posture spoke of a tenderness beneath the surface. He didn't lounge in the chair so much as he *curled* his body into it, like a housecat perched on top of a pillow.

"What are you doing here, Lord Briarwood?" she asked.

Angelica uttered a quiet gasp at his name.

"I'm searching for something." He unfolded his long legs and stalked from the shadows. The flickering firelight cast an orange hue over the sharp planes of his cheekbones, wide lips, and slightly crooked nose, making him appear even more devilish. She stood her ground, her hands buried in her skirts, heart thundering in her chest. She tilted her head up and met his gaze.

"Searching for what, my lord?"

"Something that doesn't belong." His lips twitched. "Rather like you, Miss Summersby. You do not belong here, dressed like..." He trailed off, running his gaze down her body.

Her stomach churned and for a fleeting moment, she wished she'd chosen something other than the plain but serviceable gown of brown wool unadorned with lavish ribbons or ruching. Combined with her coal-black hair and pale complexion, she probably looked more like a scullery maid than a lady.

Angelica glided around her and dipped into a curtsey, a picture of grace and beauty. "It is lovely to make your acquaintance, Lord Devil."

Briarwood's eyes crinkled at the edges. Then Angelica rose from her curtsey and smacked him in the chin with the crown of her head. Saffron tensed, expecting an outburst, but as the viscount staggered back, rubbing his chin, he laughed. "What is in that head of yours, my dear? Rocks?"

The tension that had seized Saffron's lungs drained away. She turned to her sister to examine her escaped curls and clucked her displeasure. "You must have more care. If you lose another curl, I will not forgive you." She dug her fingers into the tangle of her own hair and pulled out a pin. A lock of black hair tumbled free. Before she could tuck it behind her ear, cool fingers brushed her temple.

"I have it," Lord Briarwood said, his voice soft. "Don't worry."

The feather-light touch on her scalp sent pleasurable tingles down her back and a wild part of her wondered what it would feel like to have his fingers on other parts of her body. She imagined his long fingers trailing up her inner thigh and untying the ribbon holding her stockings in place. She thrust those wayward thoughts aside and grasped her sister's head in both hands, twisting the curls that had come free around the length of the pin and tucking them away. That done, she released her sister and inspected her work. It would not pass muster in daylight, but in the dim light of the ballroom, it would suffice.

"Now that we have been introduced, albeit in a highly unusual manner," Briarwood said, "please allow me to accompany you back to the ballroom. Perhaps we will find what I have been searching for along the way."

She hesitated. What was worse—walking in on Lady Jarvis in *flagrante delicto*, or entering a ballroom on the arm of a rake?

The viscount's lips twitched. "Propriety. Of course." He cleared his throat. "Marie? If you will."

A short, gray-haired woman wearing the uniform of a servant separated from the shadows and curtsied. "I will accompany you, my lord."

"Marie is one of Lady Jarvis's servants," Leo explained. "Our generous host assigned her to attend to me tonight. I required a servant's perspective."

The tightness in Saffron's shoulders eased, and she held out her hand. Warm fingers enveloped her own and drew her closer. The intensity in his face should have sent her scurrying away. She knew what men like him wanted, had felt their lecherous gazes lingering on her in every ballroom she'd graced since her brother's death. It was as if they could sense her imminent fall from grace and were waiting to claim her as their mistress. Those looks always made her long for a bath. Not Lord Briarwood's. His gentle gaze caressed her skin like the finest silk and made her long to slip into his arms and bury her nose in his neck.

She had never felt such wild impulses with any other man. She felt like a character in one of the romance novels she'd read.

His wicked smile would haunt her dreams for months.

"Let us return before anyone raises a fuss," Briarwood said. He pushed back a heavy drape from the wall and revealed another door. They passed through the doorway and into a wide hallway, Angelica and Marie following behind.

He squeezed her hand. "I thought you might flee rather than take my arm. I sometimes forget how imposing I must seem." He waved his free arm up and down his body.

She kept her lips shut and her gaze focused on the swirling shapes at the end of the hall. Her traitorous mind, which recalled facts and figures with ease but forced her to write down her daily tasks no matter how many times she repeated them, had already memorized every line of his body.

"Why do you wear the black?" Angelica asked. "Did someone you know die?"

"My sister." His tone had a brittle edge.

"We lost our brother, too," Angelica said. "He left us to go traveling and they found his body washed up on the shore. Aunt Rosemary says it is his fault that we must marry for money and not for love."

Hearing her sister speak of their bleak future in such a fashion twisted Saffron's heart. She pulled away from the viscount to place a hand on her sister's arm. "I don't think the viscount wishes to hear about our troubles."

As the man smothered a laugh, Saffron noticed a painting behind her sister's head. Something about it called out to her and she stepped closer, taking in the scene of a ship. The hull was primarily black, with a line of white near the top and a hint of red beneath the waves. A bearded figure graced the front of the ship, holding a round shield in one arm and a sword in the other, facing forward as if charging into battle.

It can't be.

A man stood on the deck, wearing brown, cotton overalls. One hand was on his hip, and the other buried in his mass of chestnut curls.

"Sister, no!" Angelica cried.

She jerked her hand back. Without realizing it, she'd touched her fingers to the canvas. "Look at this," she said. "Do you see it?"

Her sister crowded in beside her, but Saffron kept her gaze on the man on the deck of the ship, afraid if she looked away, he would disappear, as he had vanished from their lives nearly three years prior. She hadn't believed he was dead until a body was found wearing her brother's clothes.

"Ravenmore," Briarwood said, uttering the word like a curse.

The back of Saffron's neck prickled. She'd been so focused on the painting, she hadn't noticed him moving to stand behind her. If she took a step back, she would bump into his chest. Would he be as warm and solid as he looked? She ached to find out but didn't dare move.

Angelica peered at a metal plaque mounted on the wall beneath the painting. "He's right. It says, 'Ravenmore.' What does it mean?"

Saffron didn't respond, having noticed the slanted, silver print near the corner of the canvas.

It's only a few days old.

The world slanted on its axis as several years' worth of grief churned inside her chest.

One thought rang clear in her mind.

She had to find the artist and ask how he had painted a picture of a ghost.

Chapter Two

LEOPOLD MAYWEATHER, VISCOUNT Briarwood, lurked at the fringes of Lady Jarvis's ballroom, clutching a half-full glass of the bitterest lemonade he'd ever tasted. At his side was a plant set on a white marble column. The long, green leaves draped over the edge and waved in the breeze made by passing, tray-laden servants.

He focused on Saffron, standing in the shadow of a velvet curtain outside the refreshment room. She reminded him so much of Sabrina, with the same hair, black as a raven's wing, and the same defiant eyes. When she'd pulled back her sister's hair, tenderness written across her features, he'd felt a spark of something deep in his soul.

"Hello there," a cheerful voice said.

He turned to see the grinning face of his cousin. Simon Mayweather was dressed as fashionably as any of the other young dandies in a dark-burgundy jacket with a plum-colored waistcoat over a patterned silver vest and burgundy trousers. His dark hair was held back with a ragged strap of leather and his cravat was lopsided, as if he'd rolled out of bed moments before dressing.

Knowing Simon, that's exactly what happened.

Simon clinked his glass against Leo's. "As cheerful as ever, Briarwood."

Leo grunted. "I wouldn't want to disappoint you."

Servants dodged around Simon, who sipped his drink. "I did not expect you would ever leave that old house."

Leo put a hand on his cousin's arm and pushed him out of the flow of foot traffic. "What do you mean?"

"You're stuck in the past," Simon said, exchanging his empty glass for a flute of champagne from the tray of a passing servant. "After the accident, I was certain you would never leave. I thought I might see an article about you in the newspaper one day, that they'd found you dead in that tomb of a house. But enough of that. What are you doing here?"

"I don't know," Leo said honestly. "I didn't intend to stay this long."

He had not seriously considered that his housekeeper's gossip would hold a kernel of truth. The plan had been simple: inspect each of the paintings to disprove the rumor, then retire with a willing woman or two. He'd completed the first phase of his plan, with the help of Marie, and had been well on his way to completing the second phase when the Summersby sisters had stumbled into his hiding place. As a result, he knew the rumors were true. Somehow, Lady Jarvis had acquired a rare piece of artwork that belonged in a museum.

Simon peered through the crowds. "What has caught your interest? A new fish?"

Leo nodded to the refreshment room entrance. "Not new, but newly discovered. What do you know about the Summersby family?"

Simon tugged his cravat. "Where to start? Old family, distantly related to royalty. Or so I hear. Tragic story, really."

"Tragic?"

"Consumption, both the baronet and his wife in the same year. Over a decade ago. The widow of the baronet's brother took them in."

Leo cracked the stiffness out of his neck and shoulders. That explained the haunted expression Saffron wore, and the way she'd hovered over her sister.

He remembered how it felt to have someone to protect. To care for a sibling like a parent. When that bond had been torn away, something vital inside him had withered and died.

He understood why Saffron had stood up to him in that cramped room, defiant and trembling beneath his stare.

They had more in common than she realized. "It gets worse," Simon continued. "The eldest child died, and with no male heirs, the Crown awarded the baronet title to a distant cousin. The family title, fortune, even the lands. From what I understand, the ladies barely keep above water." He leaned closer. "Rumor says they have pinned their hopes on a suitable match for the younger sister, Miss Angelica Summersby."

Leo downed his lemonade and turned his gaze to Angelica, standing next to her sister. If he had not been told, he would never have guessed they were related. Saffron's dark hair was confined in a tight bun, set with tiny gems that sparkled like the night sky. She wore a severe gown more suitable for a housekeeper or governess and clung to the shadows like a footpad.

Angelica, on the other hand, wore her spun-gold tresses piled atop her head, with small ringlets dangling at her nape. Her brightly colored gown was high in the rear and low at the bodice. When she laughed, the surrounding crowd joined in.

The Summersby plan was likely to meet with success. The *Ton* valued beauty and charm in a lady above most other characteristics.

His cousin stared in the same direction, his mouth turned in a scowl. But it wasn't Saffron who had caught Simon's eye.

"Angelica Summersby is rather young for you," Leo said.

Simon coughed. "She's of age, although she often acts as if she were still in short skirts. Despite that, she's gathered a horde of suitors. Poets and artists."

The disapproval in Simon's voice made Leo smile. "Not unlike the horde of fanciful ladies you string along."

"It's not the same," Simon protested.

Leo snorted, then asked, "What about the elder sister? Is she also seeking a match?"

He didn't know what had prompted the question. The lady had nothing to do with him. Long before his sister's death, society had lost its appeal. He was content to languish in hedonistic delight, or so the newspapers reported. He had no intention of telling them that most of his waking hours were spent at an easel.

The image of Saffron standing between him and Angelica flashed into his mind again. Her heaving chest, showing off an expanse of creamy skin. The way she licked her bottom lip, the tip of her tongue flashing in and out. Her shapely form disguised within a poorly fitted gown.

He flushed and adjusted his stance so as not to embarrass himself. Who was this woman, to summon from his barren heart such passionate desires?

Simon blew out a breath, then shook his head. "No. Miss Summersby does not dance. There is something odd about that girl. The way she stares, like she can see right through you. It's unnatural."

He watched Saffron adjust a curl on her sister's cheek before melting back into the shadows. She didn't seem odd at all. Captivating, caring, and skittish, but not odd.

"Why do you ask?" Simon waggled his eyebrows. "Are you seeking a new mistress? Or has the bachelor finally decided to take a wife?"

Leo stared into his glass. It was true that he was expected to marry and produce an heir, even though he had never expected to inherit. His father had succumbed to poor health two summers past and, soon after, an accident with a horse had claimed his unmarried brother's life. The trauma of those deaths had damaged his mother's mind and he had resolved never to allow himself to care for anyone again.

Simon smacked Leo on the back with his open palm. "Don't look so dour, cousin. There are worse things than marriage."

"Indeed," Leo said, upending his glass and letting the last few drops fall to the floor. "I can think of several things that are worse."

Chapter Three

S AFFRON LEANED INTO the plush, velvet curtain that framed the window, tearing small pieces of paper from the leaves of her fan and letting them flutter to the floor like flakes of snow. A few feet away, Angelica smiled and laughed at something the Duke of Canterbury had said. The heavy-set man's cheeks were stained the same ruddy color as his coat, and his bushy, black mustache was covered in crumbs of yellow cake.

She couldn't stop thinking about the painting.

After Lord Briarwood had vanished like the devil Angelica had branded him, Saffron had dragged her aunt Rosemary over to the painting. She'd expected her aunt to gasp or cry, but Rosemary had met her excitement with cool indifference. It was nothing more than coincidence, she had argued. They didn't even know the name of the painter, only that the piece was titled *Ravenmore*, and it was new, impossibly new.

"Come away from there before you sprout roots," Rosemary said as she lounged on a red, leather divan against the wall. "I did not raise a wallflower."

The woman was as attractive as she had been fifteen years prior, when she had taken in Saffron and her siblings. Perhaps with a touch more silver at her temple, and new wrinkles at the corners of her eyes, but with the same single-minded determination that had earned her reputation as a fearsome matchmaker.

Saffron stepped from the window and sunk into the plush cushions beside her aunt, prepared for another long night of watching her sister flit from one suitor to the next. Whereas Angelica thrived in social settings, Saffron was more withdrawn, preferring to spend her time with her family or alone.

"Your sister is shining tonight," Rosemary said. "My dearest wish is that you would shine as brightly."

Saffron tucked her mangled fan into her pocket before her aunt could comment on it. As much as she longed to wear the same beautiful fabrics and jewels that Angelica donned night after night, they did not have the funds. It took all of Saffron's careful planning to keep them from being cast out of their home. Her childhood dreams of finding a love match had been crushed under the weight of responsibility.

She glanced at the painting on the other side of the ballroom.

What if there was another option?

"It is a passing resemblance, nothing more," Rosemary said, as if reading her mind. "Now stop fidgeting. You are so distractible."

Saffron stared down at her clasped hands. "You're wrong." She remembered her brother's face as clearly as if she'd seen him that morning. "We only assumed the man that we buried was Basil."

The constables had not let them see his face, claiming it had been too gruesome.

"Your brother is dead." Rosemary shook her head. "Do you not remember how we suffered after he left? After he abandoned us? I cannot see what will come of this fantasy of yours, other than opening old wounds best left closed."

Her fingers ached from clenching them. She tore her hands apart. What mattered was the money. If Basil were still alive, and he returned, they could petition to reclaim the family's baronet title and the fortune that came with it. Angelica's dowry would be restored, giving her the freedom to choose a husband.

Rosemary hissed in a breath, and Saffron realized that a man had joined the circle of admirers surrounding her sister.

"Who is that?" she asked.

The new suitor towered above Angelica, but when he smiled, it held none of the arrogance of many of the titled men present.

"Mr. Simon Mayweather," Rosemary said. Her lips twisted in a moue of displeasure. "His father was a merchant."

"Ah," Saffron replied.

Translation, respectable enough to stay in Angelica's assembly, but with neither requirement of title nor fortune.

Mr. Mayweather made some comment, and a flush spread over her sister's cheeks.

"What is she doing?" Rosemary whispered.

The young man leaned in closer, one hand snaking around Angelica's back. Canterbury drew himself upright, scowling fiercely. Before the situation could escalate, Saffron bolted from her seat and reached through the gap between her sister and Mr. Mayweather, forcing the man to retreat.

"Sister, your glass," she said, plucking the empty champagne flute from her fingers. "I'll fetch you another."

As Saffron stepped away, Rosemary slid into her place, ensuring that Mr. Mayweather would not attempt to get nearer Angelica again.

She hurried off to the refreshment room, ducking under elbows and lifting her skirts to avoid a spilled glass of wine. Then a path opened in front of her, leading straight to Briarwood. Under the bright light of the chandeliers, his hair shone like liquid gold. He'd buttoned his waistcoat and tied his long hair back with a blue ribbon.

His gaze met hers, and warmth flooded her stomach.

She staggered back, shaking her head. He raised an eyebrow. The crowd on either side was impassable. The muted sounds of conversation floated around her.

He prowled across the gleaming, marble floor and bowed before her. "Miss Summersby."

The words slithered across her skin, as intimate as a caress. He took her hand and breathed a kiss over her knuckles, squeezing her gloved fingers a tad too tightly.

The gall of the man for taking her hand unoffered.

"Lord Briarwood," Saffron said. "I thought you had left."

Another lie. She had not lost sight of him for a second since leaving his side. A crowd three times the size of the one currently occupying the ballroom would not be sufficient to dim the intensity of his presence. She wished she knew what it was that caused her to fixate on him, to seek out his shape amid countless others.

"Call me 'Leo,'" he said.

"Certainly not. That would be highly improper."

He chuckled. "I would not dare offend your delicate sensibilities. My cousin encouraged me to stay and engage you. I suspect he wants more time to speak with your sister. Dance with me?"

Her already racing heart thudded painfully in her chest. How long had it been since anyone had asked her to dance? She had grown so used to every would-be suitor's gaze passing over her, drawn to the radiant beauty of her sister.

The screech of a violin announced the start of a new set. The crowd pressed together, forming more space in the center of the room for dancing. The candles above them sputtered as wind breathed into the room. The footman had thrown open more doors to the terrace.

"Is your dance card full?" Lord Briarwood asked. He lifted her sleeve with his other hand and tugged out the circle of paper tied to her wrist. She wrenched her hand back before he could leaf through it and discover that not a single name was written on the pages.

"I-I don't know the steps," she said. It was a terrible excuse, not believable in the least, but he only quirked an eyebrow.

"Then I shall have to show you."

The light of the viscount's attention gave her newfound courage. She took his hand, and they merged into the flow of dancers. Their first set was silent and awkward, but it didn't take long before the rhythm of the music unlocked the steps from her forgetful body. It was glorious, like she was flying free after years of watching in silence. She didn't even care that people were staring. Their leering eyes could not disrupt her excitement.

She stomped to the beat then hooked her arm through Briarwood's and spun in a tight circle until she was so dizzy, she thought she would faint. But then large hands clasped her waist and her head stopped spinning.

I could learn to enjoy this, she thought, her hopes rising. Perhaps it was not too late, after all. She did not have looks to attract a husband, but her mind was sharp, her instincts true. Briarwood was far too scandalous to be suitable, but if she could find a wealthy man to agree to marry her, then Angelica would be spared the injustice of a marriage of convenience.

Lord Briarwood's palm slid down her side and squeezed her hip. It happened so quickly that she didn't have time to gasp or pull away—not that she wanted to. The pressure of his fingers sent tingling sensations down her thigh.

If she pretended to trip, would he do it again?

He handed her off to a new partner and the distance brought her back to reality. She chastened herself for her foolishness. As tempting as Briarwood was, he was a rake, not a suitor.

When she returned to his arms, he immediately drew her closer than was proper, causing several other of the ladies dancing to throw them sidelong glances. She could not tell if they were scandalized or jealous.

"You're drawing attention to us," she said, squeezing his hand.

He shrugged. "Let them gawk. I am only doing what they all wish they could." They whirled past a line of stern-faced matrons along the wall, who tilted their heads together and muttered. The words *strange* and *disgraceful* were spoken loudly enough for her to hear and dug into her heart like daggers.

"You dance well," the viscount said. "Yet they reject you. Why?"

"I have no dowry," she said, concentrating on moving her feet in tune with the music. She could not embarrass her sister or aunt by falling on the dance floor. "That is reason enough."

"I am not interested in your dowry. And unless I am mistaken, your sister is also without dowry, yet she has several admirers."

"I have more pressing concerns," she said, thinking of the pile of gowns sitting in her room, waiting to be modified so that the *Ton* would not notice that they were last year's fashions. That was assuming they could find the funds to make the payment on their townhouse. She woke up most nights in a cold sweat, plagued by nightmares of burly, faceless men carting trunk after trunk out of their house while Angelica sobbed in Rosemary's arms.

"What could be more important than marriage?" Briarwood asked mockingly. "I believe my mother once said those exact words to me some years ago. A ridiculous notion." He caught her as she stumbled on a puddle of spilled wine, lifted her off the ground, and returned her to her feet in a smooth motion.

"You disagree?" she asked, breathless from her momentary flight. The large hand splayed along her back provided a pleasant distraction.

"I'll share a secret with you. Several of the works on these walls were painted by unmarried women." He spun her about and nodded to a large oil canvas behind the chaise of disagreeable matrons. It depicted several women in flowing gowns sitting on prancing horses. The frothing, light-colored garments distracted from the wicked eyes of the horses, who looked about to buck their riders.

"It's lovely," she said. "Who painted it?"

He flashed a grin. "A darling cousin of mine. She has no head for household matters but is a master with a brush. Finding and supporting artists is a personal project of mine. I don't think I need to tell you how challenging it is for a woman artist to sell her work under her own name." He scowled. "There are limited opportunities for women, even in the Royal Society of Arts." Saffron remembered Lord Briarwood's reaction to the painting. "Is the *Ravenmore* one of those paintings?"

He stumbled but caught himself before they careened out of position. Then he drew her a touch closer. "Ravenmore is the name of the painter, not the painting. You haven't heard of him?"

Before she could respond to that, he handed her off to a different partner. She smiled up at Mr. Pennyworth and responded demurely to his idle conversation, while at the same time trying to rein in her spiraling thoughts.

Ravenmore is the name of the painter. What did that mean? She'd never heard that title before, and she had *Debrett's Peerage* memorized, to better guide Angelica in her choice of suitor.

When she finally returned to the viscount's arms, she was bursting with questions. Unfortunately, every time she tried to bring it up, he stopped her with a pointed question about the weather, her sister, or the refreshments. Then it was too late, and he handed her off to the next man in the set.

She had only a moment to school her features before realizing whose arms she was in.

The Duke of Canterbury.

Beady, brown eyes narrowed, and for a moment, she was afraid he would step away, leaving her floundering. But then he sniffed and roughly grasped her hand.

"So, girl," he said after they had completed half a rotation. "What manner of gift might sway your sister's affection?"

She swallowed the instinctual, crass response that flew to her tongue and instead smiled prettily. It was tempting to lead the man astray and suggest he buy a bouquet of violets, but that would only punish Angelica when she broke out into hives.

"Red roses, my lord," she said instead. "The color suits her golden hair."

"Roses? Yes, a splendid idea," the duke said. He lifted his hand from her for a moment to scratch his thick neck with his black-gloved hand. "Perhaps you are not so useless, after all. If you can keep this up, you might yet find a husband." He lowered his voice to a whisper and narrowed his eyes. "Unless you've already spread your legs for the viscount?"

Her cheeks burned, and she could not find the words to form a response. She'd met a fair number of uncouth individuals, but no one had ever spoken to her so crudely. As the music faded, Lord Briarwood came to her side like an angel of grace, taking her hand and placing it on his arm.

"Lord Canterbury? If I may?" he asked the uncivilized man.

"Of course." The duke had the audacity to raise a brow at Saffron and chuckle, as if the viscount's arrival proved his point.

Saffron refused to meet his gaze. She feared if she did, she might not be able to hold her tongue. Thankfully, Briarwood did nothing more than offer the duke a stiff smile before he whisked her out of the crowd.

"What did he say to you?" he asked. "You looked like you were going to faint, or scream."

She shook her head. "I could not possibly repeat it."

"I apologize for leaving you," he said, his words tight.

The buzzing inside her intensified, and she had to concentrate on taking each step without stumbling.

"You cannot remain by my side the entire night, my lord," she said, with only a slight waver.

"I wish I could. Your company is far more pleasurable than that of anyone else here."

She swallowed a sudden lump in her throat. Did he really mean it? The man was an enigma, with the reputation of a rake but words that melted her heart. She remembered the beautiful woman who had kissed his cheek.

It is none of my concern whom he associates with.

She clung to the thought, refusing to acknowledge the trickle of jealousy that welled up and soured the back of her throat.

They were halfway across the room when a young woman in a fawn-colored gown crossed their path. She gave a sly smile and fluttered her fan. "Lord Briarwood, there you are. You owe me a dance."

"As much as I would love to, Miss Tilson," Briarwood replied, "it is stiflingly hot in here."

The woman giggled. "Lady Jarvis is not known for her planning. But I enjoy the other pleasures she provides. Perhaps you would accompany me for a walk in the gardens. I hear there is a lovely pergola at the center of the maze. Very private." She peered around the viscount. "But first, you simply *must* dispose of that creature that clings to your coattails."

The words peeled off the scabs of old wounds in Saffron's heart, and the room spun. Beneath her gloves, her fingers were gritty where the sweat had dried, rubbing against her skin like rough stone.

"Excuse me." She pushed away before hearing Briarwood's response. "I need some air."

She hurried out of the ballroom and onto the terrace. Once she was outside, she rushed down the ornate, curving staircase and around the side of the house, her heels first clicking against the smooth stone and then stamping on the stone walkway. Bulbous lanterns hung from the low branches of the trees, casting circles of sickly-yellow light on the ground.

She searched for a dark alcove where she could hide from the prying eyes of the guests and found it near the rear entrance to the house, beside a gurgling cherub fountain. Water bubbled out of the angelic figure's pupil-less eyes and ran down its cheeks like tears.

She fled to the darkest part of the alcove, taking great, gasping breaths as the world spun out of control. Her head fell back against the wall as she pushed away the darkness that creeped in from the sides of her vision. The lilting sounds of the orchestra, combined with the occasional shriek of laughter, carried to her.

"There you are."

Saffron spun to find Lord Briarwood leaning against the stairs. His coat was unbuttoned, his cravat missing. The triangle of skin showing beneath his chin was enough to make her knees wobble anew.

She scuttled back until her hands splayed against the brick exterior of the house. "What do you want?"

"Only to help." He held his palms spread out at his sides. "But I will leave if you prefer to be alone."

"Why would you want to help the 'creature that clings to your coattails'?"

The pain of the words struck her anew.

The viscount's jaw ticked. "Don't listen to them. There is nothing wrong with you. My sister used to panic around crowds as well. She hated parading around in front of them." He paused, then held out a hand. "Let me help you?"

Heavens, he was temptation personified. Her instincts blared, demanding that she run before anyone caught them together and assumed the worst.

Saffron stared over his shoulder. Although her heart still raced, her legs no longer felt like rubber and her hands had stopped prickling. As dangerous as it was to be alone with a man, she liked the idea of being by herself even less. With nothing to anchor her, the chains of panic would draw her into a sobbing mess.

"You can stay."

He approached her with small, measured steps, stopping when he was a foot away.

"Focus on my voice. I'm right here with you. I'm not going anywhere." He placed his hands on the wall on either side of her, sheltering her with his body. The sound of the ballroom faded into the background until all she could hear was her own breathing, harsh and uneven.

"I'm here," he said, leaning closer. "Nothing else matters but this moment, right here, right now."

The soothing words filled her with fizzing bubbles like she'd drunk an entire bottle of champagne. Warmth surrounded her, pushing out the cold. The sweet smell of cigar smoke clung to his shirt, and there was an echo of brandy on the breath that caressed her cheek. She longed to reach out and tangle her hands in his shirt, draw him close. She glanced up through her eyelashes, and the heat in his eyes made her stomach flutter.

"Thank you," she whispered, her voice husky. The tendons in his neck tightened, and his nostrils flared. He pushed away from the wall, took several staggering steps back, and fled.

What was that?

For a fraction of a second, she'd thought he might kiss her. But that was ridiculous, of course. She never would have allowed it, not the least because she looked terrible, drenched in sweat, with her hair flying around her face.

Still, her heart thundered at the idea.

Chapter Four

L EO WET THE tip of the finest, most delicate paintbrush he owned and dipped it in a tub of charcoal-colored paint. A fuzzy ball of gray fur danced at his feet. He picked the kitten up and briefly cuddled her against his cheek before setting her down. A footman had chased her into his studio, and he had not had the heart to send her away. Much like he could not close his eyes without seeing Saffron Summersby's face. The way she had stared up at him, her wide eyes filled with tears, her hair drooping onto her pale neck. She had seemed so fragile, like a glass sculpture that would shatter if not handled with care. The urge to gather her up in his arms and spirit her away somewhere safe had overwhelmed him. Rather than face what that meant, he'd fled.

Coward, the voice in his mind whispered.

At least he had made progress on the Ravenmore. All it had taken to convince Lady Jarvis to relinquish the painting was a strongly worded letter threatening to expose her to the press.

But the woman could not tell him how she had acquired it, as the seller had routed the transaction through several intermediaries. Worse, he'd reached out to his museum contacts and learned there were no reports of theft.

"My lord, your cousin is here."

Lady Jarvis's Ravenmore should have been hanging in the British Museum. It still *was* hanging in the museum. A second, identical painting.

There was only one conclusion.

Someone is stealing Ravenmores and replacing them with forgeries.

He set his brush against his canvas, forming the hull of a ship. The same ship from the painting that had caught Miss Summersby's interest. It was familiar, somehow, although he could not remember ever seeing it before.

"My lord?"

His hand cramped, slashing black ink through the gentle waves of the blue sea.

He threw down his brush. His butler, Sinclair, stood solidly by the door, waiting for a response. The kitten, who he had not yet named, sprinted across the room and clawed up Sinclair's leg. The butler disengaged her and held her by the scruff in one hand far from his body, the way Leo might have held a rodent. "Shall I tell him you are not receiving?" Sinclair asked.

Leo sighed. "Send him to my office."

"Your office, my lord?"

Leo swirled his paintbrush in a cup of water. "What's wrong with my office?"

"Nothing, my lord. The dust gives the room character."

A book flew from Leo's hand and hit the door as it closed.

Leo removed the stiff, gray apron splattered with paint and hung it on a peg jutting from the wall. The apron, and his clothing, were so restrictive. Given the choice, he would have painted in the nude, but the one time he had done so during the day, his housekeeper had caught him and nearly fainted.

He capped the small bowls of oil paints and rubbed sand on his hands to remove the flecks of paint from his skin.

The latest letter from his mother sat unopened on the windowsill. He had stopped reading them years ago, when she had accused him of being the cause of his sister's death. He didn't need her to remind him of what he already knew.

He set his painting out of the sunlight then closed and locked the door to the one room in the house that still held some of the life and warmth that had once filled the estate. Once, he'd considered filling the house with the sounds of laughter. Back before his family had shattered, before he'd retired to his ancestral home and buried himself in art.

Those days were long past.

He followed the cold, barren halls to his office and stepped inside. Although it was just as dark and brooding as the rest of the estate, this room held something of the man he had once been. The walls were covered in paintings. Not portraits, but colorful landscapes. His sister's early works.

Simon sat in a chaise by the crackling fireplace, holding a cut-crystal glass in one hand and a cigar in the other. He was impeccably attired in a double-breasted frock coat and striped trousers. A significant amount of spirit was missing from the bottle of brandy on the table.

"Helping yourself to my spirits already, Simon?" Leo asked as he sat across from the man. "It can't be that bad."

Simon waved a hand. "Good afternoon to you, as well. I must ask, where are all your servants?"

Leo handed Simon an ashtray. "The noise was making it difficult to paint."

Even after he'd issued instructions that no one should come near his studio, the sounds of footfalls and murmuring conversation had still reached him and disrupted his focus. Finally, he'd instructed his housekeeper to dismiss all but the most essential of the staff.

Simon set his glass down on the table. "I came to ask you to join me in town for a Season."

Of all the things he'd expected his cousin to say, that was not one of them. "Why come to me?"

"You rarely leave the grounds, I know," Simon said. "I had thought after the ball last week, you might have changed your mind."

Leo snorted, and Simon winced. "Right. Yes, poor excuse. Well, straight to it, then. I do not have the means."

Leo nodded. This was more in line with what he'd expected his cousin to discuss. He crushed a twinge of disappointment to dust as he calculated the amount he should give the man that would send him away without setting expectations for further funding.

"You can use my townhouse and carriage in the city," Leo said, "and I will open an account for you to use at your leisure."

Simon beamed. "Excellent. Will you be joining me?"

Leo looked at the pile on his desk and shuddered. He had no desire to re-enter society, but he had to figure out who was stealing the paintings. Writing to the collectors would be a pointless exercise. Even if he trusted them to tell him the truth, knowing who had purchased the paintings did not help him track down who had stolen them in the first place. There were thousands of artists in England alone who were skilled enough to create a forgery that would not be detected as false except by the most skilled appraisers.

But he couldn't tell his cousin any of that without risking the entire *Ton* learning his plan by week's end.

"I thought I would host an event here," Leo said. "A country party, for perhaps three days."

It would be a challenge to organize such an event on short notice, and it would require Mrs. Banting to hire many more servants, but he was more concerned about the disruption to his studio. He would have to relocate his supplies, and there would be few opportunities to paint, but he was not willing to threaten his sister's legacy. He would find the thief, recover her paintings, and restore them to museums, where they belonged.

Simon fell back into a chair. "At this mausoleum? Wherever will you find space for all the eager ladies?"

Leo crumpled a vellum invitation to an afternoon tea and took aim at his cousin's head.

"Better luck next time," Simon said as the projectile landed a foot away. He kicked it into the fireplace, where it hissed and sparked with greenish flames. A foul odor wafted out of the fireplace and wreathed around them.

"I hate the scented ones," Simon said, waving his hand in front of his face. Then he pointed to the wall above the fireplace, where a painting was mounted. "That's it," he said, "That is how you lure your guests."

Leo looked at the painting. In coarse brush strokes, it depicted a group of cherubs clutching small golden harps in their chubby fingers. Streams of warm, golden light shone down on their fluffy, white wings.

Simon tilted his head. "What is that monstrosity worth? A hundred pounds?"

Leo shrugged. "Perhaps. My father imported it from Germany."

Simon inspected another painting. "I don't know much about art, but I know many of your fellow lords are collectors. They would love to have a chance to peruse the Briarwood collection, and the matrons of society adore an exhibit. If you host one, they will demand to come and bring their daughters. You will have the whole of the *Ton's* marriageable ladies under your roof."

Leo looked at the horrid cherubs glaring at him from the wall. As a child, he'd thought they looked more like trolls than angels. He'd had nightmares about the winged creatures flying out of the clouds and bludgeoning him with their harps. He would be glad to be rid of the piece, and there were hundreds more dusty paintings in storage.

"An auction it is," Leo said.

LEO CLENCHED HIS fingers around the railing of the ship as the calm water of the Thames washed against the hull. Gulls squalled overhead, diving into the murky depths near the rocky shore.

Being on the water was an uncomfortable reminder of everything he had lost. He would never forget the hundreds of bodies bobbing in the waves amid the flotsam.

The blare of a horn pulled him from his thoughts. The boat shuddered as it docked, making him break out in a cold sweat. He shoved past the other passengers to the gangplank, clutching the railing in a white-knuckled grip. The lapping waves beneath his feet made his stomach perform somersaults. It did not help that so close to the water's edge, the sour smell of what the river had washed ashore was overpowering, like a slop heap left to rot.

He inched across the narrow bridge until at last he was free. Nothing had ever felt so sweet as the solid and immovable earth beneath his feet.

The clip-clop of horse hooves drew his attention. He searched until he found the source, a hansom cab meandering down the street. He raised a hand in salute. The driver chirruped at his horses, nudging through the crowd.

Leo flicked the driver a guinea. "Sheffield and Sons. I am late for an appointment with my solicitor."

The cabby, a grungy-looking man in a dusty, black coat and bowler cap, tested the guinea with his few remaining teeth then pocketed it. "Right, guv', git in."

Leo opened the door and settled inside to rattle down the London streets. How many years had passed since he'd sworn never to return? The weeks had blurred together, punctuated by moments of brilliant clarity in his art. Painting was the only light in his life, distracting him from the utter silence of a home that should have been filled with the chatter of managing relatives.

Family. He could have it again if he wanted. But the edges of his soul were still ragged and bleeding, unable to bear another loss. Better to keep to himself and avoid further hurt. He did not want to become like his mother, so damaged by grief that she could no longer participate in any of the social activities she had once loved.

The cab hit a rut, and his teeth clacked. He closed the drapes tighter, keeping the revolting sights from his view. He longed for the serenity of his studio, but there was something he had to do first.

Finally, the cab rattled to a stop, and the driver rapped on the roof. "'Ere we are, guv."

Leo jumped out, placing his feet to avoid the piles of horse manure that covered the road. He stepped inside the white building, then held up a hand to greet his solicitor, who was sitting at a desk on the other side of the room, wearing a dark-green suit jacket with bronze buttons.

"Lord Briarwood!" The man rose quickly, scattering papers to the floor. "I did not expect you." He gathered the papers in his arms and returned them to his desk, then pulled out a smooth, glass container and tilted it back and forth so the rich, amber liquid inside sloshed around. "Drink?"

It was a tempting offer, but Leo's stomach had not yet settled from the trip. "I will get straight to the point," he said, going on to explain his theory.

Percy paled, making the hollows around his dark brown eyes even more prominent. Between that and the sharp lines of his cheekbones, he could have passed for a specter in the dark of night. "Stealing? How is that possible?"

Leo examined his solicitor's expression and judged that the man's surprise was genuine. He had not wanted to believe his most trusted advisor could have betrayed him, but Percy was one of the few who knew his secret, that the paintings he supplied under the alias "Ravenmore" were his sister's creations. Had she lived, the paintings might have slipped through history unnoticed. But with the help of the pseudonym Ravenmore, her work finally had the acclaim it deserved.

34

It was the least he could do, considering he was the reason she was dead. He only wished he had thought of the idea before the accident.

He cracked the joints in his hand. "I don't know. I recovered a painting from a private collector and confirmed its authenticity, but the museum did not report it missing."

Percy's brows knitted. "If the thief, or thieves, are selling to private collectors, it will be difficult to catch them."

"I have decided to host an auction at the Briarwood Manor," he said. Then he withdrew an envelope with Percy's name scrawled on it from his pocket and held it out.

Percy took the envelope and stared at it. "How can you be sure your quarry will attend?"

"My family has an extensive collection of artwork, and to ensure our thieves will make an appearance, I will add a Ravenmore to the docket."

He had one left, the final painting his sister had created before her death. Parting with it would be difficult, but once the collectors learned the mysterious Ravenmore had allowed a painting to go up for auction, they would swarm the viscount with demands for invitations. Every private collector in the country would be at his doorstep, and he'd interrogate each of them until he got to the truth.

They won't get away with it.

His sister's paintings belonged in museums, where they could be seen and enjoyed by all. Private collectors did not deserve to have Sabrina's works gracing their walls, not after they had rejected her from their ranks.

He sighed. "It is time for Ravenmore to retire."

Percy sloshed brandy over the edge of his glass. "My lord, I must insist that you not act so rashly, and leave this matter to me—"

A crash from outside interrupted them. Percy set down his drink, then scurried to the door, throwing it open as a familiar feminine voice shrieked, "Release me, you beast!"

Leo was on his feet and at the door before he could think.

Saffron Summersby stood on the sidewalk, holding the front of her skirts in both hands, attempting to tug it out of the snarling jaws of a mottled, brown-and-gray mutt.

It took all his strength not to lunge forward and scoop her into his arms, away from the danger. What was it about the woman that called forth his protective instincts that had remained dormant for so long? He resolved to keep his distance.

Then she pinned him with an accusing look. "What are you waiting for? Help me!"

Propriety be damned.

He shoved Percy aside and clasped his hands around her waist, lifting her off the ground, out of the reach of the dog yapping at her heels. She struggled in his grip, the feathers in her hat brushing against his face as he breathed in the smell of cinnamon and vanilla, like baked apple pie, straight out of the oven. It shocked him enough that he held on to her longer than was appropriate, and she struggled harder.

He moved her away from the door, then set her down on the floor behind him.

You didn't want to let her go. What would you have done if you were alone?

"Lord Briarwood." She dipped into a quick curtsey without lifting her head. "I didn't expect to find you here."

He chuckled. "I could say the same, Miss Summersby. I am unaccustomed to the role of savior. Perhaps I should accompany you home, lest you find yourself in another difficulty."

"Ah, thank you," she said. "That will not be necessary."

"Odd thing for a mongrel to do," Percy said, having chased the dog away with shouts and claps of his hands.

"It's my fault," Saffron said, falling on the bench near the door. She picked at the tattered remains of a petticoat, which was, by Leo's estimation, damaged beyond repair. "I passed a butcher on the way here and stepped in something dreadful. The hound must have smelled it."

Percy cleared his throat. "Miss—"

She fluffed her skirts, rose to her feet, and curtseyed. "Summersby. I apologize for the intrusion. I would not be here if it were not a matter of some urgency."

"You'll have to return another time, Miss Summersby," Percy said. "I am otherwise occupied with a client."

She turned her head so her bonnet obscured her face. "Then I will wait here." The spray of golden feathers bobbed above her head. "Go on. I have important matters to discuss, and I do not have all day."

Percy frowned. "Miss Summersby, I cannot assist you today. Perhaps you could return tomorrow with an appropriate chaperone?"

The glare she gifted Percy was so venomous that Leo had to pretend to muffle a cough to hold in his mirth. She was like a lioness stalking an injured prey, determined and unwilling to back down. Percy withered before her ferocity.

Is this the same woman who shuddered in my embrace not two nights ago?

"That is unacceptable, Mr. Percy," she said mulishly. "I have come all the way from the other side of London. You will not throw me out because this man demands all of your time." She folded her hands in her lap. "I must speak with Ravenmore."

The rush of panic that followed those words choked Leo's throat. She couldn't know, not unless Percy had done him a disservice. It had to be something else. But what?

Percy smoothed his cravat. "I do not know what you are talking about, miss. I don't know anyone by the name of Ravenmore."

She straightened. "I spoke with the curator at the Royal Museum, and I know you negotiate on behalf of Ravenmore. You are his solicitor. Sir, I must speak with the painter. It is of the utmost importance."

Masterful. She played him like a violin.

His respect for her increased further. The woman knew what she was about.

Percy worried his hands together. "I am sorry, but I cannot help you."

Before she could mount a new line of attack on his beleaguered solicitor, Leo stepped closer. "Why is it so important you speak to this painter?"

She faced him, her eyes fixed on his cravat. "That is no concern of yours."

The way she avoided the topic only made her more interesting. Did it have something to do with how she'd reacted to the painting at Lady Jarvis's ball?

Percy flapped his hands about ineffectually. "Lord Briarwood is acquainted with Ravenmore. Perhaps he can help."

Leo sent a baleful glower his solicitor's way, to no effect. Percy returned to his desk and refilled his brandy, then downed it.

Saffron stepped toward him, clutching her hands together in front of her, and his reason was once again swept aside.

"I must speak to Ravenmore," she said. "Please. I beg of you."

He ran his eyes down her form. Her plain gown, though fashionable, was a clever re-tailoring of a different dress. The scuff marks on her shoes and the tarnish on her buttons suggested she was not from a wealthy family, as his cousin had said.

"Well?" she asked. Desperation tinged her words. If he did not help her, she would find some other way to accomplish her goals.

For a fleeting moment, the image of his sister overlaid her. Sabrina had shared Saffron's impatience, demanding his attention when he was busy, pouting and raging, until he'd acknowledged her.

He remembered her accusing eyes staring up at him from her swollen, blue-tinged face.

Sabrina had trusted him, and he'd betrayed her. He could not go through that again. A chill settled over him, and he took a step back. As alluring as Miss Summersby was, his sister's legacy came first.

Nothing else mattered.

"I apologize, but I cannot help you."

She leaned forward, beseeching him with her wide, brown eyes and pouting lips. "Surely, you could pass on a letter, at least."

Her bosom rose and fell in a way that made him long to sweep her back into his arms and capture her wind-chapped lips. He remembered how she'd felt pressed against his body.

"It's not that," he said, scrambling to recover his scattered wits. "Ravenmore has... retired."

Saffron paled. "Retired? No, that cannot be. I must speak to him. If I can't..." She trailed off, staring at the ground. She looked so distraught, like a child separated from her parents in a crowded market, that he could not stop himself.

"There might be a way."

Her lips parted on a soft gasp, and her cheeks bloomed with color. "Truly? What is it?"

The pure, innocent hope in her words slayed the last of his reluctance and the words tumbled out of him like marbles released from a jar. "I am holding an auction at the Briarwood estate. There will be a Ravenmore for sale, so it is likely that the artist will attend. If you wish, I could invite your family."

He bit the inside of his cheek to stop himself from taking the offer back. Not only because it would be rude, but because he was surprised to find he liked the idea of her wandering the halls of his home. She would be a ray of light in the otherwise bleak house.

She folded her arms over her chest. "You would do that?"

The blatant skepticism scratched at his pride. What had he done to earn such distrust? She was so flighty around him, ready to bolt at any moment. When he moved, she flinched, as if she expected him to strike.

"My lord, if I could make a suggestion?" Percy asked timidly.

He jerked his head toward his solicitor, having forgotten the man was in the room. "Yes?"

Percy held out the invitation Leo had handed him earlier. "I regret I cannot attend."

Leo accepted the envelope and flipped it over in his hand. He brushed his thumb over the unbroken wax seal. "A pen, please, Percy."

As Saffron shuffled by the door, he took a seat and drew a line through Percy's name, then wrote in "Summersby." With that complete, he stood and held out an open hand to Saffron. She narrowed her eyes, then placed the tips of her fingers against his palm. He folded his fingers over hers and kissed her knuckles.

Her hand trembled. "Lord Briarwood, that is not—"

"Appropriate? I so rarely am these days." He released her and she whipped her hand back to her chest. A minute later, she left with the envelope clutched in her hands.

Chapter Five

TWO SLEEPLESS NIGHTS later, Saffron admitted defeat. No matter how much she tried to think about anything else, her mind returned to Lord Briarwood and their moment at the fountain. In her dreams, he didn't run away. He wrapped his arms around her and pulled her close, stealing her lips.

He was just being a gentleman, Saffron thought as she lifted a water-stained box from the set of wooden shelves against the wall. *It meant nothing.*

A cloud of coal dust drifted up and made her cough. The only light in the windowless basement came from a small candle she'd carried down with her. The floor beneath her was beaten earth, and there was coal piled up against the stone walls. Black soot covered her dress, and the ashy smell of coal clogged her nose.

She was sure she wouldn't smell anything else for days.

She tilted the lid of the box on its side so that the remaining dust slid into a pile. After hours of searching the windowless basement, she was no closer to her goal. She set the lid aside and sorted through the contents.

Before her brother had vanished from their lives, there had been paintings of him all around the house. After he'd left, Rosemary had ordered the staff to put every painting that included his face into storage. Which made it difficult to prove to anyone that her brother was the man in the painting she'd seen at Lady Jarvis's house.

She vividly recalled his mop of unruly curls, and the way his green eyes had glinted when he'd laughed, the dimples in his cheeks when he smiled at her. Despite his many flaws, Basil was still her brother, and she would not give up on him while there remained the smallest chance that he lived. Whatever he'd done, whatever trouble he'd gotten himself into, she would find him and put things to rights.

Saffron shifted her stance, sore from slouching. Gravel crunched beneath her soft slippers, cutting into her feet. She replaced the lid on the box and placed it back on the shelf. Something moved in the corner of her eye, but she refused to look, fearing it was rats or worse. She could hear them moving around her, squeaking and scuttling through the earth.

In the next box, she found a painting of her parents.

As she touched her fingers to their faces, she remembered how her father had allowed her to watch him auditing the estate accounts when she'd been young. She'd marveled at the way he'd balanced the columns of numbers, which had seemed like magic to her. But as she'd grown up, her father had pushed her into embroidery and music, activities he'd considered more suitable for a young woman.

That rejection had hurt more than anything that had followed.

She pulled a clean square of linen from her pocket, covered the painting to keep away the dust, then replaced the lid on the box and moved on to the next.

Finally, after what seemed long enough that she would become part of the clutter herself, Saffron found a portrait the size of her hand. It was something a parent commissioned for a child, a wooden frame with scalloped edges and an oval of canvas in the center.

Saffron's brother looked to be in his early twenties, and the painter had been talented enough to capture the boyish charm in Basil's eyes.

"Perfect," Saffron said, rubbing some coal dust from the frame. It would serve as a comparison when she confronted Ravenmore. She reached through a slit in her gown and stored the painting in a pocket she'd sewn into her chemise.

One never knew when a pocket would be useful.

The floorboards above her creaked, sending a spray of dust onto her head. She placed the boxes back where they had been, shook as much of the dust from her skirts as she could, then padded up the stairs to the main floor.

The ever-present clatter of wheels filtered in through the window, a consequence of their townhouse being located on the fringes of the fashionable Mayfair district. The proximity to the Thames also meant it was impossible to avoid the stench, a rotten egg smell that seeped in through the heavily scented curtains.

Saffron held her breath and scurried up the steps to her bedroom.

Angelica was lying on her stomach on the narrow bed with her legs in the air. Saffron clenched her fingers on the doorknob, scanning her room for changes.

Three logs were missing from the grate near the fireplace. The wool blanket that she kept folded in the trunk in the corner lay in a pile at the side of the bed. The chair tucked beneath her dressing table was pulled out, and the lid on the metal box that contained Saffron's few pieces of jewelry was askew.

"What took you so long?" Angelica asked, rising on her elbows. "I was falling asleep."

Saffron pulled her eyes away from her dressing table. "She hid them in the storage hutch below the dining room."

Angelica patted her palms on the bed. "Of course."

Saffron removed her gown with slow movements, to keep the dust from rubbing onto her chemise. "She must have thought it was the last place I would look."

"Was it?"

Saffron laughed. "Yes. She knows me too well."

A ruffle on Saffron's skirt snagged on a hook of her corset. Rather than tug on it and tear the fabric that she could not easily repair or replace, she began the arduous process of untangling herself.

Angelica bounced off the bed and came over to help. Soon they had the soiled garment off and discarded in a corner. She would take it to a washerwoman for cleaning in the morning.

She selected one of the many plain gowns from a leather trunk in the corner and slipped it on.

"Let me see it, then," Angelica said. "I hardly remember him."

"You could not possibly have forgotten already," Saffron said, pulling the painting from her pocket and handing it over.

"Look at that face." Angelica laughed. "It's no wonder he was a troublemaker." She set the portrait on the bed. "Do you really think he's still alive?"

Saffron unraveled her hair, shaking out black flakes of coal onto the carpet. "If he'd posed for an artist while he lived with us, I am certain he would have told us. So perhaps he posed since last we saw him. The body we buried must have been someone else. Perhaps our brother was robbed, his clothing stolen."

"If he didn't die, why would he stay away?" Angelica asked.

"I think our brother is neck deep in trouble. Maybe he owes someone a lot of money and is afraid that if he comes forward, he'll end up in debtors' gaol."

Angelica groaned. "That sounds like him. But no letter? No sign at all?" Her voice wavered. "Why would he let us think he was dead?"

Saffron set the brush on the dressing table and wrapped her arms around Angelica, feeling her sister's shoulders shake. In the mirror, she could see the tears gathering in her sister's eyes.

"Wherever he is, I am sure he has a good reason for staying away. I am sure he feels he's protecting us. We have to believe that."

Angelica sniffed. "How are we going to find him?"

Saffron pulled back and squeezed her sister's shoulders. "Leave that to me."

A booming sound made them both jump.

"The door," Angelica said. "Should I—"

"I'll get it," Saffron said firmly.

They had not received afternoon callers for weeks. If someone wanted to pay court to Angelica, then Saffron would gladly let them in, but the increasingly loud knocking suggested their visitor was not a caller.

As she descended the steps to the foyer, her corset seemed to tighten around her chest. The banging continued, shaking the old oak door on its hinges. She was tempted to retreat and wait for whoever it was to leave, but her feet continued moving until she was in front of the door, her hand on the knob.

She cracked the door open to see a short, rosy-cheeked man in a tweed suit clutching a sheaf of papers in one hand. He lowered his fist and straightened his shoulders. "Miss Summersby?"

"Yes?" She did not open the door any further, fearing he would shove his foot inside. This was no gentleman to offer his card. He looked vaguely familiar, but she couldn't place where she had seen him before.

He shoved his bundle at her. "You are in default."

She stared at the stack of papers. "Excuse me?"

The man snapped his fingers and two burly men in workman's clothes climbed the steps and stood behind him with their arms crossed. Neither of them would meet her gaze.

Please, no. Not now.

"Sorry, miss," one of the burly men said, in a grating baritone. He splayed a hand on the door and pushed it open, sending her staggering back. The door slammed against the wall and the three men sauntered inside.

That was where she knew the short man from. He was the bank manager. Basil had held a few meetings at the house when they'd encountered financial difficulty in the past. Her charming brother had always been able to wheedle a few extra weeks out of the man through flattery and bribery. Saffron had watched her brother subtly press bank notes into the man's hands when greeting him. She hadn't understood the necessity.

Until now.

"Paintings and any small items of value first," the short man said to his henchmen. "Pay particular attention to shiny baubles. Those items will fetch the best prices."

This cannot be happening.

Saffron gaped as strangers trod all over her carefully washed floors with their dirty boots. What could she do to stop them? She barely had enough notes for a carriage. The shop that had bought her mother's jewelry was not open until the morning.

She rushed to the bank manager's side. "P-Please..." She searched her memory for a name. "Mr. Grummet. I am sure we can come to some kind of understanding."

The man ignored her. He was too busy barking commands at a cart driver outside.

Saffron's head pounded. She wasn't a man and therefore was not worth his attention. She clenched her back teeth together. If he would not listen, she would *make* him. She had to get all of them out before Angelica or Rosemary came downstairs and discovered they were pillaging the house.

"Mr. Grummet," she said loudly.

The man spun around, scowling. "Cease your screeching, woman. The terms of the mortgage your brother signed are clear. Upon default, the bank has the right to auction the house and everything inside it. If you have a grievance, you can apply to—"

She stepped forward, donning her best smile. "There will be no need for that, my dear Mr. Grummet. Have you seen our..." She searched the house in her mind for something that would convince the man to leave, something of value she could give to him to stop this madness. She could not remember what she'd eaten the previous day, but she could recall every word of a conversation that had happened more than three years ago. Mr. Grummet had expressed a desire to purchase several of Basil's books, but Basil had insisted they had not been for sale.

"Our library," she said. Her face felt as stiff as starched linen. "My father was a collector, you understand. There are several very rare volumes." She leaned forward. "They could be yours, Mr. Grummet. Not the bank's. Are you a collector?"

The man narrowed his eyes. "What manner of volumes?"

She knew what she had to say, but she choked on the words. It went against everything that was important to her.

"What are those men doing?"

Saffron jerked her head around so fast that fire erupted in her neck. "Angelica, return to your room. I will deal with this."

The fear on her sister's face broke Saffron's heart anew. Her task was difficult enough without Angelica there to witness it.

Angelica flew down the stairs and linked her arm with Saffron's, then faced the bank manager.

Mr. Grummet shuffled his feet. "The books?"

"We have never read any of them, of course," Angelica said before Saffron could speak. "What use do we have for books?" She sniffed. "Take the entire library. It will give us more room for dancing."

Saffron's eyes burned, but she refused to let the tears fall. She would mourn the loss later, with Angelica tucked in her arms. The most important thing was to evict the strangers from their home so they could regroup.

The bank manager stuck out a hand. "Might I see those papers, Miss Summersby?"

Saffron realized they were stuck beneath her arm. She hadn't looked at them. She was too afraid to see what they would say. She shoved them at the man.

Mr. Grummet leafed through a few pages, then nodded. "I must apologize, Miss Summersby. It appears I read the date wrong. You have another month—"

"Three months," Saffron said. "Many of the books are first editions."

Mr. Grummet clenched his jaw. "Very well. You have three months to pay what is due before we can legally claim the property." He snapped his fingers again. The workmen set down the pieces they were carrying and made their way toward the steps.

"An understandable mistake," Saffron said tightly. The floor dipped and bucked beneath her as if she was on the deck of a ship. She clung to Angelica to keep upright. She could not waver until the awful man was gone.

Only then would she allow herself to feel.

⁕

THE MEMORY OF men carrying armfuls of books down the steps would haunt Saffron for the rest of her life. They had treated those precious items like any other trinket, letting the covers flop open without a care for the spines. It was enough to make her bite her tongue to keep from screaming. Saffron peered out the small window of the hired carriage. Water droplets flicked the glass and trailed away in long lines, clinging to the window before whipping away into the night. The woods on either side of the road blurred past, a stream of brown and green like two paints that had spilled together. The rain hammered against the roof and drowned out the rattling of the wheels.

That morning she had penned letters in response to three families seeking a governess, but she had little hope they would respond. There were many young ladies applying, and not enough positions available.

A situation more suited to her skills was that of a lady's companion, but the few women she knew who might have need of one had no interest in employing her.

They prefer to look down their noses at me. Regardless, she doubted she could ever earn enough to support her family.

The gold-toned parchment in her valise bearing the Briarwood seal was their only hope. She had to find Ravenmore and demand where he had met her brother. When she had proof that Basil still lived, she would convince Aunt Rosemary to refuse the duke's suit of Angelica and give her time to find their brother and restore their fortune. Then things would go back to the way they had been.

Angelica deserves better, she thought, remembering how Lord Briarwood had rescued her from Canterbury's scorn in Lady Jarvis's ballroom. The two men could not have been more different. The duke's reputation was sterling, his manner acidic. Meanwhile, ladies clutched their daughters close whenever Viscount Briarwood passed, and yet she had never met anyone who had treated her with such gentleness.

"I feel as if I am being dragged along the road," Angelica said, rubbing her back. "What will the other guests think if we arrive in such a poor state?"

The carriage was sparse, without warm bricks to heat them or even padding on the bare wooden seats. Saffron had given over one of her few gowns to Rosemary, who had tucked it around her legs. Every time the carriage hit a rut in the road, all three women knocked into each other.

"It is the best we could afford," Saffron said, breathing on her chilled fingers. It didn't seem possible, with the oppressive heat in London, that it could be so cold only a day's drive into the country. She flicked the shade on the window shut. "We should be glad we found any transport."

They had left town late, held up by the difficulty of finding a conveyance. It seemed every family on their street had left on the same day to escape the heat and stench of London.

She had managed a few fitful hours of sleep, woken by every creak and howl of the wind, certain that brigands or highwaymen surrounded them.

Not that they had anything of real value. They had sold most of their jewelry to pay their debts.

The carriage rattled to a stop.

"Are we there?" Angelica asked.

Saffron pulled back the shade from the window. "I don't think so." They were at the edge of a river. The dark, surging waters lashed against the shore and sent up a cloud of spray that spattered the side of the carriage.

"We've arrived at the gates of hell," Angelica said, looking over her shoulder.

"I did not hear that," Rosemary said. "My niece does not speak like a common sailor."

"I'll ask our driver," Saffron said. She steadied her nerves, then opened the door and stepped out. The rain soaked her gown in seconds. Wind buffeted her hair, and before she could reach up, her bonnet whipped from her head and flew off into the trees.

She sheltered against the side of the carriage and looked up at the hulking man atop it.

"Why did we stop?" she yelled.

The coachman slid down off his perch and peered at her from beneath his hood, grinning a gap-toothed smile. He pointed toward the water. "We wait to cross."

She held a hand to her head to keep her wet hair from lashing against her face. There was a small craft approaching them, little more than a bundle of logs lashed together. "That is hardly a ferry."

The coachman shrugged. "The boat doesn't run in the squall."

I guess we have no choice.

They had not passed an inn for hours, and she did not wish to spend the night in the cramped quarters of the carriage.

She backed up and opened the door. Rosemary and Angelica stared at her with wide eyes, like two owls in a burrow. As Saffron stepped inside, the rain splattered into the interior, but when she turned to close them in, the storm tugged the door out of her grip.

Angelica's hands joined hers on the handle, and together, they pulled until the door slammed shut, sending them falling to the floor.

Saffron flicked the water from her hands. "We're at the river crossing. Not much longer now."

Rosemary huffed. "If our host has any sense, he will have hot towels waiting for us when we arrive. I can't understand why anyone would live in the frigid country."

Saffron peeked out the small window as the ferry docked against the shore. The coachman navigated the carriage onto the contraption. It was not a ferry, more like a barge that floated from one side of the river to the other. There was a small, enclosed area in the center where passengers could shelter from the rain, but Rosemary and Angelica were determined to stay inside the carriage. The coachman muttered his annoyance at their choice, as he had to stay with them in the sheeting rain, lest the horses spook.

The surging waters lapped against the sides of the ferry, causing it to pitch and sway. She huddled into a ball on the floor. There were so many things that could go wrong. The barge could sink. They could be tossed overboard. Lightning could strike them and set the carriage aflame.

It will be fine, she thought, forcing herself to believe it.

Angelica gasped, and the ferry bucked, throwing them in the air. It happened half a dozen more times before they finished the crossing.

"I do not know how you enjoyed that," Saffron groaned. Her head throbbed and there was a bitter taste at the back of her throat, like she had sucked on a penny. It had taken all her concentration not to cast up her accounts all over the floor.

The wheels thumped onto the earth as the coachmen led them off the barge. Then they were off again, the horses plodding along a narrow path that was surrounded by dense forest.

As she chewed the inside of her cheek, there was a deafening thunder crack, the sound of splintering wood, and the shriek of horses. The carriage listed to one side, sending all three women sliding into the wall.

"I say!" Rosemary banged on the roof with her fist. "Watch where—"

A low creaking filled the carriage, and then it toppled over.

Saffron's shoulder hit something hard, and she tumbled onto her back. As she struggled out of the heavy embrace of her skirts, Angelica grabbed for the door high above them. Rosemary lay slumped on her side, her head lolled back.

A jolt of pure fear shot through Saffron. Rosemary looked like her mother, flushed and pale on her sickbed.

"She's okay," Angelica said, grasping for the door. She got her fingers around the handle and pushed but couldn't open it.

"Let me try," Saffron said, holding her hands against the carriage walls. As she reached up and grasped the handle, something smacked against the side of the carriage.

"Hang on, 'ere," a rough voice called.

Saffron lunged for Rosemary as Angelica clutched the seats. The carriage groaned again and shifted upright, then settled with one corner lower than the rest. She threw open the door to see the remains of a broken wheel scattered across the road.

"What do we do now?" Angelica asked, clutching her arms around herself.

The driver was standing by the horses. Saffron struggled through the sucking mud to his side, only to realize he was removing the ropes that held one of the two horses to the carriage.

She reached out to grab his cloak, shouting words that were whipped away by the wind. Her fingers tangled in the fabric, and she took a firm grip, pulling with all her strength.

"Miss, it's every man for himself!" he shouted. Then he waved an arm, and she fell back into the mud, the thick cloak in a heap on her lap. By the time she'd recovered, the coachman was on the horse departing down the road.

They were on their own.

Hold it together, she thought. *The others need you.*

She struggled out of the mud and pulled the heavy cloak around her shoulders. Although it was as wet as the rest of her clothing, it was wool and provided some warmth. She flipped up the hood and trudged over to the carriage. Their cases had broken open and spilled their clothing all over the interior. Angelica kneeled in front of Rosemary, pilling fabric onto the older woman.

"The coachman fled, didn't he?" Rosemary asked, frowning.

Saffron shrugged the cloak into a more comfortable position around her shoulders. "He took a horse."

Angelica made a low, keening sound and slumped at Rosemary's feet. "What are we going to do? We'll die of cold. I was right, this is hell!"

"Calm yourself," Rosemary said, kicking at Angelica with her leg beneath the many layers of fabric. "Hysterics will not help us."

The remaining horse bucked and carried on with its terrible shrieks.

Saffron looked at her family, huddled together in the cold. Water dripped down onto the seat from a crack in the roof. Even if the storm ebbed in the morning, it might be several hours before anyone came down the road. They would catch a chill from the cold and be bedridden for weeks. Or worse, the next person to come by would find three frozen bodies.

They were stuck, and it was her fault. If it were not for her delay in getting transportation, they would have arrived hours earlier. A dizziness worse than the seasickness she'd felt crossing the water washed over her. Panic was setting in. She had to act fast.

"Sister, you have a plan, don't you?" Angelica asked, her voice pitched higher than usual. "You always have a plan."

"O-Of course," Saffron replied, forcing herself to speak with confidence she did not feel. The weight of the situation bore down on her, and a thousand ideas flooded her mind all at once.

Take shelter and wait it out. No. Build a fire, keep warm. No. Take the horse.

She seized upon the last. "I'll go ahead. Stay here and try to stay warm."

Before Angelica or Rosemary could argue, she closed the shattered carriage door and strode toward the horse, hoping she wasn't making a mistake.

Chapter Six

A CRASH WOKE Leo from a fitful sleep. He threw aside the sweat-soaked sheets and ran out into the hallway without bothering to don a robe. He knew, instinctually, that the sound had come from his studio.

Had the thief or thieves attempted to break in? Or had a canvas jostled free and fallen to the floor?

Shouting followed him, but the residual fear from his dream propelled him forward, as if he were running from the past. The lamps along the walls were cold, and moonlight filtered through the windows. The air was stale, and the carpet beneath his feet was thin and slippery.

He reached the closed doors of his studio and tugged the handles. They stuck firm. His butler skidded to a stop and put a hand on the door. In his other, he clutched a long, white robe, which he thrust at Leo.

"For God's sake, cover up, my lord," Sinclair said, between gasping breaths. "Think of the maids!"

Leo shrugged on the robe, then grasped the handle again. The doors rattled but stayed firm.

Sinclair held up a ring of keys. "Locked, as it is every night, my lord."

Leo snatched the keys and splayed them in his open palm. In the darkness, they were identical. "I need more light."

A footman rushed forward with a lantern and Leo held the keys to it, selecting the correct one and inserting it into the latch. He turned the key, and it unlocked with a dull click. He threw open the doors to the studio as a flash of lightning illuminated the room. At first glance, nothing seemed disturbed. The large windows showed the dark night sky beyond, and a gentle breeze flirted with the end of his robe.

"What did that noise sound like to you?" he asked Sinclair. Servants rushed around him, carefully maneuvering canvases to light the lamps in the walls.

"It sounded like glass breaking, my lord," Sinclair said.

Leo stepped over a paint-splattered carpet to inspect the easternmost window, which had a corner smashed out. On the floor, a broken branch the size of his forearm lay in a bed of shattered glass.

He held his hand out the gap and the wind sprayed a fine mist over his skin. The boughs of the nearest tree thrashed against the side of the building.

His butler lifted the branch. "Our perpetrator. Straight to the lumber pit for this one for having caused so much trouble."

"Maybe not," Leo murmured as he touched some black flakes on the window frame. He rubbed his fingers together and held them to his nose, then stuck his head through the hole. A trail of footprints retreated into the brush.

He pulled his head inside, slicking back his wet hair with a hand. A footman hovering nearby offered him a towel, and he accepted it, ruffling his hair, then draping it around his shoulders.

"Let me see the branch," he said, holding out his hand. Sinclair passed it over, and Leo examined the broken end, finding it smooth. The intruder had been clever, but not careful enough.

"Send for the constable," he said. "This branch was cut, not broken. This was more than an act of nature."

Sinclair bowed. "As you wish, my lord. Now please, return to your chambers. I will ensure the window is boarded up."

Leo stepped away from the window, then paused. The room was full of paintings. Hanging on the walls, stacked on the ground, balanced on canvas stands. What if the intruder had taken off with one or more? How would he know? Each painting held a piece of his heart, and he would feel their loss keenly. The few he had selected for the auction were ones his father had purchased before his death, and even those, he'd struggled to release.

"We will perform an inventory, my lord," Sinclair said. "Please, return to your bedchamber."

Setting the branch on the ground, Leo left his studio, trusting his staff to take care of the damage. But as he walked through the chilly hallways and into his chambers, he abandoned any idea of sleep. He hastily pulled on trousers, then summoned Sinclair by pulling the thick, braided rope in the corner of the room. The man arrived in moments. "Yes, my lord?"

"Have someone guard the studio," Leo said, pacing the room. "In case our uninvited guest returns."

Sinclair quirked an eyebrow. "I've already taken care of it. Two footmen will take shifts. The thief will not catch us off guard again."

Leo rubbed his face with his hand. Of course, he should have expected Sinclair to handle the situation. It had been months since he'd actively managed the affairs of his estate. His butler and the housekeeper oversaw the day-to-day needs of the household. Only through their weekly reports did he learn the stairs were rotting, the kitchen understaffed, the servants' quarters drafty. Dozens of trivial household concerns that would otherwise have kept him from pursuing the one activity that gave him a semblance of peace—painting.

And now someone is trying to take that away from you, too.

"Tomorrow, move the paintings in my studio to a different wing," Leo said. "Somewhere that is not accessible from the outdoors. Perhaps on the third floor. We do not want to give our intruder another chance."

"And your… supplies?"

Sinclair's hesitation was not a surprise. Leo had, on more than one occasion, reminded the maids not to clean around his brushes and oils. He did not have the patience to set everything back to rights every day.

"I will gather them myself," Leo said. He would package up the least used of his materials into crates and move the rest somewhere close so that none of his guests would stumble upon them.

But even with plans set in motion, he still felt like a caged lion, tensed to bite the next hand that approached.

There is only one thing for it.

He walked over to his wardrobe and rifled through the frippery, scowling. Hundreds of pounds spent at the tailor, and not a piece of it was waterproof.

"My lord, do you intend to go out into the storm?" Sinclair asked, alarmed. "I would advise against such action. It is not safe."

He shrugged on his thickest coat and tightened the belts about his waist. "I cannot rest until I investigate myself. Bring me my hunting boots."

His butler sniffed, then stiffly walked out the door, returning a minute later with a pair of heavy boots clutched in his arms. Leo sat in a wingback chair near the cold fireplace and allowed his butler to lace them to his feet.

"I beg you to reconsider, my lord," Sinclair said, following him as he made his way down the hallway to the entrance. "I do not wish to send a team to recover your body. Wait until morning, at least."

"It'll be too late," he said, tugging his hood tightly around his head. "Our trap has sprung early. In a few hours, there will be no evidence to speak of."

He wouldn't let them get away with it.

A footman opened the main doorway and Leo stepped outside. The rain pelted his face, spurred on by a roaring wind that cut straight through his coat. He descended the stairs, then slogged through the thick mud surrounding the outside of the building until he reached the point around the house where the intruder had tried to enter.

When he found the footprints, he crouched down for a closer look. Once, when he'd been a young lad, he had tried to get past his nursemaid by sneaking out the same back windows. The mud had been so thick that he had lost a shoe.

After a few moments, he found what he was looking for: a bare, trampled area of ground surrounded by trees denuded of leaves. Evidence of a horse.

He returned to the front entrance, where Sinclair waited. The butler crouched to undo the laces on his boots, but Leo shook his head. As nice as it would have been to rid himself of his sodden shoes, there was more to do, and it would take too long to dry off.

"Have the stables prepare a mount," he said.

"At least wait until you are properly attired," Sinclair begged.

"We don't have time for that. There was a horse tied nearby. Its rider is escaping as we speak. I must pursue now or not at all."

He spared a moment to exchange his waterlogged coat for another, then charged back out into the tempest.

An hour later, he regretted his decision.

He was on horseback, following the tracks, wincing through the sleeting rain, and trying to remain astride as his horse picked its careful way through the muck. Branches lashed him, breaking off and littering the forest floor.

Sinclair was right. This is madness.

But having set out on the task, he was determined to finish it. It was not as if he had anything to look forward to. Sleep routinely brought the same nightmares he'd suffered with each night since Sabrina's death. Only through painting was he able to escape his demons.

Another reason to find the intruder who had violated his sanctuary.

The tracks led through his property to an old groundskeeper cottage, a small, thatched-roof structure with an attached stable that showed signs of recent use. He resolved to tell his staff after this was over to either demolish the building or install a tenant to keep it from acting as a waystation.

He continued until he reached a hill overlooking a view of surging ocean waves in a small bay. A blot on the water suggested a ship, but it was too far away to gleam any recognizable details.

Too late.

He turned his horse and made his way back through the woods. As he rounded the last bend, he spotted a rider in a black cloak at the treeline bordering the road.

The thief?

He waved his arm. "You there!"

The rider turned his mount, then took off down the road. Leo kicked his heels into his horse's sides. The thudding of the animals' hooves on the gravel path kept pace with the erratic pounding of his heart. He kept close behind his quarry but did not overtake. The road was pitted, and one misstep could send him flying.

His brother, the viscount before him, had died in just such a manner. They had found his body the next morning, crumpled in a heap at the bottom of a cliff. A victim of his own poor judgement.

And here I am about to repeat his mistakes.

The rider maintained an even distance, and Leo was considering giving up the chase when the man skidded to a halt. The viscount had to pull hard on the reins to stop from soaring over the neck of his horse as she dug her hooves into the slick earth and threw her head up, whinnying sharply.

Then the rider lifted his hood to reveal the blazing, brown eyes of Saffron Summersby, her mouth set in a tight line.

The shock of seeing her nearly unseated him, and he had to clutch the reins.

What the devil is she doing here?

"You scared me half to death!" she shouted. The words were bare-ly audible over the rumble of thunder. He urged his horse closer until his thigh pressed against the heaving sides of her mount.

"What are you doing?" he shouted. "It's dangerous out here."

She glowered at him, her hair tangled around her face, her body shaking beneath her heavy, water-logged cloak. She gestured with her hands, and her lips moved, though he could only make out a few words.

Carriage, River. Help.

"An accident? What happened?"

She pointed to her ears, then to the road, the way they had come.

He nodded, all thoughts of the thief gone from his mind, and then brought his horse around to follow her, hoping that she would not be foolish enough to take off again.

What she does with her time is no concern of yours. If she wants to run about in a storm, you cannot stop her.

Hypocrisy aside, he could see her trembling from three horse lengths away. If they did not get warm and dry soon, the consequences might prove dire.

He remembered the groundskeeper cottage and imagined putting on dry clothing and sitting in front of a warm fire. They might even find some old jerky, hard and salty but wholesome. He urged his horse closer, then grabbed Miss Summersby's arm beneath her cloak. "Let's take shelter," he shouted. "I'm soaked to the bone."

She tried to speak again, but when he shook his head, unable to hear, she scowled and resorted to nodding her head up and down in an exaggerated gesture.

Relieved, Leo turned his horse toward the cottage.

When they arrived, he jumped down from his mount, clutching on to the saddle to keep from slipping onto his back in the mud. Saffron followed his lead with a much more elegant dismount. Without asking, she took his reins and her own and led their mounts into the small stable attached to the side of the cottage.

Trusting her to see to the needs of the animals, he gathered his saddlebags then entered the dark structure and took a cautious sniff.

Smoke.

As he examined the remains in the firepit, the roaring wind buffeted the sides of the cottage, and the thunder crashed overhead.

The cottage was a single room with stone walls and a wooden floor that creaked as he stepped. The only window was boarded over, letting in a sliver of cold air through the gaps in the wooden planks.

By the hearth were two wooden stools, which he broke apart with his heel and assembled into a pile, grateful for the first time in his life for his father's lectures on keeping his saddlebags fully stocked. He retrieved a box of matches, then nursed a small flame in the hearth with numb fingers, hoping the chimney was clear enough to allow the smoke to pass through.

The door creaked open and then shut with a bang.

"We can't stay here," Saffron said.

"What were you doing out in that storm?" he asked, pushing down his temper as he fed the small fire with more splinters. "You could have broken your neck if that horse had thrown you. I could barely keep astride."

She stayed stubbornly by the door. "I left my aunt and sister. Our carriage lost a wheel at the riverside and our driver abandoned us. We can't leave them alone!"

Leo cracked a branch harder than he'd intended, spraying splinters onto the floor. The damned woman was going to get herself killed. "I'm not letting you leave this cabin until the storm calms down."

She scowled and looked like she was going to argue, but then a bolt of lightning struck, illuminating the room in a burst of light. When Leo could see again, her shoulders had slumped, all the fight drained out of her.

"My butler was set against me leaving," he said, compelled to reassure her. "They'll have sent out a search party by now."

"If anything happens to them, I won't forgive you," she said, coming close to kneel beside him. She reached out her hands toward the fire, and he glanced at her face, highlighted by the flickering light. Even drenched, she was beautiful, with long eyelashes and rosy cheeks. He could not see much of her through the cloak, and for that, he was grateful. Thinking about her wet gown plastered to her curves made his loins stir.

Then she closed her eyes and sniffed. "I feel so helpless."

He reached for her knee and squeezed. "My staff know these woods."

"I hope you're right."

She relaxed against his touch. He jerked his hand away and reached for his saddlebags, glad that Sinclair had filled it with additional supplies before he'd so recklessly taken off into the storm. He found a woolen blanket that was damp but not wet and shook it out.

"Here," he said, draping it over Saffron's shoulders and tucking it around her. "We'll wait for a break in the storm, then return to the manor. It shouldn't be long. Storms here burn themselves out quickly. We'll be back before your family knows we were ever here." He slammed his mouth shut before he could babble further.

"Thank you."

The next ten minutes passed in a tense silence broken only by the crackling, popping fire and whoosh of rain coming in from the gaps in the window. A prickling numbness crept from the tips of his fingers and toes up to his elbows and knees.

That was when he realized something was wrong. There were dark bags around Saffron's eyes. Her shoulders shook, and her fingers were tinged blue.

Fever.

The word hit him in the gut. She'd been out in the rain, but was sickness even possible so fast after exposure? He'd seen his sister come down with a chill once, after a swim on a windy day. She'd spent a full night shivering in her bed, shoving the heavy blankets away even after the doctor had insisted what she needed was warmth. Sabrina had barely survived the incident.

He wouldn't let it happen to anyone else.

He removed his overcoat and wrapped it around Miss Summersby's shoulders, then pulled her tightly to him.

Chapter Seven

L ORD BRIARWOOD'S BREATH grazed Saffron's cheek, smelling of brandy and cloves. The light of the crackling fire cast his slightly crooked nose and stubbled cheeks in a golden tinge. Her stomach filled with swirling butterflies, and she almost forgot her feet were soaked and her fingers numb from the cold.

When she'd walked into the cottage, she'd felt a searing rush of nerves at the sight of him, water dripping from his hair, shirt plastered to his chest. She'd dreamed of him every night since they'd met, replaying every scene, languishing in the comfort of his arms. She'd never met a man who had treated her as anything more than an annoying accessory to her sister, who didn't make her feel like she needed to hide some part of herself away.

She realized she was staring and hurriedly turned her gaze to the fire. "What are you doing?"

He pulled her tightly against himself. "You've caught a chill from the rain."

"What? No." She tugged away and looked into his face. The worry she saw there made her eyes burn with tears.

How can he care so much when he barely knows me?

"I'm fine," she said, enunciating the words. "I don't have a chill. I'm sure of it."

He moved his arms to her shoulders. "Your cheeks are flushed, and your hands shaking."

"It's nothing, Lord Briarwood," she said, glad when her voice came out evenly. Being so close to him was enough to send flickering tendrils of electricity across her skin.

"If not a fever, then what?" A slow smile spread across his face.

She licked her lips, unsure of how to respond. She'd never desired a man before. Should she tell him of her fantasies? The dreams she had, replaying their moment by the fountain?

"Call me 'Leo,'" he said.

She startled, bumping her arm against his. "What?"

He turned his head so that his nose was only inches from hers and gave a boyish smile. "I told you to call me 'Leo.' Not 'Lord Briarwood.'"

"As I told you before, it wouldn't be proper," she whispered. Not that anything about their situation was proper. If anyone found out they had been alone together for so long, and in such a state of undress, she would be branded a lightskirt.

It might already be too late, she thought, with a frisson of fear. How was she going to explain arriving with the viscount, soaking wet, without a chaperone? Every minute they waited increased the chances that someone would stumble upon them, or that more guests would arrive and further complicate their return.

I've all but ruined myself already.

It was not that she cared about her own reputation. Three years of failing to find a man willing to marry her had chased away her childhood fantasies of securing a husband. But she could not allow her actions to reflect poorly on her sister and aunt.

"Are you still cold?"

Belatedly, she realized she was trembling again, and her breath came in gasps.

"I—It's not—" She swallowed a huge amount of saliva that had collected in her mouth and then groaned and thumped her forehead on her knees. "It is a problem I have. When things happen that I can't control, my mind tries to predict every possibility, and I get trapped in a cycle I cannot escape."

Leo chuckled. "You are so much like her."

She tilted her head to the side so she could see his face. "Who?"

His soft smile turned down. "My sister. She died three years ago."

Her heart ached for him. She knew how it felt to grieve a sibling. Losing Basil had torn her apart.

"My advice," he continued. "Do whatever feels right and don't worry about the consequences. I never do." Then he tilted his face toward her and dropped his eyes to her lips, as he had done in every fantasy that she'd had of him.

The temptation was too much to resist.

She fluttered her eyelids closed, angled her face, and pressed her lips to his.

It was nothing like she'd imagined.

His mouth was hard and unyielding, like cold stone. She tried again, desperately reaching for the warmth she'd felt when he'd protected her by the fountain, whispering sweet words that had made her insides feel like jelly. But aside from the muscles bunching in his neck, he gave no reaction.

Disappointed, she pulled back, tucking her arms against her chest and lowering her chin, not wanting him to see the tears forming at the corners of her eyes. She had trusted her instincts, and they had failed her.

"I'm sorry," she said. "I thought…"

"You thought what?" His voice was as cold as his lips.

That you wanted me.

"Nothing." Her voice broke, and she tried to pull away, only to find his arm anchoring her in place. "My lord, what are you doing? Let me go."

His rejection was embarrassing enough. It simmered in her mind, another reminder that she wasn't normal, would never be normal.

She'd been so sure he had wanted her, but she'd imagined it, seen a spark where there'd been nothing. Facing the depth of his scorn tore at her already fragile confidence.

He's not different, after all.

"Let me go," she said again, struggling in his grip as tears dripped from her eyes and slid down her cheeks. "It won't happen again."

He uttered a strangled curse, then moved his hands from her arms to frame her face. With his thumbs, he brushed away the tears.

"You think too much."

He pressed a soft kiss to her forehead, her nose, then her lips.

She melted beneath his feather-light touch and wound her arms around his neck. Her pulse skittered, making her dizzy with relief. Was it really happening? Or was she dreaming?

One hand cupped her breast, and she gasped. His tongue swept into her mouth and tangled with hers, sending a jolt of heat to her pelvis. He tasted smoky sweet, like a rich brandy, but more intoxicating.

He broke away briefly to pull her into his lap, straddling him. His hands grasped her rear and squeezed, his fingers tantalizingly close to her most sensitive area. It was as she'd dreamed, and so much more. Wetness pooled at the apex of her thighs, and she arched her back, aching for him to touch her there.

He drew back with a muffled curse and pressed his lips to her cheek in a chaste kiss. His heart pounded beneath her curled fingers and the hard ridge of his desire pressed into her thigh. Her skin prickled with sensation where he had touched her, and his taste lingered in her mouth.

"That was nice... Leo," she whispered.

Using his name felt so intimate, but it seemed fitting after what they had shared.

He nudged a strand of wet hair out of her face. "So, I am 'Leo,' at last?"

She flicked her tongue across her lips. "Yes."

He cupped her cheeks in his hands and squeezed. "As much as I would love to continue this moment, the storm has stopped. We should get back before they come looking for us."

❧❦❧

SAFFRON STUMBLED OUT of the sheeting rain through the large doors of the manor, held open by footmen, and shrugged off her purloined cloak. It fell with a wet *thud* onto the marble floor, splattering the marble tiles with a brownish-gray liquid.

Everything around her screamed opulence, from the grand, marble staircase carpeted in a rich crimson to the gilded-gold frames of portraits hanging high on the walls.

Despite her fears, they had not encountered a soul on the road, nor had any guests arrived before them. She felt both amazed, and somewhat guilty, by her fortune. It was as if the moment in the cottage had been a dream.

"My servants are very discreet," the viscount murmured, coming to stand beside her. "No one will ever know. Your honor will remain intact."

If only that were true. Honorable women did not throw themselves into the arms of rakes, no matter how gorgeous they were. But she was relieved that her lapse in judgement would not reflect poorly on her family.

A heavy blanket dropped onto her shoulders, and she looked up to see Leo's hands falling away.

"Thank you." She pulled the blanket tighter around her. Her eyes trailed down his silk shirt, plastered to his body. He had rolled his sleeves up to his elbows, exposing his bulging forearms, covered in a fine layer of golden hair. She had the sudden urge to reach out and stroke him like a cat. She could still feel his lips on hers, his tongue swirling around her mouth. His firm hands kneading her breast, cupping her rear.

This spark of attraction is a distraction. Nothing more.

She would not abandon her quest to find Basil. Not when she was so close. Somewhere among the guests attending the auction was the painter who had captured her brother's likeness. When she found Ravenmore, she would demand to know where he had met her brother. She couldn't be more than a week behind him, given the date on the painting. Things would go back to normal after she'd chased him down.

"Are you even listening to me? Not now, man!"

Saffron jerked her head around to see Leo struggling with a fluffy, pink towel that someone, probably his butler, had draped over his head.

"That's a good look for you," she said, laughing.

Then she remembered the sound of the carriage wheel cracking, Angelica and Rosemary screaming. How long had it been since she'd left them at the side of the road? It had gotten colder by the minute, and the rain had fallen from the sky in endless buckets.

What if it's too late?

She would never forgive herself if something happened to them.

Leo was still arguing with his butler, their voices rising in volume. The only other person in the room was a young footman with sandy-blond hair.

She charged toward him, filled with a renewed sense of urgency. "Have any other guests arrived? A young woman with golden hair, and an older woman?"

The boy gaped at her as if she'd turned into a dragon and breathed fire. "N-No, madam."

She followed his gaze to Leo, who was approaching them, having divested himself of the offending towel.

"Get the coachman," he said to the servant. "Make sure he sends a carriage to the riverside."

The boy scuttled off through the open front doors and into the rain. A footman in identical livery entered from the adjoining room and pushed the door closed, then took up a position against the wall.

She returned her eyes to Leo, who had his arms crossed. She fidgeted. He had the look of a man waiting for an answer, but she couldn't remember if he had asked a question. "What did you say?"

A muscle worked in his jaw. "You should have stayed with your aunt and sister. A storm is no place for a lady."

She snorted. "I shouldn't have to remind you I am not exactly a lady."

He cupped her cheek in his hand. "You could've been killed. Didn't you think about that? What would your family do if you got hurt?"

Before she could respond, a plump, bespectacled woman rushed them, her arms outstretched. Although she wore the same livery as the rest of the servants, the large ring of keys knotted to her belt with a thick rope marked her as a housekeeper.

Leo dropped his hand from her face and ran it through his wet hair. "Yes, Mrs. Banting? What has gone wrong now?"

"It's the grocer's bill, milord," the woman said between gasped breaths. "They've sent a beater of a man to collect payment."

"Then pay the man. What's the problem?"

The woman clutched her hands together at her waist. "I swear I left payment in the usual place. But it's disappeared! Oh, milord, I don't have a clue where the funds have made off to."

Saffron could not stop herself from interjecting. "Surely, this can wait until morning."

The housekeeper balled her fists at her sides, opened her mouth, and wailed. There was no other word for it. She sobbed, her head tilted up, mouth wide open.

Saffron gaped, then turned to Leo, surprised at his lack of response. Most other men she knew would have burst into a temper and fired the woman on the spot. No self-respecting lord tolerated such actions from those under his employ. Certainly not from his housekeeper, a position of considerable power within a household.

But Leo only groaned and buried his head in his hands, muttering something about responsibilities. The other servants slunk silently away, as if accustomed to such outbursts, and in short order, it was only the three of them in the cavernous entryway.

The opulence that had blinded Saffron on first seeing the grand estate shattered, and she saw the cracks in the façade. All was not well at the Briarwood estate. She filed that information away for later as a potential opportunity to assist with her search.

"Fine!" Leo shouted over the wailing. "Cease your caterwauling. I will handle it."

The woman paused, her mouth still agape, her cheeks flushed. "You will?"

He smiled tightly. "Allow me a moment to exchange my clothing, and then I will send Sinclair to the coffers to retrieve the funds you require." He grabbed Saffron's shoulders and shoved her toward the housekeeper. "Miss Summersby is our guest. Please see she is comfortable."

With that, he ran from the room, leaving Saffron standing next to Mrs. Banting while water dripped from her clothes and formed a puddle at their feet.

"Come, madam," Mrs. Banting said, tugging on her arm. "I will show you to your room."

Saffron followed the housekeeper up the central staircase and onto the first floor, then down a hallway decorated with red damask wallpaper in a swirling, floral pattern. Her feet made dark footprints in the thick red-and-gold carpeting that shared the same swirling pattern as the wallpaper. Chandeliers hung in even intervals between each set of doors, burning enough oil to supply the Summersby townhouse for a year. Yet despite the lush appointments, there was ample evidence of neglect. Black soot marks on the walls, wear patterns in the carpet, and an acrid odor that suggested the chandeliers had not been cleaned in some time.

So much wealth, and yet such commonplace issues have not been addressed.

The house was as much a mystery as its master.

"Here you are, ma'am," Mrs. Banting said, stopping at a door and opening it with a key from her keyring. "I hope you'll be comfortable here. I'll be off to the kitchen to deal with the beater from the grocer now."

She bustled Saffron inside before departing, leaving her to stare, open-mouthed, at the luxury surrounding her.

The suite was composed of three adjoining rooms. The first bedchamber contained a bed larger than any she'd seen in her life, piled high with blankets and pillows. She punched one experimentally to confirm it was filled with feathers. Two smaller bedchambers connected through single doors on either side of the room, each with its own color palette and expensive furnishings. It was startlingly like the home in the country she had grown up in, and she had to clear the tears misting her eyes.

We'll have it back.

Thus determined, she began the laborious process of shrugging off her wet clothes. She had made small progress when a young maid with bright-red hair exploded into the room without knocking, sending the doors banging against the walls. She let out a string of rapid-fire words in a language Saffron didn't recognize but thought might be Gaelic, then charged her.

"Madam," the maid said, in a scandalized Scottish accent. "You need not do such work on your own. Mrs. Banting let me know you were in need and assigned me to help. My name is Lily. Don't mind the doors, they're always a-slamming here."

Too tired to argue, Saffron allowed Lily to peel the wet clothing from her body, then shivered while the maid arranged for a large, copper tub and buckets of steaming water to be brought up. The backbreaking work was done by the sturdiest of the manservants, rather than the lowest on the household hierarchy. Seeing that raised her opinions of Leo a notch.

Once the tub was full, she sunk into the frothing, scented water with a sigh of pleasure.

Lily wasted no time pulling up her sleeves and scouring Saffron's long hair with a brush.

"Oh, madam," the maid said. "Your hair is beautiful but naught treated well. You must not shampoo dry hair such as this more than once a month. A wash of eggs and oat bran is what you rightly need to make it shine. I have done so since I was a lass."

Saffron kept her lips sealed. There was no point in telling the maid that any eggs she could afford went right onto their breakfast plates. She could not fathom wasting good food on beauty.

Then Lily disappeared, and Saffron dried and put up her hair at the small dressing table. She was about to begin the tortuous process of putting her still-damp garments back on when the maid returned, her arms full of fabric.

"Oh, no," Lily said, dumping her load on the bed and gathering the old clothes out of her hands. "You canna wear those. Mrs. Banting told me to bring you these."

The fabrics were lovely, and she knew she should refuse, but the thought of stepping back into her sodden clothing was too much to bear. Instead, she allowed Lily to hand her the most beautiful under-things she'd ever worn. First a chemise and drawers of sheer silk and knitted wool stockings for the cold. Then the maid pulled back the covers on the bed, but Saffron stopped her with a wave. She was too anxious to sleep, especially when Angelica and Rosemary had yet to arrive.

Lily smoothed the bedspread. "As you wish, madam." Then she brought over Saffron's old corset with an apology. "Would not want you to use one that was not properly fit, and the lady who owned this gown was a fair bit taller than you. This was the only gown we could find."

Saffron could not argue, although she hoped the clothes had not belonged to one of Leo's light ladies. She wasn't sure how she would feel about him looking at her the same way he would a woman he had bedded. It was difficult enough maintaining her composure around him after what they'd shared in the cottage without imagining him intertwined with the previous owner of her dress.

A snowy-white petticoat came next, and a blouse instead of a corset cover. Then Lily spread out a bodice and skirt on the bed for her to admire. The emerald-and-cream day dress was made of silk taffeta and velvet, with a low, square neckline, an open skirt, and dropped waist trimmed with a wide, cream, silk ribbon.

"It's lovely," she whispered as Lily helped her into it. "I haven't worn something this beautiful in my entire life."

To finish the ensemble, Lily presented her with a pair of emerald gloves, only slightly too large, and a pair of pale-green slippers. Her toes bumped up against the tips, but it was better than walking around in stockinged feet.

When she was finally dressed, she stared at herself in the mirror, breathless. Proper attire was a kind of shield, invisible to most, but jarringly obvious when done cheaply. She had spent so long patching her old gowns until they were so thin as to be transparent that wearing proper, sturdy clothing filled her with a renewed sense of purpose.

I can do this. First, Ravenmore, then Basil.

"Much better," Lily said, her hands on her hips. "I will have your garments cleaned and returned to you, but if you'll be asking me, I think these suit you more."

Saffron dismissed Lily with thanks, then without a plan for what to do next, walked over to the window by the small writing desk and looked outside.

The storm had passed, leaving behind a rose-tinted sky as the first rays of the sun peeked over the tops of the trees. If she squinted through the scratched and dirty glass, she could make out the dotted shapes of staff working on the grounds, busy at their tasks, despite the remaining trickle of rain. How many people did an estate the size of Briarwood Manor employ?

She checked the ornate clock on the mantel, surprised that it was early morning. She did not know how long she had been on horseback. Had it been minutes or hours? The time spent in the cottage had passed with tremendous speed. She paced her room in a knot of worry. Every time she closed her eyes, she imagined the worst-case scenario of Angelica and Rosemary beset upon by brigands or highwaymen. Or, even worse, braving the storm themselves and falling victim to a flood or landslide.

What she needed was work. Something to keep her busy. But she had no garments to repair, or letters to write.

Remembering the incident in the entryway, she searched the room for a bell and found it in the corner. She grasped the heavy, braided cord, pulling it down in a quick motion. It wasn't long before there was a soft knock at her door.

"Enter," Saffron said.

A young maid with brown, plaited hair and a spattering of freckles opened the door. "Would you like a hot meal, madam? It's a few hours still before we'll be serving in the main parlor."

"No, thank you. Please tell Mrs. Banting I would like to speak to her."

The maid bowed and departed, closing the door with a soft whisper, in defiance of Lily's previous claims.

Left alone again, Saffron took a seat at the small desk and tried to calm her jittering nerves by organizing the contents of the drawers.

Twelve jars of ink. Fifteen sheets of vellum. Three fountain pens.

What if Angelica had set out after her? Would Leo's coachman even find her?

One bag of setting powder. Two wax seals.

There was nothing left to sort, but her mind refused to settle. Aunt Rosemary was sensitive to the cold. Would she take ill after being exposed for so long?

A gentle rapping at her door startled her. The housekeeper opened it when bidden, her hands tucked behind her back. "Terribly sorry to bother you, madam. You wanted to see me?"

"Yes," Saffron said, standing so fast that she rattled the table. This was her chance to begin her investigation. "I was hoping to speak with Ravenmore. Do you know if the painter has arrived yet?"

Mrs. Banting frowned. "I apologize, madam. There is no one with that name on the guest list."

Well, it had been worth an attempt. "Perhaps you might show me to the paintings for the auction? I find I am restless."

The housekeeper's lips thinned. "Lord Briarwood has made it clear that no guests should be allowed access to the items for the auction." She twisted her hands together at her waist. "Is there anything else you require?"

She could prowl the corridors, but what would it accomplish? Her time would be better spent making herself useful.

"Yes," she said. "You need help. I can provide it."

The housekeeper blanched. "Begging your pardon, but it would not be proper."

Saffron smoothed her hands along the bodice of her gown. "You would be doing me a kindness. The only family I have ever known is out there." She waved her hand toward the window. "I find myself thinking of them incessantly, which pains my heart."

The housekeeper seemed to struggle with something for a moment before her shoulders dropped. "A lady, cooking and cleaning? No, madam, I won't allow it. But there is something..."

"Whatever it is, I can help," Saffron said, more confidently than she felt.

Mrs. Banting nodded. "Well, you are right. I am in desperate need, madam. There is much to be done, and I am in a fluster on how to get it complete in time."

Finally. Something I can do that's not sitting around.

She was well acquainted with work, and it would force her mind to focus on something productive. She straightened. "You might as well avail yourself of my help while you can. When my aunt and sister arrive, I won't be able to assist you. What do you need?"

Chapter Eight

L EO STOOD IN front of a mirror in the small dressing room attached to his bedchamber and tugged his cravat from his neck. He dropped it onto a growing pile of colorful fabric, then kicked the pile into a corner.

His butler stood behind him. "Are you certain you wish to dress yourself, my lord?"

"Do you have to ask me that every time?" Leo asked.

Sinclair's eyebrows rose. "You do not have a valet, my lord."

"Then I'll hire one. As soon as the auction is over. For now, I do not wish to be disturbed."

The butler's lips thinned, but he nodded, then left.

Is this what it is like to be a viscount? Leo stared at his reflection in the scuffed mirror hanging from the wall, and another cravat that didn't match the waistcoat he wore. *To have not a moment for yourself?*

When he'd inherited the title, he'd issued instructions that any matters pertaining to the viscountcy continue as they had. He'd been so mired in grief that it had seemed a sensible decision. But with a parade of guests about to descend upon a house that was, by all reports, in a serious state of neglect, he wondered if he'd made a mistake.

The only rooms you ever cared about were your bedroom and studio.

His mind flickered back to Saffron, and he wondered how she had gotten on. The last time he'd seen her, she had worn an expression of betrayal as she'd been shuffled away by the housekeeper. He remembered what it felt like to hold her, steal her lips. It had taken every ounce of his self-control not to tumble her onto the bare floors of the cottage.

He couldn't wait to do it again.

A knock came at his door. He sighed and chose a cravat at random, hastily knotting it before opening the door. Sinclair stood in the hallway, clutching a key in both hands.

"I instructed you not to disturb me," Leo said. "Although I suppose it is too late now. What is the problem?"

"You must come at once. The-The woman, Miss Summersby, she—" Sinclair, normally stolid and unflappable, stuttered. "You must come at once."

It had been a long time since he'd seen anything get under Sinclair's skin, and it made him unaccountably amused, and even more curious about what Saffron had done to earn such a reaction.

He followed his butler out the door as the man continued to babble about Miss Summersby's unspecified, unacceptable behavior. By the time they'd stopped at the entrance to his office, he half-expected to find her laid out in the nude on the settee.

Not unless this is a dream.

"Please, my lord, rectify this before your guests arrive," Sinclair said, pointing to the closed doors. "It is unseemly. For a lady to indulge in such matters."

Leo leaned closer. He could make out muffled voices coming from within. When he touched a hand to the door, it was warm.

"I hardly know what to expect," he said, fingering the deep grooves on the door. "What could one woman do that would cause you such distress?"

Sinclair huffed, then turned on his heel and stormed away.

Pushing aside his amusement, he opened the door and peeked inside. Saffron was seated at his desk, bent over an open book. Long strands of black hair hung limply by her cheek.

He closed the door as softly as he could, then stepped into the shadow of a wardrobe.

His eyes burned as he watched her. She wore one of Sabrina's old gowns, which was a surprise, as he hadn't known there were any left in the house. It was a significant improvement from the gray dresses she had worn before. The emerald hues made her look every bit the lady of the house.

Her color was better, too. Given her slender physique, he had worried the rain might have left her drained.

"What would you say for luncheon, then, madam?"

His housekeeper sat on a stool before the roaring hearth, clutching a small, leatherbound notebook in her hand and a pencil in the other. As Saffron spoke, Mrs. Banting frantically scribbled.

Saffron tapped her fingers on the desk. "A light fare for the ladies. Bread and cold meats."

His housekeeper's hand flew as she jotted down notes, her feet kicking back and forth.

"Do you have a seating plan for dinner?" Saffron asked. Then she sniffed. "No, of course not. Well, I believe there was something…" She shuffled through the papers on his desk, then selected a sheet and raised it in her hands. "Ah, here it is." She bent over a piece of paper and sketched something out. "It is best to keep the quieter guests spread out between those who are more social. In that way, we can ensure a better experience for all."

She patted the ink on her parchment dry with some setting powder and then passed it over to his housekeeper, who gripped it as if it were a ten-pound note. In less than an hour, Saffron had secured the trust of one of the most important members of his household.

Wasn't that interesting?

"It seems as if you have everything under control here," he said.

Saffron jumped out of the chair at the sound of his voice. Her hands flew to her face, tucking the stray strands of hair behind her ears. He wished she hadn't. She looked adorably distracted and rumpled. His loins stirred at the thought of her splayed beneath him on his bed, her dark hair an inky blot on his white linens.

"I'm terribly sorry," she said, pushing her chair back from behind his desk so quickly, it squealed on the floor. "You appeared to need someone to handle the logistics, and I was free."

"I appreciate the help," he said. "Share with me your magic so I may continue the excellent work you have done. Surely, you are my fairy godmother come to grant my wishes before the ball begins."

She slapped a hand over her lips to hide her grin. A flush spilled over her cheeks, and his eyes dropped to the cream lace at her bust.

He would buy her pearls, he decided. A string of pearls to wrap around her neck and trail down into her décolletage. Then he would follow the path of those pearls with his lips and tongue.

As if reading his thoughts, she spun around. All the better. He gazed at her back, imagining the curves that lay beneath her many layers of clothing. The lobes of her rear fit perfectly in his hands, and she was tall enough that when he held her close, her head tucked just beneath his chin.

She clasped Mrs. Banting's hands. "If you require further help, please know that you can call on me."

His housekeeper adjusted her spectacles on her nose, repeated her thanks, then made for the door.

"If you don't mind me saying so, milord," she said to Leo, holding her precious notebook to her chest. "Hold on to that one. She has a right smart head on her shoulders. If she has not yet been taken, swoop her up."

"Mrs. Banting!" Saffron said, her tone scandalized. The housekeeper giggled as she scurried out of the room, leaving them alone and unchaperoned. The air between them seemed to spark with electricity.

Saffron rubbed her hands together, then ripped them apart and walked over to the desk. She lifted some papers that hung over the edge, then set them down in a pile. "If that is all—"

"Wait," he said. He'd assumed that his staff had everything they needed to prepare for the event, but Mrs. Bantings's transparent happiness shamed him. He had ordered them to do whatever was necessary to ready the house for the auction without considering how much work that might entail.

How long have they been covering for my lack of action?

Even more worrisome, what else had he forgotten? If he wanted to find the person who was stealing Sabrina's paintings, it was in his best interest to ensure the auction went smoothly. He could not investigate if he was busy dealing with one disaster after another, and here was a solution packaged neatly before him.

"I have a proposition for you," he said, finally.

"W-What?" She stumbled back a step, holding out her arms as if to ward him off.

He splayed a hand over his face to muffle a groan. "Not like that."

"What is it, then?" she asked sharply.

He had intended to approach the matter more delicately, but her stiff posture made him fear she might flee, so he blurted out the words, "Someone tried to steal the Ravenmore."

She gasped. "What? When did this happen?"

"Shortly before I met you in the storm. I tried to follow but lost the trail."

In a way, he was thankful for the thief. If the crash had not woken him, he might not have met her in the forest. He did not want to imagine what fate she might have met otherwise.

She chewed her bottom lip. "Could it have been the driver who abandoned us by the crossing?"

That would explain the evidence he'd seen of a horse outside his window. "Perhaps." The man could've intended to use the Summers-by family as an excuse to approach the house and then used the carriage to transport the painting back to whoever had hired him.

Her shoulders slumped. "Then I brought a thief to your door."

The guilt in her voice bothered him. "You were not the one who invited them here. I am certain one of my guests is behind the attempt."

As she considered his words, he felt as if his nerves were stretched taut. He could manage without her, he was sure, but a part of him wanted to keep her close.

She sighed. "What do you need me to do?"

A powerful sense of relief washed over him. "I can trail the men, but I need someone to watch the women while I do so. I could use your help. Discreetly, of course."

Surprise flashed across her face. "Then we are agreed. I will help you find your thief, and I will assist you in organizing this auction. But I have a condition of my own."

He remembered their encounter in Percy's office. It was easy to guess her goal. "You want to talk to Ravenmore?"

Saffron smiled. "Precisely."

He buried his hands in his hair. Was it worth it? As long as his sister's paintings remained in museums, Sabrina's legacy was secure. No one would forget the anonymous painter who had taken the London art scene by storm. Then there was the fact that Saffron had her own motives. Ones she refused to reveal. Left to her own, her attempts to uncover Ravenmore might hinder his plans. She would be furious when he told her the truth, but he would deal with that when the time came. Life was much easier when one focused only on the present.

"I accept your terms," Leo said. "After the auction, I will introduce you to Ravenmore. I will tell my butler, Sinclair, to give you access to everything you need. In exchange, I need you to tell me why this is so important." He stepped closer. "Why are you so damned determined to talk to Ravenmore?"

Chapter Nine

S AFFRON BACKED AWAY from Leo, hitting a chair in the process and nearly tumbling over. She wanted to tell him about Basil and the painting, but every time she tried to get the words out, they wouldn't come. If he knew the truth, would he still agree to help her? Or would he, like Aunt Rosemary, insist that she was wrong, and Basil was dead?

She couldn't take the chance. Not when Angelica's future was at risk.

"So quiet, suddenly," Leo said, closing the space between them with frightening speed. "That's okay. I have my own ways of getting information I want."

He wrapped his arms around her. "Stop thinking," he breathed, touching his nose to hers. "I can see the fight in you. Just give in and do what feels right." He tilted his face and met her lips with his in a gentle kiss. It lasted only a moment before he pulled away, then kissed her again.

"Take what you want," he said, brushing his palm over her breast. "Take it."

She sank into Leo's deepening kisses, opening her mouth to him. He murmured his enjoyment into her lips, but it wasn't enough. She needed to feel more of him, needed his hands on her skin. She pulled at the strings behind her dress, but he stopped her. Then his face came down on her neck and his tongue swirled in the whorl of her throat, making her gasp.

"So lovely," he said. He tucked his hand beneath her bodice and fondled her breast, tucking his fingers under her corset and tweaking her nipple with his fingers. Then he moved his attention from her neck to her earlobe, taking it into his mouth and sucking gently.

She bumped into his desk and fell onto it. The desk screeched as it slid under the force of her weight. His hand crept beneath the many layers of her gown and underthings, rubbing small circles on her bare flesh. He ripped her stockings free from their garters in one swift tug. Then he trailed his palms along the inside of her thighs, up and down.

"Leo, please." She didn't know what she was asking for, but her pelvis throbbed, and she ached with the need for his touch.

A guttural growl and his mouth was on hers again. Then he slid one finger inside her sheath, rubbing in a way that made her back arch like a cat. Pleasure ebbed and flowed, building up to a crescendo, then slipping out of her grasp.

"That's it," he coaxed, moving his fingers faster while kneading her breast. "Come apart for me."

The rising tide rolled over her and a piercing, delicious sensation rippled out from where his hands touched her. The waves of pleasure radiated all the way to the tips of her ears and her toes, leaving her panting.

"God, Saffron," he said, smoothing her clothing back into place. "You do not know how much I want you." He took a shuddering breath, then stepped away.

Her eyes fell to the prominent bulge tenting his trousers. She was not innocent. Three years spent pinching her pennies, seeking any deal with the butcher, grocer, and others in less-than-savory areas of town to prolong her funds, had opened her eyes. She'd seen men taking women against tavern walls, moaning and thrashing. Her torrid romance novels had described the act in detail and had kept her awake at night imagining what it might feel like to be with a man.

She'd had no idea.

But despite how pleasurable it had been, she couldn't push aside how scandalous her actions were.

"I... cannot do this," she said, edging her way to the door. "We are not wed."

She was not opposed to the idea of marriage if it meant saving Angelica from marriage to Canterbury. It was clear they were compatible on some level, and it would allow her to support her family. Even if he remained a recluse, she didn't mind living outside of London.

Then Leo scowled. "I am not the marrying kind."

His words stung more than she'd expected, but she forced her emotions aside. "You do not wish to produce an heir?"

He snorted. "I never wanted to be Viscount Briarwood to begin with. Besides..." He stepped closer and smirked. "We do not need to be married to enjoy each other's company."

She gave a startled sound and fled his office as if he'd thrown a bucket of cold water over her head, then flew through the halls of the house. She'd never been so close to a man who wasn't a blood relative. A man who looked at her like a woman and not a piece of furniture, or an extension of her sister or aunt, and he was not interested in marriage.

At least she'd finally experienced what her romance novels described.

Her skin still burned from where he'd touched, and her body thrummed with pleasure.

No wonder the ladies swoon before him.

She flushed at the memory of their bodies intertwined on top of his desk. Despite knowing she had truly ruined herself, she couldn't bring herself to care. Leo had brought her something she hadn't even known she'd wanted.

"It will be fine," she said, pausing in front of a suit of armor to fix her torn stockings. The deal they had struck complicated her plans, but not irrevocably. She had already come to play the detective.

The only difference is that I am searching for both a thief and a painter.

No matter what she'd promised, it was in her best interest to continue her investigation alongside what he had tasked her to do. Thanks to Leo, she had a list of attendees to analyze and interrogate.

First of the Ravenmore suspects on her list was Simon Mayweather, Leo's cousin. She could imagine the charismatic man taking up his time painting. He had the casual, artistic air of a man who kept secrets.

Second was the Lady Olivia Allen, the beautiful widow of the late Earl of Allen. Saffron had never met the woman, but rumor held she was a collector of artwork. She also had a reputation for being mysterious and coy. Leo had suggested at Lady Jarvis's ball that women were not generally accepted as painters by the Royal Society of Arts. Could Lady Allen have chosen the alias Ravenmore to tweak the noses of the upper elite?

Third and fourth were Mr. and Mrs. Morgan. She'd learned through talking to the housekeeper that both were late additions to the event. One or both could be Ravenmore. She did not know enough about them to judge if that was likely.

Then there was Leo himself. As much as she didn't want to believe that he would keep such a secret from her, it was Leo who had put her on to the idea that Ravenmore was an alias. She would not remove him from consideration until she was certain he was not the painter.

There remained a chance that the artist was someone else attending the auction, but she would not consider them without cause until she had ruled out the others.

She slowed her steps as she approached the front entrance, comporting herself into the genteel lady she had to project to the world. Her head tilted higher, and she schooled her expression into one of mild interest. The act was tiring to keep up, but she had learned over the years that she could not show her real self without facing derision. She checked her coiffure in the reflection of an ancient Roman shield mounted on the wall, tucking a few curls back into place. Then she scowled at herself. Whom was she trying to impress?

"I know what I am doing," she said to her reflection.

A footman standing by the door smothered a laugh. She hurried past him before she embarrassed herself further and arrived in the entryway to find Mrs. Banting arguing with Leo's butler, Sinclair.

"It is not proper," the housekeeper insisted. "The ladies with maids cannot stay in the rooms in the east wing. I will not be responsible for any more injuries on that staircase. We will have to move the paintings."

Paintings?

Sinclair shook his head. "Let's not forget the gentlemen and their valets. Would you subject them to that staircase instead? My lord was quite clear on this matter. We are not to touch the items for the auction."

Like a bloodhound scenting a trail, Saffron leaped into the conversation. "May I be of assistance?"

Mrs. Banting pursed her lips. "Madam, this matter is not your concern. We will find a solution."

The two servants turned toward each other, closing her out.

She cleared her throat. "I have never met a maid who would avoid a simple staircase."

That did the trick.

Both servants gaped at her for a moment, then stories poured out of them both. Tales that chilled her blood.

"We've had three scullery maids quit this month," the housekeeper said. "They can't avoid it, madam, as it's right by the kitchen. There is no other staircase in the east wing."

Sinclair elbowed her aside. "The footmen refuse to use it. They go around to the other side of the estate, which takes twice as long."

Saffron held up a hand, silencing them as she recalled the floor plan that she'd found in Leo's office that morning. The estate was a three-pronged building with a set of servants' stairs in each wing. The kitchen was in the east wing on the main floor. Most of the guest rooms were in that wing, including her own room. From what she'd overheard, the paintings were somewhere in the east wing. That was a useful piece of information.

"What about the rooms in the west wing?" She remembered the small writing on the sheet of paper. Those rooms were reserved for use by the viscountess, but given that the viscount was unmarried, she did not think they were being used.

Mrs. Banting blanched. "We have not yet cleaned those rooms. They've remained closed since…" She shot the butler an anxious look.

"Quite," Sinclair said. "The viscountess's rooms will not do."

Their nervous reactions made her curious, but Sinclair's tone brooked no argument, so she let the matter go and turned her mind to alternatives. She'd always had a fantastic memory, ever since she'd been a child. She collected and cataloged everything she saw, and if she was lucky, she found cause to use the information rather than let it clutter up her head.

If only such a skill were valued by the Ton.

"The rooms near the nursery in the north wing," she said. "That is the only other option."

Mrs. Banting fidgeted with the keys at her belt. "I suppose we could move the furniture around."

Before they could argue the point further, Saffron clapped her hands. "Excellent. Then Mr. and Mrs. Morgan can take the first bedroom, and…" She called out the remaining couples and unattached guests, working from her memory of the guest list she had found in Leo's office.

She was so preoccupied with sorting out the problem that she only barely registered the increasingly loud clattering coming from outside.

BOOM.

She jumped at the sound. A footman hurried from his post to pull the doors open as a bedraggled figure burst into the foyer, spraying water all over the freshly waxed floors.

"I thought we would never arrive," Angelica said, shaking the water from her hair.

Saffron rushed across the room to wrap her arms around her sister, forgetting her new gown until the cold pierced through the thick fabric.

Angelica squeezed her back. "I thought you had perished," she whispered.

"I would never leave you," Saffron replied. Then she grasped Angelica's shoulders and pushed her away, analyzing her with a critical eye. Although her skin was a shade too pale, and her clothes sodden, her eyes had none of the cloudiness she'd feared. In fact, even with her hair plastered all down her back and pins falling to the floor like a concord of music, Angelica was beautiful.

"Do not cause a scene, dear," Rosemary said, strolling into the foyer at a more sedate pace. Unlike her niece, she stood still while several servants plied her with towels.

"Just wait until you see the rooms," Saffron said, clutching Angelica's hands. "They are simply gorgeous."

Rosemary sniffed. "I would hope so."

Angelica lifted her foot and her muddy slipper made a sucking sound as it split from the tile floor. She grimaced. "Right now, I would settle for dry clothes and a warm bath. It feels as if we've been through Shakespeare's tempest."

"Of course," Saffron said. "I will see to it at once."

She looked around for Mrs. Banting, but finding her gone, she touched the sleeve of a passing maid. When the girl turned to her, eyes wide, Saffron gave her what she hoped was a reassuring smile. "Please arrange for my sister's and aunt's trunks to be taken up to the rooms next to mine."

"Yes, madam," the maid said.

"I didn't realize you were the mistress of the house already,"

Rosemary said. The servants had divested her of her outer clothing and were ushering them up the stairs.

"You know our Saffron." Angelica laughed. "If she weren't constantly helping someone, she might actually learn how to relax."

Chapter Ten

L EO LEANED BACK in his chair in his office and stared up at the ceiling. Exhaustion burned in every muscle, but at the thought of Saffron, his body came alive.

He reached beneath his desk to where his cock stood at attention, freed from the fall of his trousers, and imagined her in his arms. The light-pink flush of her skin over her bosom drawing his mouth closer. He would love to kiss that pert nose, see her smile.

She would bend over his desk, and he would flip her skirts back and dive into the sweet heat of her entrance, riding her until she came apart. He would stay anchored inside her and wait the few moments she needed to recover, holding on to his passion with iron control. When she stopped shuddering, he would plunge into her again and empty his seed inside her.

Other men have mistresses for such a task, Leo thought, panting hard. He finished into his neckcloth and threw it into a corner for some maid to find in the morning and giggle.

With some tension drained, he tucked himself away and pulled open the middle drawer of his desk to reveal a collection of dusty glass bottles that wobbled and clinked together. He selected one at random, pulled out the cork with his teeth, then took a long swig. When it was empty, he replaced it in the drawer, then knocked the drawer closed with his knee.

He thought about returning to his newly relocated studio and working on his latest piece, but a distant thud and murmuring of voices reminded him that his time was no longer his own. As host to the event, it would be rude if he was not present to greet his guests as they arrived.

He straightened his waistcoat, then strolled out of his office and down the hallway to stand at the top of the stairs and observe the chaos erupting in his entryway. When he realized it was Saffron's aunt and sister arriving, he turned around and took a longer route to the front door. It took an extra few minutes, but he did not want to interrupt their reunion.

By the time he'd navigated the creaking stairs and cold halls to return to the foyer, Saffron and her family were no longer present. He waited for a moment, unsure of what to do next, when the front doors creaked open and two men entered, engaged in conversation. The first was Simon, dressed in a dark-blue waistcoat and trousers. In one hand he carried an enormous umbrella, and with the other, he gestured to his companion, a man in his late forties with streaks of silver shot through his black hair and a matching salt-and-pepper mustache. The man wore a tall, domed hat and an ankle-length, dark-blue, wool coat. He kept his hands on a black, leather belt high on his waist.

Leo had almost forgotten that he had sent for the constable.

Simon spotted him and raised a hand in greeting, then turned to his companion. "Can't say I've ever heard of mischief around these parts before."

"A nuisance, I'm sure," the constable said. "I'll get this sorted out as soon as I can." The man caught Leo's eye and straightened. "You would be the Viscount Briarwood, Lord Leopold Mayweather?"

The use of his title sent gooseflesh pricking up his arm. "The viscount" was his father, then later his brother. But both were dead, and the title was his responsibility.

"Indeed," he said, his voice echoing as he descended the stairs.

Simon removed his hat and handed it off to a servant. "I met Detective Jansen on the ferry. He told me of the nasty business of the break-in."

"I am surprised you arrived so soon," Leo said. "Did the storm not wash out the bridge?"

The detective removed his hat. "It was in working order by the time I passed over, but I'd rather not tally long. The surging waters can wipe out logs in a moment, and my wife would not be happy if I did not return for supper."

"Of course," Leo said. "Follow me and I will show you to the scene."

As he guided the detective to the room that had once held his studio, Saffron appeared at his side.

He tucked her hand into the crook of his arm, then turned to his cousin. "Simon, I believe you've met Miss Summersby. She came to some trouble along the road."

His cousin removed his hat and bowed. "I am sorry to hear that, Miss Summersby. Is your sister—"

"Angelica is well," Saffron said, interrupting. "She accompanied me, along with my aunt."

Simon tugged at the bottom of his waistcoat. "Excellent. Well, cousin, we should not keep the detective waiting."

Leo guided the group to the sitting room. He had relocated all the implements and products of his craft, leaving a cavernous room that was occupied by a single, horsehair sofa, an oval, walnut table, and a gilded-bronze lamp. It was so different from the sanctuary he had established that he hesitated on the threshold, horrified by the transformation. The very soul of the room had been sucked out, leaving behind a hollow shell.

That's what society does, forcing out all uniqueness to emphasize only what is acceptable.

Simon and the detective crossed the bare floor to inspect the boarded-up window. Saffron, however, split from the group and conversed quietly with a maid, who then rushed away.

"I asked them to move in some additional seating and a few paintings from other areas of the house," she said when she rejoined him. "This room is near the entrance, and you want to ensure that it gives the right first impression to your guests."

He could've kissed her, but she flitted out of his grasp.

"Be careful." He pointed to the tips of her feet, peeking out from beneath her gown, covered in silk slippers. "There may still be shards of glass on the floor. I would not want you to injure yourself."

"I am sure your staff has done a thorough job," she said. He searched the floor in front of her as she went, his heart pounding with every step, expecting her to let out a high-pitched cry as a shard cut through her thin slippers. When nothing happened, he forced his attention back to the problem at hand.

The detective crouched by the window, one hand on his chin, the other holding a small notepad. "You say nothing was disturbed?" He peered out the window, where long branches scraped against the sides of the house in the buffeting wind. "Might it have been one of them branches that done the deed?"

"There was a branch, but the end was cleanly cut. There was also mud on the carpet inside, and evidence of a horse sitting for some time nearby," Leo said, as Saffron surreptitiously used a corner of her gown to remove a streak of mud from the window frame. "I searched the woods but lost the track by the cliff. I suspect he had a ship docked nearby."

The detective scribbled on the notepad. "Well, I'm not sure what we might do. Destruction of property, that's a crime, but it will be blasted hard to catch the man, what with the storm. I would guess any evidence is long gone by now."

Leo sighed. Although he had expected as much and had already moved his canvases to a secured room where only his most trusted servants could enter, he had the overwhelming urge to rush to the room and count the canvases and make sure there were none missing.

"What do you suggest, then?" he asked, doing his best to keep his tone even as Saffron wandered away to direct the newly arrived Mrs. Banting where to position more chairs, oblivious to the potential danger beneath her feet.

"You might hire some locals to keep guard," the detective said. "This isn't a case for Scotland Yard, my lord. Chances are, you spooked the thief right off and he won't soon return."

Leo had his doubts, but he understood there was little the law could do, even if he revealed the priceless pieces of art that had been present in the room on the night of the break-in. Better to take matters into his own hands.

"Thank you, Detective. We will consider your suggestions."

He walked the man out, partially to ensure he didn't wander around on his own, but also to remain occupied and unable to answer questions for some time longer. As expected, once the doors closed, his butler and housekeeper were at his side.

"Milord, the roast—"

"No room in the stables—"

He took a deep breath. Before he could settle their concerns, Saffron swept between them.

"Calm down, both of you," she said. "Now, Mrs. Banting, you start. What problem is so serious that you must accost your master mere moments before the guests arrive?"

Sinclair and the housekeeper plied the woman with a deluge of problems. As he watched, bemused, she triaged a new main course for the dinner and arranged for a new paddock with a temporary stable to be built that same afternoon.

"Your skills are wasted," he said once his servants had quit her side. "You would be a remarkable mistress of a household."

The moment he'd said the words, even in jest, he regretted them. He had no intention of ever marrying. A dalliance was acceptable, but taking a wife would make him vulnerable. He could not risk feeling the kind of pain he'd felt after Sabrina's death again.

Saffron's jaw trembled. "Indeed."

"If only there was a way to manage the lives of those around you without marriage," Angelica said from the stairs. Dressed in a silver-and-lilac gown with an overdress of white, pleated flounces and silk rosettes, she descended to stand beside her sister. Her curls were piled atop her head and decorated with iridescent beads.

"Are you sure you are recovered?" Saffron asked, touching her sister's cheek with her fingers.

"Stop fussing," Angelica said. "I'm fine. Aunt Rosemary is fine. You can stop worrying about us."

"If only that were possible," Saffron said.

Hoping to forestall a fight, Leo bowed before Angelica. "You are radiant, Miss Summersby. Nearly as radiant as your sister."

"You are too kind, Lord Briarwood," Angelica said, waving her fan in front of her face. "I must admit that a maid supplied us. Most of our gowns were soiled in the crash."

Well, that will not do.

"I will rectify that situation at once," he said. "My coachman will accompany you to the nearest dressmaker at your convenience. You may use my account." Angelica squealed.

"That wouldn't be proper," Saffron said, putting her hands on her hips. "You presume too much, Lord Briarwood."

Hearing her use his title bothered him, even though he knew she had to use the proper form of address around others. He looked forward to making her moan his name. Assuming he got a chance. He would not blame her if the next time they were alone, she insisted on maintaining a proper distance.

"As we have already established," he said, "I am entirely improper."

Angelica grabbed on to Saffron's arm. "Oh, please, sister, please say *yes*. It has been so long since we had new gowns."

He kept silent as the sisters argued, hoping that Saffron would realize his offer was practical, as much as it was his own secret desire to see her dressed in finer clothes. If she was going to help him in his search over the coming days, he needed her able to blend in. If she wore another gown like the one she'd worn at Lady Jarvis's ball, she would attract too much attention.

"If Aunt Rosemary agrees," Saffron said at last.

"I will ask her," Angelica said. She turned and rushed back up the stairs.

As Leo laughed, a loud boom sounded through the hall for the third time.

A footman hurried from the sitting room to pull the door open. A woman in an indigo day dress stepped over the threshold, her hand on the arm of a large man with a bulging stomach. The difference between the two was striking. The woman's brightly painted lips and low-cut bodice suited a woman half her age, whereas the man, with his mottled complexion and deep-set eyes, seemed like he might drop dead at any moment.

Three servants dressed in dark-brown livery hovered around the couple, holding overlapping umbrellas to keep the rain from touching their masters. On entering the hall, they bustled away, dragging the soaking wet umbrellas with them.

Saffron stood behind Leo, and as much as he wanted her by his side, he respected her choice.

"Mr. and Mrs. Morgan," Leo said, forcing a smile. "Welcome."

Mr. Morgan frowned. "Lord Briarwood. Didn't expect you to be the one to greet us."

Leo was growing rather tired of having to explain the state of his house. He was looking forward to the conclusion of the auction when he could return to his solitude.

"My butler is occupied with a more pressing matter," he said.

Mrs. Morgan inclined her head, making the peacock feathers in her bonnet bounce.

"Girls, present yourselves to Lord Briarwood," Mr. Morgan said before coughing into a handkerchief.

Two young ladies scurried forward, dressed in nearly identical bell-shaped gowns that differed only in shade.

"Miss Morgan," Leo said to the girl in lilac, bowing over her hand.

She gasped. "Lord Briarwood, you know my name?"

"Of course, and your sister." He clasped the hand of the girl in peach and bowed. "Miss Beatrice Morgan."

The girls tilted their dark blond heads together and giggled. Both were young, beautiful, and heiresses in their own right.

"Oh!" Mrs. Banting said, as she rushed into the room. "I apologize, my lord."

As she took charge of showing his guests to their rooms, Leo watched Mrs. Morgan order her daughters about. Mr. Morgan kept shooting glances down the hall. Could the Morgans have come to steal the Ravenmore? With two young daughters, he didn't think they had the time or privacy.

"Too young for you," Simon said, appearing at his shoulder without warning, making Leo jump.

"You're like a damn ghost," Leo said. "Must you sneak around like that?"

Simon shrugged. "Perhaps rather than my stealth, you might say it was you who had your mind in the clouds." He glanced around, then smiled at Saffron. "Hello, Miss Summersby. Will your sister be joining us this evening?"

"I could not keep her away if I tried," Saffron said.

Then the door creaked, and Simon turned. "Ah, my favorite of your guests has arrived."

A tall, raven-haired woman strolled through the front doors wearing a sleek, crimson gown with a low neckline and cinched waist. Lady Olivia Heather, the Countess Dowager of Allen. He had not spoken to her in months, but she was as beautiful as the day they had met, shortly after the death of her husband, the Earl of Allen.

Simon stepped forward to greet her. "Lady Allen. As lovely as always."

The woman's rouged lips curved into a smile as she accepted Simon's greeting. "Mr. Mayweather. I look forward to renewing our association."

Leo heard Saffron gasp and reached out to take her hand before she could retreat, pinning him to her side.

"What is she doing here?" Saffron hissed.

Leo squeezed her hand. "It's not what it seems."

Saffron huffed. "Really? You didn't invite your mistress to this event? The same woman who was fawning over you at Lady Jarvis's ball, when we first met?"

Lady Allen met his gaze and raised one sleek eyebrow. He shook his head slightly, then took a step backward, forcing Saffron along with him. He led her out of the room and into a dark corner before realizing she was tugging at her hand.

Look what you've done now. You'll be lucky if she doesn't hate you.

He released her, increasing the distance between them before he could do something stupid, like kiss her. Her eyes were wide and misty, her lips twisted, her brows drawn together.

"Trust me," he said. "Please. Let me explain."

She bit her lip, crossed her arms, then nodded, once. "Fine. Explain."

He took a deep breath, exhaled. "Yes, Lady Allen was my mistress, but I severed our arrangement years ago."

He could see the suspicion in the hard lines of Saffron's face, and the indecision in her eyes. She wanted to believe him; he just had to give her a reason.

"Why is she here?" she asked.

"Our parents were friends," he said.

"Could she be—"

"Olivia is too refined to stoop to theft," Leo said, interrupting Saffron's accusation. Of all his guests, he suspected Lady Allen of being the thief the least. Seduction, trickery, and blackmail were Olivia's weapons, not theft.

"See to your guests," Saffron said. "I-I must make sure my sister and aunt are settled in their rooms. I will return shortly."

"Of course." Leo bowed, and when he straightened, she was gone.

At least she didn't reject you.

He had feared that exact outcome, a termination of their agreement, and the weight of it still rested heavily on his shoulders. In the short time he'd known her, Saffron had become important to him. That was the most terrifying thought of all.

Restless, he returned to the entryway, where Olivia was waiting. She met his gaze and smiled, but the expression held none of the heat that he'd expected.

"Lady Allen, I apologize that you were not greeted properly."

"A trifling matter." Her eyes sparkled. "I am far more interested in your relationship with Miss Summersby. I saw the way she looked at you. Quite the mess you've landed yourself in, Leopold. You will give me the entire story when it is over." She held out her gloved hand, and he pressed a kiss to her fingers, then handed her off to a footman, who took one look at the mountain of trunks being loaded from her carriage into the foyer and paled.

"I would suggest you consider a household bonus after this event," Olivia said as they watched the footman struggle to carry a trunk up the stairs. "Unless you want to hire a new staff."

Leo closed his eyes. It was only three days. He could manage three days of disruption.

Chapter Eleven

AFTER SEEING TO her family's health and comfort, Saffron was reluctant to return to the entrance.

I should observe each of the guests as they arrive.

How they interacted with their host might provide clues as to their motives.

Her reluctance had nothing to do with her dislike of meeting strangers, however, and everything to do with the memory of Leo's face as she'd left him. She'd been angry at him at first, when she'd seen Lady Allen, but the softness in his eyes had nearly undone her.

With a mere glance, he shatters me.

She paused at a corner and straightened her back. It was a lapse in judgement, nothing more. He had made his view on marriage clear. The physical attraction between them would soon fade, and they would go their separate ways.

Solidifying that idea in her mind, she returned to Leo's side and plastered a wide smile on her face through a dizzying array of arrivals. Thankfully, there were enough people milling about that her presence at Leo's side was not commented upon. Most of the well-dressed couples entering through the grand entrance skimmed their gazes over her as if she were invisible and plied their attention on the viscount.

That is fine with me, she thought. Their disinterest was to her advantage because she could listen in on conversations without being noticed.

Then the footman flung open the oak doors and revealed a sight that made her stomach churn.

What is the Duke of Canterbury doing here?

Leo tightened his hand on her arm. "Your Grace. I was not expecting the pleasure of your company."

The duke's black coat was slick with rain and his cheeks were flushed, although how much of that was from the unpleasant weather, Saffron could not guess. Distantly, she realized her legs were trembling. Canterbury's presence threatened to derail her plans, as it certainly meant the man intended to continue his pursuit of Angelica.

"Briarwood. I heard about your little soiree and decided to pay a visit," the duke said. "I have a particular fondness for beautiful things, you understand."

A horde of servants streamed in behind him, heavily laden with trunks and boxes. Each one kept their eyes carefully downcast, like a pack of abused dogs with their tails between their legs. It was another subtle sign that the duke was not what he appeared. What kind of man treated his servants like pack animals?

I cannot let this beastly man marry my sister.

Finding her brother would not help her if Rosemary convinced Angelica to marry the duke first. She would have to keep him occupied and far away from her sister.

The first step was to ensure his rooms were not in the east wing. She inched back, set on finding Mrs. Banting and arranging things to her advantage, but Leo kept an iron grasp on her hand.

"There are several pieces on the docket that would suit your preferences, Your Grace," Leo said. "If you would excuse me, I must speak with my housekeeper about preparing a suitable set of rooms."

Canterbury's brows furrowed, and his gaze dropped to land on Saffron. She tensed and shuddered as the duke's eyes swept down her body to her toes and back up again. He did not leer, but she felt uncomfortable, like she needed to bathe to remove the stain of his lecherous interest. "Miss Summersby."

She curtseyed just slightly. "Your Grace."

"Come, Miss Summersby," Leo said, his tone as hard as granite. "I must introduce you to the Duke of Hawthorne."

She allowed him to lead her out of the room, her hand clenched on his arm. When they were out of earshot, she forced herself to relax, one muscle at a time.

"Believe me when I say that I did not invite that blackguard," Leo said. A vein pulsed at his temple. "I wish I could throw him out on his ear."

The repressed anger in his words somehow made her feel better. Perhaps because she had expected him to shrug off her concerns, as so many others did.

"He will attempt to secure the closest rooms to ours," Saffron said, running through the options in her head. Where could she put him such that he would cause the least amount of damage? What if he was already talking to the staff, arranging things to suit his plans? She thrust away from Leo. "Please excuse me. I must speak to Mrs. Banting."

She scurried away, but before she could find the housekeeper, she ran into her aunt, who pinned her with a stare.

"There you are. Your sister requires your assistance in her room."

A dozen awful scenarios flitted through her mind, all at once, and she abandoned her task to join her aunt's side. "Was it the cold, after all? Has she come down with fever?"

Rosemary huffed. "Of course not. It is her attire. I checked in on her, and she is not dressed appropriately. She must look her best for His Grace tonight."

Saffron sighed. "I would rather she stay as far away from that man as possible. He is much too old for her."

Not to mention cruel.

"Spare me your dramatics," Rosemary said. "I am glad I sent off that missive before we left, or he might not have arrived in time."

Saffron stopped dead in the middle of the hallway. "You did *what?*"

It had not been a coincidence, after all. Rosemary had sabotaged her.

Her aunt opened the door to her room, then stood in the doorway, one eyebrow arched. "What did you expect me to do? We have mere months before we lose our home. Angelica must get engaged as soon as possible."

"But Basil might still be—"

"Your brother is dead, Saffron. You are no longer a child. Put your fantasies away."

It's not a fantasy.

The proof was in the painting. All she had to do was find Ravenmore, and he would confirm that Basil lived.

While there remained a chance, however slim, that she could restore their family, she would pursue it. She would not give up her task, even with her aunt and Canterbury standing in the way.

No matter the cost.

Chapter Twelve

L EO PACED THE length of his office in a black temper. After greeting his guests and sending them off to their rooms to prepare for the afternoon's activities, he had searched the estate for Saffron and come up empty. She'd agreed to aid him in his search, but she had said nothing about reporting her efforts. He should have made her promise to keep him informed of what she had planned.

Instead, the woman was traipsing all over his property.

What he wouldn't admit was that he *longed* for her company. She was a breath of fresh air in a world too dark and stifled for his liking. When she was around, a weight lifted from his shoulders.

A mental image of Saffron falling down a rickety set of stairs flashed into his mind, and he shuddered. If something happened to her because he had failed to keep the house in good repair, he would never forgive himself.

He took a swallow of courage—brandy—and stormed out of his office. As he passed, his staff moved out of the way, pressing themselves against the wall.

Lady Allen stood at the top of the main stairway, examining a painting hung on the wall. He wanted to rush past her, but that would have been considered intolerably rude. Olivia was willing to forgive some transgressions, but rudeness was not one of them. Since she was among the least likely of his guests to be his thief, it was in his best interests to stay in her good graces.

"How are you finding your accommodations?" he asked.

"Exquisite, as always," Olivia said. "I wondered when you would come to me." Then she smiled at him. He recognized that smile from when he had engaged the beautiful woman as his mistress.

"You have other things on your mind, my lord, do you not?" Olivia asked with a wink. "Such as the location of a certain raven-haired lady?"

How does she know?

Gooseflesh pimpled his arms. "I am indeed looking for Miss Summersby. We have unresolved matters to address."

Olivia giggled. "'Unresolved matters.' I am certain I do not know what you are talking about, my lord."

He shuffled his feet. The woman always made him feel like a schoolboy begging for favors from a teacher. Rather than face her wiles, he turned to the painting she had been examining. It was one of the few he'd selected for the auction, an old piece from Italy depicting a group of peasants crowding around a woman holding a swaddled baby. A maid kneeled on the floor, holding out a cloth to the child. The painting was tinged with deep red, giving the scene a sense of morbidity, which was only aided by small cracks in the fresco.

"Enough with the games, Olivia," Leo said. "Have you seen Miss Summersby or not?"

Lady Allen touched her fingers to his shoulder. "Such passion. How I long for my days of adventure. Alas, they are long past. I wish you the best, Leopold."

With that, she swished her skirts and set off down the hallway.

Ambiguous, as always, and entirely unhelpful.

Frustrated, he glared at the painting in front of him. His eye was drawn to the maid, holding out a cloth to the child while being spurned and kicked by the uncaring people surrounding her.

Maybe that was the key. Saffron was incapable of stopping herself from barging into the lives of others, as she'd done when she'd inserted herself into his household. Somewhere, he was certain, she was engaged in solving a problem.

The kitchen.

Mrs. Banting and Sinclair had previously reported that the cook had complained about the state of the larder. It was as good a guess as any.

Rather than take the grand staircase and risk running into more of his guests, Leo slipped into a servants' hallway and ran into his housekeeper, approaching from the opposite end.

"Milord!" She fluttered her hands. "Whatever is wrong?"

He ground his teeth. The woman filled the hallway such that it was impossible to pass.

"Have you seen Miss Summersby?" he asked.

The housekeeper beamed. "Oh, yes. She sorted out a disaster in the stable. I think I may have even seen Mr. Sinclair smile. It was quite a sight. The woman is a marvel. I am terribly glad she is here to assist us. I wouldn't know what to do without her. Just this morning—"

Leo groaned. "Mrs. Banting, we can discuss Miss Summersby's charms later. You said you saw her in the stables. When was this?"

He had no hope of catching her if she had taken off on horseback for whatever foolish reason. The thought of her on a horse after he had chased her in the storm made his palms sweat. The trails were still slick with mud. She could easily break her neck.

"Only a few moments ago, milord," Mrs. Banting said. "Then a footman came and summoned her to the laundry. I am on my way there myself. Not as quick as I once was. Miss Summersby went ahead. I am sure she—"

He spun around, leaving Mrs. Banting to sputter behind him. He would apologize when he wasn't filled with a foreboding sense of dread and worry.

By the time he made it to the laundry, to the shock of his servants, who squealed and grabbed at the washing, Saffron was gone.

"Let me guess," he said to a stuttering laundry maid. "Miss Summersby. A footman summoned her elsewhere?"

The maid shook her head. "No, my lord. It was Mr. Sinclair who came and fetched the lady. He was in a right fuss about something."

It was as if the woman remained one step ahead of him on purpose.

He shoved his hand in his hair. He had known his house was a mess, but he never would have realized how bad the situation was without Saffron's ruthless efficiency. Any emergency would have her coming at once. He paused mid-stride before a window that overlooked the grounds and gardens.

That was the answer. If he could not find her, he would fabricate a situation to make her come to him.

A smile tugged at his lips.

That will solve the problem quite well.

Chapter Thirteen

S AFFRON STOOD IN front of the blackened, cast-iron stove with her hands on her hips. Smoke billowed from a hunk of charred meat sitting in a pot on top of the oven and filled the rafters, escaping out the open doors to the garden. She'd spent the morning flitting from one emergency to the next, doing anything she could to avoid Leo. Being around him made her feel helpless, like a ship without a rudder, and it terrified her.

Her plan to divert the Duke of Canterbury had borne fruit, at least, and the man was preoccupied with explaining the finer points of horse breeding to Mr. Mayweather. She was proud of herself for that feat—because it had been Leo's own staff that had given her the idea. She had caught them gossiping about the huge number of stallions Canterbury had brought along with him. All it had taken had been a word in Mr. Mayweather's ear when Canterbury was present that Angelica adored horses, and the duke had done the rest. She had even convinced Mrs. Banting to secure the man in the rooms farthest from theirs.

Now if only I could be as successful with Ravenmore.

Keeping Leo unaware of the reasons for uncovering the painter's identity hinged upon the auction progressing smoothly, but every time she turned around, there was another problem to deal with.

She touched the wooden handle of a hanging pot. "It cannot be that bad. They appear serviceable." Her eyes burned, but she didn't want to wipe the tears away because her hands were filthy.

"I've been cooking my entire life," the cook said, dabbing her rosy cheeks with the handkerchief Saffron had handed her. She stabbed a finger at the oven, making the thick, brown curls that framed her round face bounce. "I've never had this trouble. The devil's in this kitchen!"

It was bad. Saffron could not argue otherwise, but she was not one to give up on a challenge. The time in the kitchen had at least convinced her that the cook was not likely to have played a part in the break-in. The woman had difficulty standing on her feet for any length of time, owing to the more than thirty years she'd spent as a maid of all work. She did not have the stamina to ride a horse or sneak around in the rain.

"Do you have pigeons in the larder?" Saffron asked, her mind searching for alternatives that would suit the diverse preferences of the guests in residence. "A cold pigeon pie will do in a twist."

And few will object to pigeon, unlike fish.

The cook patted at her swollen eyes with the corner of her apron. "Aye, we've got pigeon, madam. Me mam made a mean pigeon pie. That'll do if you say. I can have one ready within an hour."

Saffron shook her head. "This is too much work for one woman. Where are the scullery maids?"

"I've had a miserable time hiring. A dozen girls never showed up for their first day! This darn house chased them away. So many who've worked here have been injured that they call this place haunted. 'Tis just me in the kitchen most days, and hardly a larder at all."

There was something very wrong in Briarwood Manor. It would have been unusual enough for one or two girls to abscond, but a dozen was highly suspicious.

"Show me the pantry," Saffron said, using a tone she reserved for when Angelica complained.

The cook led her to a small closet, and when she stepped inside, she felt a sense of growing dread. She'd never seen a house in such disarray. The foul smell of rotten meat permeated the room, and when she checked the sacks of flour, there were small flecks of black.

Weevils.

The bags would have to be tossed or carefully sifted through to remove the bugs.

She plucked at a strand of onions hanging from the rafters. When she flicked it, the strand hit its neighbor with a wet thud.

"The onions, too," The cook moaned. "Last week, it was the carrots. What will we do? There's a haunt in this house, I swear on it!"

Saffron considered the onions, chewing the inside of her cheek. So much discord in such a short time. An unorganized staff created an opportunity for theft. Was it just that Leo had lost control of his house? Or was it something more?

"You need assistance," she said. "Offer the girls whom you hire a bonus if they stay until the end of the auction." Hopefully, that would be enough of a lure to keep the thief from drawing the staff away. "By the way," she continued. "Last night, did you hear anything unusual? Lord Briarwood mentioned that his studio was broken into."

Mrs. Banting shook her head. "I can't sleep without my nightly draught. I'm afraid I missed all the excitement."

Suddenly, a young girl came flying around the corner, her cap askew. She was one of the younger between maids, or tweenys, who answered the calls of the bells in the family and guest rooms. The Briarwood estate had a plethora of tweenys, perhaps because it was a role that did not require any special training, and therefore it could be offered to local village girls to supplement their family income.

"Oh, madam, you must come," she said. "My sister took a faint and won't rise."

"Oh, goodness," the cook said, fluttering her hands. "'Tis a haunt, truly. Oh, madam, what will we do? You must call the vicar at once!"

"Focus on your duties," Saffron said, raising her voice above the cook's. "I will see to the trouble with the maid. Do you know where I might find smelling salts?" She might need them to revive the maid.

The cook clutched her apron. "What?"

"Smelling salts," Saffron repeated. "Do you have any? Or know where I might find some?"

"Oh, I... Yes." The cook bustled over to a shelf above the sink and picked up a small, white vial.

"I'll return it later," Saffron said as the cook handed it over.

What will it be next? she wondered as she followed the tweeny. *It is a wonder this household has continued in such a poor state.*

Her corset made it difficult for her to run, which meant the maid she followed had to stop several times and wait anxiously for her to catch up. The girl ran as if she had the stamina of a racehorse.

She expected the maid to lead her to the servants' quarters and was surprised when they headed toward the drawing room. She heard the ruckus before they arrived, the chaotic sound of many voices speaking at once. When they skidded to a halt, her entire body stiffened. Kneeling on the ground with a pale-faced maid draped in his arms was the man she'd tried so hard to avoid. Leo grinned. "There you are."

Saffron paused in the motion of retrieving the smelling salts from the pocket of her chemise. "What is this? What has happened?"

Leo cleared his throat. "All right, thank you, everyone. That will be all."

Saffron clenched her fingers around the bottle as the blushing maid rose to her feet, mumbled an apology, then skittered off, followed by the others. Only a single, white-haired maid remained behind for propriety. The old woman hunched over on a bench, half-asleep.

Leo dusted his trousers, then stood and tucked his hands behind his back, a wide grin still on his face.

Like the cat that has gotten into the cream.

She huffed. "What is this about, my lord?"

"It was the only way to ensure that you would appear, my dear. You must admit, it was quite clever."

He walked closer, and she remained rooted to her spot, like the gazelle frozen before a stalking lion. His slow prowl sent shivers rippling down her arms, and the gleam in his eyes made her want to flee. She had the irrational urge to throw her arms about his neck and kiss him senseless. The memory of their previous amorous encounter warmed her cheeks and had her staggering back.

"There was no need for this, Lord Briarwood," she said tersely. "I assure you I have things well in hand. You should see to your guests."

His longer legs ate up the ground between them and in moments, his chest was so close, she could feel the heat of him.

She knew she should put distance between them, but her legs refused to cooperate.

"What do you want?" she breathed as Leo loomed closer.

He raised a hand to cup her cheek. "You."

In that moment, he had her in thrall. She would've believed anything he said, agreed to any request he made. Her skin prickled where his palm touched her. She didn't know if she had the strength to step away, no matter how her brain screamed at her that what she was doing was wrong.

The realization broke her from the spell, and she jerked her face out of his reach.

"I do not wish to play your games," she said, forcing as much venom into her words as possible. "I agreed to assist you with the auction and in finding the thief. That does not include having you monitor my every move."

Leo quickly tucked his arms behind his back. "Of course. I did not—" He cleared his throat. "What I meant to say was, there are discrepancies in the latest receipt from the grocer. I would value your input as to the cause of the error."

The man was clever. She would give him that. He had already figured out her weakness. The allure of a problem to focus on, to ground her and force her imagination back to Earth, was too much to resist.

Chapter Fourteen

S AFFRON SAT CROSS-LEGGED in the middle of Leo's office on a beautiful, multicolored rug imported from India, cradling a fuzzy ball of purring warmth in her hands. A breeze entered through the open window and swirled around the room, ruffling the papers on his desk.

The white-haired maid, Mary, had followed them up from the entryway and slumped on a chair near the open window. The act did not fool Saffron. She caught the woman looking through her eyelashes twice, and her snoring was suspiciously regular.

What am I doing here? she thought, not for the first time. *I should be searching for Ravenmore, or tracking down the thief, or keeping an eye on Angelica, or...* Her eyes drifted to Leo, at his desk, one hand buried in his hair, a scowl across his face.

As promised, she had reviewed the receipt from the grocer and had quickly pointed out that the numbers quoted did not match the supplies she had seen in the pantry.

"Is there not a person in the country who is not trying to fleece me?" Leo asked, sliding the papers in front of him aside. "Thank you for your insight. I shudder to think how long it might have taken me to realize the problem without your help."

His praise warmed her cheeks and elicited a fluttering sensation in her chest. How many men would have accepted her help in a similar position, much less recognize the value of her opinion?

The Duke of Canterbury would not, of that I am certain.

"I believe it is time for a break," Leo said. "I see you have become fast friends with my painting companion."

She rubbed her nose against the kitten's gray fur and ignored the taunt. "She's adorable. What's her name?"

He chuckled. "I have not yet named her. I was thinking Cinder, because the footman who found her said she was curled up next to the remains of the kitchen fire."

She cupped her hands around the ball of fur and deposited it in her lap. The ball unfurled and stretched out both arms, claws extended. Large, yellow eyes peered up at her.

"Ow." She gently disengaged a claw from her wrist and moved both hands away before the kitten decided she was fair game as a playmate. It reminded her of how Leo treated her, although his claws were not so sharp.

Spoiled, Cinder jumped from her lap and waddled away, toward a string twitching across the floor beneath Leo's desk.

"She will be a mighty hunter," he said, pulling the string away as Cinder pounced. The kitten skidded across the wooden floor, tumbled onto her back, and was up again in a flash as if nothing had happened.

Saffron clapped a hand over her mouth but couldn't stop her giggle. Leo began laughing shortly after, and soon both were clutching their stomachs while Cinder chased a beetle on the floor, oblivious.

"Oh, she's lovely," she said, wiping away her tears. "I must tell Angelica. She will be in raptures. She loves animals."

He scooped up Cinder with one hand and deposited the kitten in a wicker basket filled with a soft blanket. The kitten made a sharp mew, as if annoyed at the restriction to her freedom.

"You know there's probably more," Saffron said, sobering at the thought. "There is rarely a single kitten in a litter."

Leo rose from his desk and extended his arm. "Shall we hunt?"

She giggled as she took his arm, the other holding the quivering basket. The kitten made sounds more akin to a wildcat. Mary rose from her chair, unbidden, and followed them down the rear stairs to the kitchen. There, Saffron explained their quest to the cook, who was engaged in hanging what she called "specter traps" from the rafters.

"Search all ye want," the cook said. "I could use more cats. They keep the mice at bay, even the wicked, black ones. I hardly have time to be watching them with a party to cook for and so little help."

And so, the hunt began. Saffron enjoyed herself so much, she ignored the small voice in the back of her head that insisted she tell Leo to return to his guests, that there were more important things for her to be doing.

I can't remember the last time I had fun, she thought as she kneeled on her hands and knees beneath the large, oaken table in the servants' dining room, listening for soft meowing. The room smelled like garlic and onions from the stew boiling away on the stove. Her stomach growled. Her knees were sore, and she was sure Lily would curse her when she saw the state of her lovely gown.

But as she was about to give up, she heard the quietest of meows and redoubled her search. She found them in an empty wooden box deep in the back of the pantry, hissing like snakes. She reached in a hand, and they swatted at her, bearing their tiny fangs. Two slate-gray kittens and a third calico with orange and black splotches and a white belly. A larger, black cat with white markings crouched a few feet away, eyes wide, but ears erect.

"Well done," Leo said, kneeling beside her.

"We should move them," Saffron said, holding out her hand toward the presumed mother cat. The feline crept closer and cautiously sniffed her fingers, then head-butted her hand.

Confident that the mother would follow them to a safer nesting spot, Saffron bundled her hands in her skirts and gingerly grabbed each of the kittens, depositing them beside their sister in the basket.

The cook shooed them out of the kitchen soon after, and they returned to Leo's office, Mary trailing behind them with the purring mother cat in her arms.

"I wanted to ask you something," Leo said, placing the basket aside.

She pulled a sheet of paper from her pocket, glad she had thought to carry it with her. "Yes, I suspected you might."

She unfolded the piece of paper in her hands and placed it on his desk, joining the other sheets of paper. "I've compiled a list of items you should purchase. Although there are significantly more, this will serve as the basis for the initial set of high-priority needs."

Leo stared at the list. "Needs?"

"Yes," Saffron said. "In order to ensure the success of the auction, I had to perform an assessment. This house is far from efficient. How you have gone on so long without a valet baffles me. Mr. Sinclair is performing the duties of both a butler and valet."

"Indeed." He picked up the paper, smoothed it out, and placed it with the other sheets. "Well, I certainly appreciate the effort."

"There is more." She straightened further. "The household turnover is significantly higher than average in this estate. I suspect that someone is trying to..." Her words faded away as Leo prowled closer, sparking fear and desire in her in equal measure.

Surely, he would not dare to ravish me with one of his staff present?

As if sensing the tension, Mary picked up the basket. "I'll return in a moment, milord," she said. "These young'uns need to be settled somewhere quiet. Don't get up to trouble while I am gone." She winked at Saffron, then closed the door behind her.

"Where were we?" Leo whispered. "Ah, yes." He tilted his head and brought his lips down to touch her cheek, a feather-light caress. His hand followed the curve of her back, and his palm caressed her rear, then squeezed tight. The burgeoning pressure in her chest threatened to explode and consume her. Never had she felt such a powerful urge, a need to be with another person. There was a hollow ache in her stomach, like someone had scooped out her insides and left her empty.

Stop this now, before it is too late, her rational mind objected. Ruining herself would not help her find her brother, and if it were discovered that she had allowed Leo such intimacies, it might bring further shame upon their family.

"You haven't finished your report," he said. "I would like to know more." He withdrew his hand and then slapped it against her rear, making her cry out. *Just this once*, she promised herself. Her aunt and sister would never have to know, and it was not likely any man would ever wish to marry her, given her reputation. The secret would be theirs, a precious memory to fuel her dark, lonely nights.

"U-Unless you prioritize renovations, you will soon pay p-premium wages for the bottom rung of s-society's house staff," she said between gasping breaths. "Oh, God, Leo! Touch me, please."

"If you insist." He hiked up her skirts to her waist and spread her thighs apart. "Wrap your legs around my hips and your arms around my neck."

She did as he asked, clinging tightly as he lifted her from the desk and carried her through an adjoining door, up a narrow flight of stairs, and then through a dark passage that ended at a door. He kicked it open, and they entered her room.

He lowered her onto the bed, grasped her wrists, and pinned them above her head. Then he captured her lips for a searing, heartbreakingly short kiss before releasing her and stepping away.

She boosted herself up on her elbow and rubbed the back of her hand against her mouth. Leo crossed the room in a few large strides. There was a click of a lock engaging before she fell onto her back and closed her eyes.

Footfalls approached, then the corner of the bed dipped down.

"What now?" she asked, keeping her eyes closed. Without sight, it was easier to imagine it was a dream, without consequences.

"Now we play."

His cool hands touched her thighs and pushed them apart. Nimble fingers removed her slippers and drawers, then peeled her stockings down and off her feet. A heady warmth pulsed from her cheeks to her stomach. Beneath her skirts, she was bare to him. At the first touch of his lips upon her thighs, she gasped and clenched her fingers in the bedspread. He inched up her inner thigh with his lips and tongue until his whiskers brushed against her quim. Then he transferred his attention to her other ankle and repeated the process until she shook with need.

"What do you want?" he whispered, rubbing his cheek against her thigh and making her shudder. "Tell me."

"Touch me. Please, Leo. Touch me."

She arched her back at the feeling of his tongue upon her. Then he slid a finger inside her sheath and rubbed his thumb against the bud of her pleasure. Heat curled in her belly, and moisture leaked and dampened the sheet beneath them.

She bucked her hips, wanting more.

"Yes." She threaded her fingers in his hair. "More!"

A second finger joined the first. The tension built, and he crawled up to capture her lips, tangling his tongue with hers while driving his fingers in and out of her sheath. She tasted her own essence on him.

Pleasure exploded and rippled out from her center, filling her with warmth and a heavy sense of contentment.

LEO RAN HIS palm up Saffron's thigh until the small shudders of her climax stilled. She was so much more than he'd expected, full of raw sensuality that he longed to push to its limits. How far could he lead her in pursuit of pleasure without crushing the fragile trust between them that he had nurtured?

He kissed her once more, then withdrew from her skirts and smoothed them down. She deserved better than a quick tumble in the sheets. When he at last had her beneath him, it would be for hours, not a few scavenged moments.

His cock throbbed with a familiar ache as he watched the rapid rise and fall of her bosom. Then her eyes flickered open, and he saw a wildness there.

"What about you?" she asked, reaching for the fall of his trousers. He knew he should stop her, step away and excuse himself, but her flushed cheeks and innocent curiosity made him hesitate, and by then, it was too late. She flicked open the fall of his trousers and his erection sprang free.

"You don't have to—" he started, but the rest of the words turned into a moan as she wrapped her fingers around him.

"It's so big," she whispered as she explored his shaft. "Will it really fit?"

He had to swallow before he could speak. "It will."

She met his gaze, then gave another wicked smile. "I saw a woman place her mouth on this part of a man's body once. The man seemed to enjoy it." She tilted her head to the side and fluttered her eyelashes. "May I try?"

Was she asking what he thought she was asking? Where had she seen such a thing? He had to clench his buttocks, lest he spill his seed over her gown like an untried youth. "It's a sensitive organ. You can try if you are careful."

She nodded, then leaned forward, clasped her lips around him, and sucked.

His vision went dark at the edges, and he momentarily forgot how to breathe. His knees wobbled, but he recovered his wits before he collapsed on her and completely embarrassed himself.

Where the devil did she learn that?

It was difficult to form thoughts with Saffron's lips and tongue dancing over his throbbing erection, but he was able to claw back some semblance of control by squeezing the muscles of his pelvis.

Unfortunately, he underestimated how determined she was, and soon enough, he had to gently take her head and pull it away. Her lips came free with an audible *pop*, and not a moment later, he climaxed, spurting his seed onto the floor, and marring the hem of her dress. As he stood there panting, holding his cock in his hand, Saffron used a corner of the bedsheet to wipe the drops of liquid away.

Then someone knocked at the door, and panic shot through him.

"Sister, are you in there?" Angelica called in a singsong tone. "Aunt Rosemary wants you to come down to the parlor."

Leo pressed one last kiss to her lips before gathering his clothing and disappearing out the door hidden behind the wardrobe.

Chapter Fifteen

S AFFRON RUBBED HER eyes with her gloved fists as she followed her sister into the shop. After the previous day's excitement, it had taken her hours to fall asleep, as her mind replayed every touch of Leo's hands and lips. She'd been so embarrassed that she hadn't gone down for dinner but had requested a plate be brought to her room. As a result, she had awoken lightheaded with hunger and had snapped at Lily when she'd arrived at their room with news that a carriage was waiting to take them shopping.

There was a bounce in Angelica's step as she approached the two raised, circular platforms set up in the corner, surrounded by tall mirrors. A group of young seamstresses scurried around the room, carrying heavy bolts of fabric, flat tape around their necks, pins in their mouths. The curtains were drawn, so the only light came from gaslights or the sunlight filtering in through the windows behind them.

The room seemed to spin for a moment, and Saffron took a seat on a plush chaise.

She had lost her senses. That was the only excuse for engaging in such wanton behavior with a man who had no desire to marry her. At least she could not be with child. Her romance novels had taught her that much. She would be safe from pregnancy as long as she exercised vigorously the morning after their engagements.

"Your sister is quite excited," Rosemary said, as she sat beside Saffron.

Angelica seemed in awe over the silks and satins in a dizzying array of colors, from lovely, maroon cambric to voluminous, jade silk. Saffron couldn't remember the last time they had been surrounded by such luxury. It was a marvel to see dresses that had never been taken in or let out, that didn't need to be modified to hide a stain or tear. The luxury of a modiste had been nothing special to them before Basil's disappearance. Her sister's transparent happiness wriggled into her heart like a sliver. Angelica deserved riches, jewels—anything she wanted.

We will have all of this again once I find Basil and restore our family fortune.

But Leo had been right when he'd insisted that she accept his support. The past day had proved that the guests treated her differently when she blended in. Her dowdy gowns were useful for infiltrating the servants, but they would not help her question Mrs. Morgan in the middle of a game of whist.

A particular shade of lavender called out to her, and she picked up a length and held it in her hands. It was soft on her fingers and shimmered in the flickering gaslight.

"That would be lovely on you," Rosemary said.

"It's so soft." She imagined herself in a gown made of the light material. Then she wondered what Leo would say if she walked down the stairs wearing a gown of such a beautiful fabric. She dropped the sample and clenched her hands into fists to keep from picking anything else up. The last thing she should think about was the man who had kissed her so ravenously in his study, who had branded her with the heat of his fingers and brought her pleasure she'd never imagined possible.

I cannot wait to see him again.

"Ladies. *Bienvenue*, welcome!" a melodious voice called. It was the modiste, dressed in a moss-colored dress. She swept into the room, a wide smile on her face. Her jet-black hair was bundled beneath a tight bonnet, and her bodice had several pockets jammed with pens and papers.

Saffron spent the next hour lifting her arms and puffing out her chest and sucking in while assistants took measurements. It was one of the few things she had not missed about their lost wealth, especially when the modiste took one look at her hands and tutted.

"Such calluses, *chérie*. It is not the fashion."

She bit down on the retort that flew to her lips. Telling the woman about her long hours sewing would not gain her anything. She kept silent until the woman moved on to shower Angelica with compliments.

Her sister wore the pinned-together panels of a dress. Even with the dress in a rough state, her sister was gorgeous. Saffron imagined her twirling around on the dance floor accompanied by some marquess or baron.

Or maybe Simon Mayweather.

The man was not entirely unsuitable and he had not shown any sign of cruelty. Her bigger concern was that Mr. Mayweather's intentions might not have been honorable. He might have shared Leo's disdain for marriage. At least Canterbury was transparent about his aim: a wife.

"Beggin' my pardon, miss," the dressmaker's assistant crouched in front of her said. "Did you be hearing the storm?"

No, because I had my arms wrapped around the viscount's neck.

"I did not," she said, dutifully lifting her foot so the assistant could measure her inner thigh. "Why, was there an accident?"

She had heard of such things happening. Lightning struck where it would and spread from cottage to cottage without thought for the occupants.

The assistant blanched before ducking her head. Although she had not responded, Saffron suspected she had been right.

Then Rosemary approached, holding a bolt of fabric in her arms, and the assistant stopped talking.

"Light colors do not suit you, my dear," her aunt said, spreading out the fabric in her arms. "What do you think of this?"

Saffron had to admit her aunt was right. The bright colors Angelica preferred made her look washed out. But the cerulean satin selected by her aunt highlighted her dark hair and eyes.

"*Oui!*" the modiste exclaimed. "You shall have a gown. And matching slippers, perhaps?"

Saffron shifted uncomfortably. How many gowns was Leo going to pay for?

"Do not look so dour," Rosemary scolded. "The viscount is a wealthy man. He can afford to outfit an entire Season of debutantes. This is but a trifling expense for a lord, I assure you."

Saffron flexed her thighs, aching from standing in one place for so long, and watched her aunt confer with the modiste. With every additional item Rosemary requested, the woman's Parisian accent thickened, until she was spouting full sentences in French.

Saffron hoped Leo wouldn't regret opening an account for them.

⁂

"I'M AFRAID IT'S the truth," Sinclair said, flipping through a small notebook in his hands. "I confirmed with your solicitor. He confirmed that the funds are missing."

Leo thumped his elbows down on top of the sturdy desk in his office and buried his hands in his hair. Beneath the desk, he stamped his feet on the floor in time with the lilting music filtering through the window. Most of his guests were in the garden, enjoying the break in the clouds. Instead of joining them, he was attempting to unsnarl yet another mess.

That is an excuse, and you know it.

He could have delegated someone else to search through the financial records of the estate or waited until after the auction was over. But he knew if he joined the festivities, he would come face to face with Saffron, and he didn't know how he would handle it.

You had the woman beneath you. You've all but ruined her.

It was odd because he felt guilty about his *lack* of guilt. He had taken her innocence. He should have done the honorable thing and offered to marry her, but the thought of marriage filled him with horror. Everyone he had ever cared about had died. He would not risk suffering the pain of loss again.

Excuses. Is that all you are good for?

He growled as he re-read a page for the third time. Hours of studying his brother's books, analyzing the sums on every page, and finally, he'd found the source of the discrepancy. Someone, his brother, maybe, or another member of the household, had systematically padded the numbers. Whoever had done the deed was an expert. The amounts were off by only a slight margin. The only reason he'd puzzled it out, instead of banging his head against his desk, was that he had found an older set of books dating from when his father had managed the accounts.

Leo didn't want to consider what it meant. For so long, he had allowed his brother to take on all responsibility for managing the finances of the estate. Once, when he'd been younger, he had allowed himself to fall into debt, and having no desire to bring shame to his family, had stepped away from the financial running of the estate. It had taken several months of working at a solicitor's office to pay his family back what he'd owed.

"Do we have any news?" he asked Sinclair, tapping his fingers on the desk.

He'd sent his butler to the bank to get an accurate sum of the household funds so he could track down the source of the errors. Instead, Sinclair had returned with worse news. According to the bank, someone had impersonated him and withdrawn a significant sum from the household account. The funds represented only a small portion of the total value of the estate, but it vexed him. If the thief could do it once, they could do it again.

"I'm afraid not," Sinclair said, with a sad shake of his head. "Your solicitor reported back that the clerk on duty insisted it was you who withdrew the money."

"Who could have done it?" he asked. "It had to be someone familiar enough with the estate to know that is the bank we use. Someone similar enough in appearance to pass as me. Percy. Simon. Who else?"

"You've left out one key suspect," Sinclair said, holding up a hand. "It was I, my lord. And now that you have caught me, I shall have to strike you down, then take off for the continent. Blast, you have foiled my plans."

Leo laughed. "If you're the one fleecing me, I have far bigger problems."

But the thought that someone close could have stolen from him made him pause.

"What about the break-in, my lord?" Sinclair asked, standing stoically by the fireplace. "Might it be related?"

Leo crossed the room and poured sherry into a glass. "I had considered it."

The coincidences were piling up in a disturbing pattern. First the break-in, then Saffron's carriage crashing.

And now this mess.

It couldn't be chance. Which meant that one person was likely at the center of it all. He sipped his drink and set his mind to the suspects. Percy was an unlikely candidate. The man was at least a head shorter than him and much skinnier. Simon, however, was a different story. They could pass for brothers, aside from the difference in hair color, which was easily disguised. On more than one occasion, he had wondered how Simon could afford the lifestyle he so obviously enjoyed. The man had a motive, that much was obvious. But if Simon needed money, Leo was certain the man would come to him and ask for it. He had done so before, and Leo had shown no reluctance in outfitting his cousin with all the funds he needed to continue his carousing. Simon reminded Leo of a younger version of himself, before Sabrina's death had turned him into a hermit.

This is ridiculous.

By spending so much time in his office, he was playing right into the hand of his adversary. He charged out of the room and strolled through the house, determined to get to the bottom of the mystery. He found his cousin playing croquet in the garden. Saffron and Lady Allen were watching nearby, their table set with an afternoon tea. Olivia caught his gaze, then waggled her fingers and gave a saucy wink. She leaned over and whispered something in Saffron's ear.

Focus, Leo thought. Saffron was not his concern.

Simon made his shot, clunking the mallet against the ball and sending it flying through the holes set up in the yard. That done, he set down his mallet and strolled over, but his smile faded when he got closer. "What is it, cousin?"

"Follow me," Leo said, pulling his cousin into the house and out of the range of prying ears and eyes. Once in the hallway, he put a hand on Simon's shoulder and looked directly into his eyes. "Money has gone missing from the estate accounts. Tell me you are not the one who did it."

Simon didn't even need to answer. The truth was written all over his face.

"I can explain," Simon stuttered. "I was going to return the funds immediately, but there were..." He glanced away. "Extenuating circumstances."

Leo squeezed his cousin's shoulder tighter. "I am listening."

Simon winced but made no move to flee.

"Gambling debts." He covered his face with one hand. "A thousand pounds. I was on a winning streak, and then I started losing, and I couldn't stop." His voice caught. "I swear to you, I tried to stop."

A memory flashed into Leo's mind. As a young man, he'd gotten drunk and gambled himself into a hole that he could not dig himself from. The owners of the gambling hall had beaten him to within an inch of his life and left him bleeding outside a charity hospital. His family had paid off the debt, but they had been so embarrassed, they'd refused to visit. Only Sabrina had come to see him, and the betrayal in her eyes had hurt him more than the beating. He'd vowed to her on that day that he would never gamble again.

Which made your inevitable betrayal that much more painful.

"I would have loaned you the money," Leo said softly.

Simon's shoulders slumped. "You're right. I was too stubborn. Pride goeth before the fall, as you know." He lowered his gaze. "I am sorry, cousin. Everything that has happened is my fault."

Leo struggled to keep his voice level. "Everything? Simon, what have you done?"

"I met a man at the cards table one night when my luck was down. He offered to forgive my debts in exchange for information about Briarwood Manor."

A cold chill washed over Leo. "Information?"

"He knew I had visited here often as a boy. He asked how to best enter the house without being seen."

"When was this? Why didn't you tell me sooner?"

Simon winced. "The night before I arrived. I know I should have said something, Leo. I feared you would cast me out. I might not have another chance to convince Miss Angelica Summersby not to marry the Duke of Canterbury."

That explained how the intruder had known exactly which window to attempt. It had to be the Ravenmore the thief had been after.

"What did this man look like?" Leo asked.

Simon shook his head. "I don't know. He wore a cloak and spoke in a low voice. He was shorter than me, though, and very thin. I did not get a good view of his face." Simon snapped his fingers. "His hands. They were clean, the nails trimmed. Those were not the hands of a laborer."

Leo searched his cousin's face for some sign that he was lying but found none. Unfortunately, the information was not as helpful as Simon seemed to think.

"We can't be sure it was the same man who broke in," Leo said. "One or both might have been hired by an unknown third party."

Simon shrunk before him. "I'm sorry, cousin. What are you going to do?"

"Nothing."

Simon's eyebrows shot up. "What?"

"I will do nothing," Leo repeated. "Other than tell you I am disappointed. I expected more from you. But if this happens again, I will visit every gambling hall in London and tell the owners that you borrowed more than you could repay, and if you appear, to summon me at once."

A nervous laugh. "You cannot be serious."

"I can be very convincing. I have no children, Simon, so as my heir presumptive, you will become the Viscount Briarwood when I die."

Simon blanched. "B-But surely, you will marry."

It was Leo's turn to laugh. "I would not bet on that, cousin."

Chapter Sixteen

S AFFRON PERCHED ON the stool in her room, trying not to dwell on her encounter with Leo the previous day and failing miserably. Every time she was certain she had put it behind her, the memory of her plaintive cries returned and brought with it a wave of embarrassment. She peeked in her mirror at the bed where Leo had crawled beneath her skirts.

She buried her face in her hands with a groan. How could she face him in a crowded ballroom without simpering like it was her first Season? A fleeting glimpse of him was enough to render her speechless.

This is ridiculous, she told herself harshly. She did not have time to be swooning over a man.

Once she left her bedchamber, she would continue her interrogations. There was only one night left before the auction and she had accomplished very little to uncover the thief or the artist.

"A TOUCH TO the right," a muffled voice said. Saffron lifted her skirt and moved it to the side as Lily finished pinning a dust ruffle to her hem, a collection of pins held in her mouth, her brow furrowed in concentration.

The lavender calico evening gown had been lying on Saffron's bed when she'd returned from a dull afternoon held hostage by Rosemary, watching the men knock wooden balls around the lawn. The woman had sent it along with a note that the others would be ready by morning.

Don't get used to this, she reminded herself. Soon enough, she would be back to her humble patchwork gowns and plain food. It might take weeks to track down Basil, and she had only a small amount of money saved for the journey. She would have to find her brother before Mr. Grummet returned to claim their home.

"That'll be it," Lily said, coming to her feet. "Madam, you are lovely, if I might say so m'self."

Saffron stood and shook out her skirts. The dress was a marvel. The gathered sleeves were decorated with French lace, and the heart-shaped neckline stopped just short of indecent. The flared skirt and lowered waist emphasized her slim figure, and the silk-covered dancing shoes that went with it were soft and sturdy.

She looked in the mirror and tilted her head to examine the intricate hairdo Lily had arranged. It was a complicated arrangement of swirls, made to look like one artful piece. A few stray curls trailed down and covered her ears, which were bare of baubles. The few pieces of jewelry she owned were entirely unsuitable for such an elaborate gown.

There was a quiet knock, and Lily rushed to open the door. Mrs. Banting stepped inside, clutching a small, brass-embossed wooden box.

"A small token of appreciation for all that you've done for us, my lady," the housekeeper said. She walked over and placed the box on the dressing table, then opened the lid to reveal a silk-linked interior and four glass bottles filled with a clear liquid.

A scent box.

Saffron gasped. "Mrs. Banting, where did you get these?"

The older woman blushed. "A former resident of the manor left them behind. I do not wish to trouble you with unpleasantries, but they will not be missed. If I may…" The woman gently touched the upper-right bottle. "My lord has a particular fondness for vanilla." Then Mrs. Banting spun around and exited the room, letting the door slam behind her.

Saffron leaned over the box. Her fingers reached for the indicated bottle before jerking to the side and selecting another. She spritzed it on her neck, then closed her eyes and breathed in the smell of citrus.

Another knock at the door had Lily scrambling, and a moment later, Rosemary and Angelica strolled in. Their new gowns were not yet complete, but Lily had helped restore two of their gowns that had been damaged in the carriage accident to what Rosemary had deemed an acceptable state.

"Oh, sister!" Angelica cried. She threw her arms around Saffron with a sob. "You are beautiful!"

Her aunt's lips twisted in a half-smile. "I have to say that you do look lovely, my dear niece."

As Angelica pulled away, Saffron smoothed the silk outer layer of her gown. "Lord Briarwood is a generous man."

"Indeed," Rosemary replied. "Angelica would be lucky to secure such a generous husband, even if he does not have the most sterling of reputations."

Angelica wrinkled her nose. "I suppose I would not mind Lord Briarwood as a husband."

A sudden image of Angelica wrapped in Leo's arms flashed into Saffron's mind and made her stomach churn. She had been concerned about the Duke of Canterbury but had not considered that their aunt might turn her attention to their host.

"It is a pity he is a confirmed bachelor," Rosemary said, with a heavy sigh.

Something wound tight within Saffron loosened, and she laughed. "Yes, of course. We would not want to impose further on our host."

"In any case, I prefer men who take more care in their appearance," Angelica said.

"Such as Mr. Mayweather?" Saffron asked.

Angelica blushed. "He is quite handsome, but he isn't interested in marriage."

It was as Saffron had feared. What was it about Mayweather men that made them resistant to taking wives?

Rosemary shook her head. "A duke is a far better catch, my dear."

Saffron avoided her aunt's gaze as they left the room and descended the stairs to the entryway, careful not to let her gown slip beneath her feet. The last thing she needed was to tumble down the main staircase and break her neck before she could begin her search.

No, she needed to blend in. That way, she could flit between groups and wait for an opportunity to ask each guest about Ravenmore.

But as they reached the entrance to the ballroom, and she realized how crowded and loud it was inside, a familiar prickling started in her neck. Six golden chandeliers hung from the ceiling, lit with so many candles that she had to wince, and when she looked away, there were shadows in her eyes.

She forced her feet forward, one small step at a time, until she was over the threshold. Then she split away from her aunt and sister and pressed her back against the wall, tucking her chin and squeezing her eyes shut.

Sound assaulted her next. Glasses clinking together. The screech of an out-of-tune violin string. Dozens of feet pounding the ground. Vibrations reverberated up her legs and sank into her bones.

Beyond caring what anyone thought, she shuffled closer to a heavy, velvet curtain and slapped her palms over her ears. What she didn't realize was that the servants had perfumed the draperies to keep out the smell of the horse pasture outside. The cloying, sickly sweet smell invaded her lungs and made her cough.

"What are you doing?" a voice hissed.

She opened her mouth, but the words stuck in her throat like sticky taffy.

It's over. I've ruined everything.

It wouldn't be long before the guests turned on her, whispering behind their fans, their wicked eyes gleaming above frothy lace. The carefully planned schedule she had worked so hard on was going up in flames.

I'll never find Basil. What was I thinking?

She distantly registered the sound of glass breaking, and then strong fingers closed around her wrist and pulled. With nothing left in her to protest, she followed willingly, her eyes still clenched shut, her feet stumbling on the smooth floor. The onslaught of sounds and smells faded, and she opened her eyes as she was shoved into a chair.

The Duke of Canterbury stood in front of her, scowling. His ruddy cheeks were stained the color of wine, and his eyes were all but bulging out of their sockets. Three servants stood quietly at the far side of the room, their eyes downcast.

"What were you thinking?" Canterbury roared. "Are you daft, girl? Another incident like that and you'll erase what's left of your sister's reputation."

A sour taste crept up her throat, but the angry words swirling inside her curdled in her stomach. The damned man was right. Her failure to anticipate her own response might have cost Angelica her future. Society already considered Saffron an oddity but had not yet associated her strangeness with anything but a quirk of her personality. If she was not careful, more dangerous rumors would start. Diseases of the mind ran in families. That was common knowledge.

The horror of what she'd almost done made Saffron want to race to her room and hide beneath the blankets.

Canterbury huffed out a breath, his arms crossed. "You are lucky that Mayweather fellow is clumsy. His accident at the refreshment table distracted everyone long enough to minimize the damage. Now..." He stepped closer, narrowing his eyes. "I will only say this once. If you wish to remain out of the poorhouse, you will refrain from making a spectacle of yourself and bringing shame upon my bride."

He wiped the spittle from his mouth with a handkerchief, then stormed out of the room—the front study, she realized—and let the door slam behind him. The sallow-faced servants followed behind him, leaving her to clutch her arms around herself in silence.

His bride.

Canterbury's words finally wriggled into her mind. He had called Angelica his bride. And there was something else, too. A veiled threat that if she did not behave in a manner that he considered acceptable, that he would prevent Angelica from providing Saffron and their aunt with funds. That was the most chilling part because it meant that Rosemary's plan had a very significant flaw. If Canterbury married Angelica, she would become his legal property. They only had his word that he would provide his wife's family with an allowance.

He intends to use it as a chain to keep us in line.

Her bleak future stretched out before her, devoid of pleasure. Canterbury would not suffer her attacks in public, nor would he allow her to pursue her own employment. If she did anything that brought attention to her condition or suggested even a tinge of impropriety, he would cut them off.

The blackguard.

She could not let him get away with it. She resisted the urge to fling herself out of the chair and rush to her aunt's side. There was no proof that Canterbury was anything but what he said he was. Considering that she'd already voiced her objections to Canterbury, she was uncertain if practical, logical Rosemary would believe her.

Leo is my only hope.

She rose from the chair, took several steps to confirm that her legs were no longer wobbly, then opened the door to the study and walked back the way they had come, her head held high. With each step, the pressure bearing down upon her increased, but she did not stop until she was back in the stuffy, noxious-smelling room. Her back ramrod straight, she strode purposefully toward the nearest group. Before she could reach them, Lady Allen swept across the room and stopped in front of her.

"I thought you would never return," the woman said, beaming. Then her smile fell, and she touched Saffron's shoulder. "What is it? What did that awful duke want?"

The polite response Saffron had prepared vanished under the weight of the older woman's concern. "H-He told me not to make a spectacle of myself."

"*What?* That—That—" Lady Allen flicked open her fan to hide her scowl. "Not here." She drew an unresisting Saffron into a quiet corner, then closed her fan. "Tell me everything."

Too shaken to resist, Saffron repeated the conversation she'd shared with the duke.

"He's even more of a monster than I thought," Lady Allen said. "You mustn't believe any of his lies, dear. There is nothing wrong with you. Do you understand?"

Saffron lifted her gaze from the floor, where she'd been staring. "But—"

"No excuses. *His Grace* is a fool." Lady Allen tapped her on the forehead with her closed fan, then linked their arms together. "Come, visit with me. We will show that beast how much you value his opinion."

They joined the small circle of guests around Mrs. Morgan. The woman wore a light-pink gown decorated with small, red flowers. The rear of the skirt rose so high in the air that Saffron had to hold her lips shut to keep from smiling. She was dressed as if she were still a debutante, and not an established matron with her own daughters to provide for.

Beside her, Mr. Morgan wore a rumpled, lilac pinstripe suit. There was a gap between where his gloves ended and his cuff began. Like his wife, the suit was decorated with small, red flowers. Together, the couple were like a faery king and queen waiting to hold court.

"Miss Summersby," Mrs. Morgan said, tilting her nose in the air. "That display earlier was quite—"

Lady Allen interrupted, fluttering her eyelashes at Mrs. Morgan's husband. "Do you have your eyes set on a piece, my lord?"

The man puffed out his chest. "The Ravenmore, of course. We wouldn't have come such a way for just *any* artwork."

"Oh, how lovely," Lady Allen exclaimed. "You will be the envy of the *Ton*."

Mrs. Morgan preened. "We shall have guests as soon as we install it. I am certain there are many who would love to see it."

Saffron flicked open her fan and waved it in front of her face to hide her grin. Lady Allen was a master manipulator, guiding the couple from topic to topic and heaping praise upon the older woman when she attempted to turn the conversation to Saffron. As vain as the woman was, it worked flawlessly.

Then Lady Allen leaned in close, lowering her fan and letting her hair droop over her décolletage. Said action captured Mr. Morgan's attention immediately. "Have you heard?" she whispered. "A thief broke into the estate. Seeking the Ravenmore, I would imagine."

Saffron froze. What was Lady Allen doing?

What did she know?

Mr. Morgan's glower at her husband's wandering eyes transformed into an open-mouthed gasp. "They did not take off with it, did they?" She pursed her lips. "We should insist that our host reveal the painting." She straightened, searched the room, then grabbed her husband's elbow and dragged him in her wake.

"What was that about?" Saffron asked with an awkward laugh.

"It was not hard to figure out, darling." She winked. "I am more observant than you might think. I heard the servants gossiping, and I've seen how you've lurked around. You are trying to figure out who broke in that night. I thought I might help."

"Oh." Saffron didn't know what to say. The speed at which Lady Allen had figured out their plan both impressed and disturbed her. There didn't seem to be any reason to lie, so she shrugged. "You are correct. Leo—I mean, Lord Briarwood and I are investigating. We suspect the thief might strike again before the auction."

Lady Allen giggled behind her fan, then snapped it shut and linked her arm with Saffron once again. "Well, I suspect you can remove at least one name from your list. Mrs. Morgan does not have the talent to fake such a reaction. I wondered if steam would billow from her nostrils, she was so worked up."

Saffron chewed the inside of her cheek to keep from grinning. "That sound she made as she rushed off did rather sound like a teakettle, did it not?"

Lady Allen burst into peals of laughter, eliciting a good number of shocked and scandalized glances from nearby guests. It was a nice change, to have censure directed at someone other than herself. Saffron had already realized that by standing at the side of the vivacious beauty, no one paid her any mind. The lack of scrutiny relieved some butterflies fluttering in her stomach. It was still a struggle, of course, and more than once, she had to fight back the urge to flee for the terrace, but it was manageable.

They stopped in the refreshment room for a biscuit and a cup of tea, then returned to circulate.

"Ah, this is wonderful," Lady Allen said. "To be young again, and full of such excitement. It has been too long." She skipped a step, then winked at Saffron. "Come, we've many more people to talk to, and the night is young. Stay sharp."

They joined a group that contained the Duke of Hawthorne and Simon Mayweather. The former was engaged in a lively political discussion, and the latter was obviously distracted, gazing above the heads of the others and occasionally tugging on his cravat.

Saffron didn't need to turn around to know what—or, more accurately, whom—Mr. Mayweather was looking at.

Better him than Canterbury.

The man did not have substantial wealth, so he could not use the purse strings as a lead to keep his wife in line.

Assuming Angelica can change Mr. Mayweather's view on marriage.

Given the passionate interludes she had enjoyed with Leo, it was equally likely that Simon's only interest in Angelica lay along those lines. Goosebumps spread up her arms, and she resolved to keep a closer eye on her sister. She didn't need Simon breaking her sister's heart.

"How are you enjoying the music, Your Grace?" Lady Allen asked, sliding closer to the duke, who wore a gray coat; gray, striped trousers; and a necktie, rather than a cravat. "I have a thought to speak to Lord Briarwood about the violin player. That screech made me cover my hair, as I thought an owl had flown in through the terrace doors."

The duke rubbed his bushy, black mustache. "Indeed, my lady. You would be doing all of us a favor. If the same musicians play during the auction, I might break the instrument over the man's head myself."

Lady Allen laughed prettily. "Oh, certainly not, Your Grace. That would be quite a feat."

The duke grumbled something beneath his breath about having to wait so long.

"I am not a collector myself," Lady Allen said. "But I've heard there are many who would give a fortune to have a Ravenmore. It's quite remarkable that one has finally surfaced at auction. I dare say many collectors are eager for a chance to buy it."

The duke perked up. "You would be correct. I'm hoping to take that one home myself."

"It's a pity we do not know the painter," Saffron said. "I would love to learn whence he gets his inspiration."

"I agree," Lady Allen replied. "*The London Times* once printed a full page, speculating his identity. I remember it because it was very amusing. I simply cannot imagine the Duchess of Killian has the time to create such masterpieces. And that it might be a common laborer was laughable. Did you read it, Your Grace?"

"Don't read *The Times* if I can avoid it," the duke said, sniffing. "Hardly better than a scandal rag. If the painter prefers to remain anonymous, the better for collectors."

"Are there any other paintings you are interested in, Your Grace?" Saffron asked.

The duke shook his head. "The walls of both my house in London and my country estate are completely filled, thanks to Mr. Morgan. I would need to buy another property to find space to hang anything else." The duke laughed, then smiled at them, inviting them to join in on the joke.

Saffron laughed prettily, then dove back in, sensing she was close to a clue. "Mr. Morgan, you mean he's an art procurer?"

"Well, I—" The duke grabbed an *hors d'oeuvre* from a passing servant and took a bite. His jaw seemed to move with incredible slowness.

"What my companion is not saying is that I am interested in procuring some pieces myself," Lady Allen said. "We would be most pleased if you could provide a reference."

The duke swallowed, then nodded. "If that is your aim, I can suggest Mr. Morgan for the job. I had a few select pieces I fancied, and Mr. Morgan fulfilled his duty. Now, if you will excuse me, ladies, I have a dance partner to engage." The duke stepped away from them and strode quickly away.

"Wonderful work, my dear," Lady Allen said. "I can see I am no longer needed. Enjoy yourself, and I expect to hear every detail of what you learn tonight."

Her mischievous smile spoke of what she had planned. As much as Saffron respected the woman, she had no desire to learn whose bed she would warm. That Leo was still in the ballroom had nothing to do with her sense of relief.

Indeed, Saffron mused, aside from the Morgans and Canterbury, her fellow guests had treated her far better than she'd ever been. Not once had she been asked to fetch a refreshment or bumped into with a snide apology. No angry debutante had spilled wine on her dress or made fun of her gown. The experience was so thrilling that when Mr. Whitewood asked her to dance, she agreed. The older man treated her with a fatherly air and answered all her questions with a gentle smile. She quickly ruled him out as a suspect because his joints creaked and moaned as he dipped her, and there was a faint cloudiness to his eyes. The man was in no shape to be riding a horse through the night, nor perching on a stool for hours on end, peering closely at a canvas.

When the music ended, the baron led her back to her aunt, who was watching Angelica like a hawk.

"Have you seen the Duke of Canterbury?" Rosemary asked, clutching her fan in both hands. "I had hoped Angelica might snare his attention with her new gown."

A powerful urge to confess what had happened in the study filled Saffron, but she pushed it away. The middle of a ballroom was not the place for such a discussion.

If she will even believe it.

"I heard him mention visiting the stables," Saffron said instead. She scanned the room, searching for a golden head. Where was Leo? She had caught only fleeting glances of him all night. She had to find him and tell him what she'd learned.

Was he avoiding her? Did he regret what had happened between them?

The room spun. Rosemary was still talking, but Saffron did not hear the words. She licked her suddenly dry lips. The prickling had returned with a vengeance, traveling down her neck and making the muscles in her back spasm.

"Settle down," Rosemary hissed. "You are squirming like a child at her first Sunday Mass."

That must be it. He wants nothing to do with me.

It shouldn't have been such a crushing blow. He was a member of the House of Lords, a disreputable rake desired by any woman with a pulse. She was an outcast, branded *strange* by society, hidden in the shadows of her much more beautiful sister.

She had to do something before she fell apart and brought Canterbury's fury down upon them.

"My throat is parched," she said. "Please excuse me."

Chapter Seventeen

S AFFRON FLED HER aunt's side and made her way around the room, sticking close to the walls. Her ankles pulsed with pain, her neck ached, and there was a ringing in her ears that wouldn't go away. Every flash of a blond head had her pulse racing.

Then Simon Mayweather caught her as she paused at the refreshment table.

"Stroll with me, Miss Summersby?" he asked, holding out an arm. "You look like you need a break."

She accepted, and as they walked away, asked, "How did you know?"

He chuckled. "You nearly stamped your partner's foot in the last set."

The orchestra started up, but he did not lead her onto the dance floor, to her relief. She didn't want to risk being partnered with Canterbury or, worse, Leo. What would she say to him? That he had burrowed his way so deep into her heart that she could not bear the thought of him courting another? They had never spoken of commitments. It was her own fault for expecting more of him than he could give.

Simon squeezed her hand. "I am surprised I got you before my cousin. Haven't a clue where our host has gotten himself off to. You'd think he'd be in the middle of this."

Saffron steered him toward the doors to the terrace. "The better for you, Mr. Mayweather. I assume you wish to discuss Angelica?"

As expected, the conversation shifted easily to her sister.

"I cannot understand why she is so cold," he said as they walked out the doors to the terrace. They were close enough to the dancers that she was not worried about calling her aunt to accompany them.

"It must be something I said," Simon continued. "The curse of it is, I can't remember what."

She folded her fingers over his arm. "If you are looking to catch a glimpse, she has been spending her mornings with the horses. She loves to ride."

Simon nodded. "Well, I'm a bit of a rider myself." After a brief pause, he added, "Has she said anything about me?"

"She said you are not seeking a wife."

Simon winced. "She might have misconstrued my intentions, but I am willing to make amends."

She squeezed his arm. "I will speak to her."

"She's a remarkable woman," he said, staring out at the dark gardens. It was easy to guess what he was thinking.

"But you are worried about the Duke of Canterbury."

The muscles of his arm tensed. "I take it you did not have the pleasure of meeting his late wife?" His lips thinned. "She was a beautiful, spirited woman—before her marriage. It was awful to see her change, night after night, retreating into herself. His Grace treated her like a wild mare to be broken and bred. I cannot see that happen to Miss Angelica."

A shiver traveled down her spine. His assessment matched with her feelings about the man. "I agree with you, sir. The problem is—"

"Money. I know. Your sister explained. I do not have the means to provide Miss Angelica with all that she deserves." He closed his eyes. "I had a fortune once. But for my hubris, she could be mine."

The anguish in his voice resonated within her. Like Simon, she longed for someone who felt out of reach. The difference was that

Simon now seemed willing to marry her sister. All she had to do was nudge them and her problem with Canterbury might be solved. She would still search for Basil, but she would not need to rush.

"There you are."

Leo stood in the doorway to the ballroom, dressed in dark-blue livery. His arms were tucked behind his back, his hair perfectly coiffed. His lips turned down as he looked beside her to where Simon stood.

"Evening, cousin," Leo said. A palpable tension formed between the two men until Simon released her and bowed.

"If you will excuse me, I promised Miss Morgan a dance." He strolled off with confidence and what Saffron thought was a new sense of purpose, leaving her to shuffle awkwardly before their host.

"I saw you dance," Leo said.

She swallowed the saliva that suddenly flooded her mouth. He had been watching her, after all. But why? To ensure she was completing her end of the bargain?

"I have not yet questioned everyone," she said. "Have there been any other attempts to steal the painting?"

Leo prowled closer. "No. What did the Duke of Canterbury say to you? I tried to follow, but Simon spilled champagne on my trousers."

She swallowed again. "He wanted me to know that if I made a scene again, he would cut us off, financially, after he marries my sister."

It would have been easier to lie, but a small part of her wanted him to get angry on her behalf. It made her feel special, wanted. Like she was back by the fountain, being comforted instead of shouted at.

But rather than explode in a burst of temper, Leo closed the distance between them and tucked her fingers into the crook of his arm, then goaded her back toward the bright lights of the ballroom.

"I won't let that happen. You are far too important…"

Her lungs seized, her heart thumped, and she nearly reached for her head for fear it would float away.

"I've never met anyone so good at solving problems," Leo continued.

She crashed back down to Earth. Of course, that was what he wanted. Practical Miss Summersby. Always putting others' needs first. Never thinking about herself or pursuing her own desires. Her entire world revolved around her family. She had no actual plan for her own future beyond finding Basil and preventing Angelica from marrying the Duke of Canterbury, because saving her siblings was all she cared about.

For once, I wish someone would put me first.

She noticed her aunt sitting with Lady Allen and was about to head toward them, when a waltz started. Leo led her to the dance floor, his hand splayed on her hip, pulling her close as they swirled around the other couples.

"I have news," Leo said. "There is an injured man in town. The constable suspects him of being the one who broke in. I thought we could question him when he awakens."

It was hard to focus when Leo clutched her so close. She wanted to drape herself over him, thrust her hands into his thick hair and lose herself in the pleasure of his kisses.

"What do you say?" Leo asked.

Saffron wrenched her mind back to reality. "I agree. As long as we set out when we will not be missed." A sudden thought struck her. "Should we be concerned that he might escape after he awakens?"

Leo shook his head. "Sinclair informed me the man has knocked his head and broken both of his legs. He will be abed for months, assuming the constable doesn't send him to the gallows for whatever other crimes he committed." The hand on her back tightened. "This is dangerous, Saffron. I am only asking you to come because I know if I don't, you will find out and follow me anyway, as reckless as that would be."

Saffron huffed. "You underestimate me, my lord."

Leo smiled and his eyes crinkled at the edges in the way that made her heart flutter. When the music faded, he took her hand and put it on his arm.

"People are going to think you've taken special interest in me," Saffron said. As they passed Mrs. Morgan, the woman gave her a frightful glare, then turned on her two daughters, barking like a seal.

"They can think whatever they want. After all, I have taken a special interest in you." They approached the musicians, who had started up again, much louder than before. As if knowing that the sound was more than she could bear, he held her tightly and did not speak again until they were on the other side of the room.

"By the way, that gown is marvelous."

"You can have it when I'm done with it," she replied tightly. "Though I don't think it would look as good on you."

His strangled response was cut off by an ear-piercing scream.

Saffron spun and raced toward the source of the noise. Memories of her parents' fevered cries in the night filled her thoughts. It couldn't be Angelica. She had warned her sister countless times not to walk too close to the gaslights. And Rosemary's bad hip made it unlikely that she had moved so far from her seat.

Still, her heart thundered as she pushed her way through the crowd, with Leo following behind her.

When she arrived at the scene, the worst of the damage was done. Lady Allen was bent over double, her hands clutching at her gown, still smoldering from where it had caught a spark from the fireplace.

Relief flowed through her like cool water on a hot day. Not Angelica. Not Rosemary.

Then she realized no one was helping. A ballroom full of men and women, and none stepped forward to aid Lady Allen. She shoved her way into the clearing and kneeled beside the woman, who sobbed loudly as two footmen stamped out the remaining flames.

"Come," Saffron said. "Let me help."

The woman lowered her hands and opened pale-gray eyes. "All right."

The crowd grew louder, women muttering to their friends and husbands behind their fans as Leo attempted to move them away. To prevent her charge from further embarrassment, Saffron hurried her off into the retiring room. Only when they were safely within the small space did she examine the damage.

It was horrific. The smell of burning fabric filled the room, and small, blackened clumps split from the dress and splattered on the floor.

"How bad is it?" Lady Allen asked, tears forming in her eyes.

"I won't lie to you. It's unsightly. But if you would allow me, I think I can fix it."

The woman let out a low moan.

Taking the sound as permission, she went to the door and asked one of the maids hovering outside to bring her a sewing kit. A young girl ran off and returned in moments with a bulging, cloth satchel.

Saffron withdrew a set of shears, as well as a needle and thread and set to work. It was not a simple task. Some embers were still fresh, singeing her fingers.

"I don't know what happened," Lady Allen said as Saffron snipped through the carnage with the shears. "One minute I was standing there, and the next, I could feel the heat of the flames licking my skin."

Saffron mumbled an apology.

Lady Allen sighed. "I have suffered no significant injury, thanks to the footman who batted out the flames. But I still do not understand where the flame came from. I was quite a distance from the fire and any gaslights, I made sure of that. But at least your aunt was not harmed."

Saffron's hands stilled. "My Aunt Rosemary was near you?"

"That's where it happened. I was sitting beside her on the couch by the fireplace."

Exactly where I would have gone if Leo had not swept me into the dance.

Were it not for his intervention, it would have been Saffron set aflame. A coincidence, or something more? In other circumstances, she would have brushed it off, but there was another fact that made her pause. After the initial shock of the carriage accident, she thought back to the moments before the wheel had broken. There had been a sound. The report of a rifle, nearly drowned out by the hammering rain. Then there was their driver. Would a man who was not a criminal have abandoned them so easily?

It couldn't have been an accident.

Someone had shot out their wheel, perhaps expecting the horses to spook and send them crashing into the river.

Her first instinct was that she needed to tell Leo as soon as possible, but then she remembered how he had hovered over her in the studio, and how he had enveloped her in his arms when he'd thought she'd had a chill. Would he continue to help her if he knew someone had tried to kill her? Or would he instead become even more protective and demand that she allow him to continue the investigation alone?

No, it was best to keep her suspicions to herself.

The rest of the work continued in silence. When all the damage was removed, Saffron turned the new, raw edge over to create a smooth hem, then set to ripping the wide band of lace from the bottom of her own gown. She would apologize to Leo later.

"Oh, no." Lady Allen gasped. "Not your lovely gown!"

"Trust me," Saffron said through a mouth full of pins. "I know what I am doing." She affixed the band to the inner layer of the gown, settled the fabric on the floor, then stood back and admired her work. The gentle sweep of the fabric fell to the floor with no sign of the damage that had been done. Without a balayeuse, or dust ruffle, the gown would not survive the night, but it was enough.

"There," she said, wiping sweat from her brow.

Lady Allen reached down and touched the work, her eyes sparkling. "You are a miracle worker. Not even my most experienced seamstress could have done such lovely work in such a short time. Can you also embroider?"

Saffron wiped sweat from her brow. "Of a fashion."

Lady Allen hummed an appreciative sound. "You would make a wonderful lady's companion."

Only a few days earlier, those casual words would have sent Saffron's pulse racing. Here was the opportunity she had been looking for, a way to support her family if her search for Basil ended in disappointment.

So why aren't I more excited?

"I hope you are right," Saffron said, with a smile that felt mostly forced. "I have been seeking a situation."

"Why didn't you say so?" Lady Allen clasped her hands. "You must join me as a companion. It would be my pleasure."

Saffron bit the inside of her lip, compelled to comment despite her situation. "I didn't help you in exchange for anything."

Lady Allen sighed. "Think about it, my dear." She fluffed out her skirts. "Now, let's return to the ball so everyone can see what a marvelous job you have done."

Chapter Eighteen

S AFFRON PERCHED AT the edge of her chair in the dining room, tapping her foot on the floor. Somehow, Leo had intercepted her plans and reorganized the seating, so she was near Leo at the head of the table. Angelica was beside her, and Rosemary across the table, to Leo's other side. They should have been spread out along the table to inspire conversation, as they had been each previous time they had sat at the table. She repositioned the cutlery in front of her until everything was perfectly aligned.

It was not the propriety she cared about, but the change in plans.

She told Leo as much, and he merely shrugged. "I'm eccentric. Plus, the three of you are far more entertaining. Indulge me." She maintained her anger throughout the first course, a decadent asparagus soup, and the second, candied carrots, but by the time they'd finished the salmon, she vibrated with excitement.

The new staff Mrs. Banting had hired had done a marvelous job.

"You've done wonders with the cook," Leo said, after servants removed the first dessert dish, milk pudding, from their plates. "I did not know she could make something without burning it."

"She had the experience and skill necessary," Saffron said. "She just needed help to get past the initial problems."

She looked around at the guests clearly enjoying the meal and felt a surge of pride akin to how she felt when Angelica was complimented on her hair. She had brought about the happiness they felt, had coaxed the seed of the event into something marvelous.

Angelica, however, stared down at her shallow bowl as if it contained a dead rat, and not a beautifully prepared trifle. A slight vibration in the floor told her Angelica was bouncing her knee. Then Angelica winced, and the vibration stopped.

Saffron glanced across the table to Rosemary, who wore a tight smile.

She waited for Rosemary to be distracted by the servants taking away the plates, then leaned closer to her sister and whispered, "What's the matter?"

Angelica shook her head minutely, then darted her eyes to the side.

Saffron straightened and, through the corner of her eye, confirmed that both the Duke of Canterbury and Simon Mayweather were watching them.

"I say, Briarwood, when will you let us see the pieces up for auction?" Mr. Morgan asked, thumping his glass on the table and splattering wine onto the tablecloth. Mrs. Morgan's cheeks pinked as she covered the stain with a napkin.

"Indeed, I should like to see them," Mr. Hawthorne said.

The rest of the guests muttered to themselves but did not speak up. Saffron cursed Leo's decision to move her. If he had placed her, as intended, near the middle of the table, she would have had the perfect vantage to overhear any conversation.

Leo finished a bite of trifle, then set down his spoon. "You will have to be patient. I have arranged for the event tomorrow to be a candle auction."

Both men wore identical expressions of disappointment but did not argue.

They will gossip instead, Saffron thought, remembering her first Season. She had not understood that smiling faces masked wicked tongues. Every mistake she'd made had been filed away, to be brought out and laughed at over tea.

"How lovely," Lady Allen said, putting her fork down. "Such a thrilling event. I simply cannot wait."

Mr. Morgan swayed in his seat. "I would rather prefer to see the works now. You could give us a small preview. Where are you stashing the artwork, anyway?"

Saffron glued her eyes to the older man. If he was Ravenmore, would he ask where the paintings were stored? Would he get drunk at dinner and demand to see them? Maybe, instead, Mr. Morgan was the thief Leo sought or had hired someone to steal the paintings.

"Let us retire," Mrs. Morgan said loudly, rising from her seat so fast, the dishes on the table clinked together. "My daughters are eager to demonstrate their musical talents."

Saffron exchanged a glance with Leo before following the rest of the women as they moved to the drawing room, leaving the men to their own affairs. The drawing room was enormous, heated by three separate fireplaces on each of the exterior walls. Tall windows stretched up to the ceiling, the curtains drawn back to reveal a stunning view of the setting sun. There were chairs set up near one end of the room, facing a set of musical instruments, which the Morgan girls picked up without prompting. Miss Morgan selected the harp and Miss Beatrice the pianoforte.

Saffron sat as far back as she could politely manage, expecting the sound to grate against her senses, but to her surprise, both girls were talented musicians. The elder Miss Morgan plucked a soft rhythm for several bars before Miss Beatrice joined her, and then both girls started to sing. Their voices formed a harmonious melody, perfectly in sync. The spell they cast lasted for three songs before Miss Morgan put down her harp. Then a beaming Mrs. Morgan loudly proclaimed, "I fancy a game of whist, if any of you ladies would like to join me."

"I would not wager a pound against that woman," Lady Allen said, taking Saffron's arm and leading her toward one of the tables the servants were setting up.

"Why not?" Saffron asked. She had been so busy rushing around solving problems that she had not yet joined the other guests for cards or other activities the previous night. This was an ideal opportunity to interrogate Mrs. Morgan when she was not bullying her husband or preening over her daughters. Mr. Morgan had expressed far too much interest in the Ravenmore for her liking.

Lady Allen sat on a chair and withdrew a pair of knitting needles and a ball of yarn from a wicker basket near the hearth. She took them up, sliding into the activity with a grace born of long practice. "The Morgans enjoy their displays of wealth, but that is all it is. I would not be surprised if the dowries on their girls were less substantial than rumors suggest."

Saffron cast a quick glance at Mrs. Morgan, already wagering with three other wealthy ladies. While the other players chatted and laughed, Mrs. Morgan dealt the cards with a purposeful, almost *hungry* look on her face.

"I see what you mean," Saffron said.

"Besides," Lady Allen said, finishing a row of what looked to be a blanket or scarf, "I believe you have more pressing matters to attend to."

"Such as?" She accepted a cup of tea from a servant and raised it to her lips.

Lady Allen hummed a tune in harmony with the clicking of her knitting needles, her eyes downcast, a small smile on her lips. "Have you noticed who is missing?"

Fear dripped down Saffron's back. She placed her teacup on the table.

"I believe I am the first to notice," Lady Allen said. "Carry on, now. I look forward to hearing all about it."

As gracefully as she could manage, Saffron performed a rotation of the room, but it only confirmed her fears.

Angelica was missing.

❧❧❧

WHEN SAFFRON FOUND her aunt, Rosemary was listening to an older woman drone on about the dessert, and so she sat beside her aunt and waited for a polite opening, all the while trying not to dance with agitation.

"Mrs. Hampshire, allow me to introduce my niece, Saffron Summersby," Rosemary said, after some time.

The woman adjusted the spectacles perched above her snub nose. "Lovely to meet you."

"We were discussing the inferior quality of the sponge cake," Rosemary said.

Mrs. Hampshire straightened her shoulders. "The strawberries were not even in season. Everyone knows it is best to pick spring fruit when it is in season and preserve it in jams or jellies."

"I quite agree," Rosemary said, her eyes sparkling.

Saffron smiled, despite her anxiety and the slight upon her menu choices. She couldn't remember the last time she had seen her aunt so happy. She took one more glance around the room before sitting beside Mrs. Hampshire. "I quite enjoyed the soup myself."

At that, Mrs. Hampshire *hmphed* and began a lecture on the proper way to harvest and preserve asparagus. While the woman spoke, Saffron cast sidelong glances at her aunt, bouncing her knee up and down beneath the small table, a nervous habit of Angelica's.

Finally, Rosemary caught on. She set her cup down on the table, then touched her head with her hands. "Saffron, my dear, I fear I have a megrim coming on. Mrs. Hampshire, it was lovely talking to you, but I think my niece should accompany me to my room for a rest."

"Oh, of course," Mrs. Hampshire said. "I will ask a maid to send you up some tea. Nothing like tea for a megrim."

AFTER SENDING HER fretting aunt to Angelica's room to see if Angelica would return there, Saffron gathered Mrs. Banting as a chaperone and then checked the retiring room, the stables, and the ballroom.

With each minute, the tension in Saffron's shoulders increased, until Mrs. Banting touched her arm. "The maids will search her out. None of my girls will tell a soul about what they see, my lady."

The unspoken warning that Angelica might be found in a less-than-respectable state made Saffron grind her teeth in frustration.

She had told Mr. Mayweather that she would speak to her sister. Had he taken that as permission to abscond with Angelica?

I should have been watching her.

What if Mr. Mayweather ruined Angelica, then refused to marry her? Saffron knew how easy it was to give in to passion.

The floor beneath her tipped and swayed as if she were standing on the deck of a boat.

"Dear me!" Mrs. Banting grasped her arms and pushed her back to fall into a chair.

I must find Leo. He'll know what to do.

He was the only man present whom she trusted not to laugh at her fears or spread rumors about Angelica behaving inappropriately. The problem was that the men had not yet joined the women in the drawing room and as a woman, she was all but forbidden to enter the male domain, the smoking room. The last thing she needed was to earn more black marks against her family.

So as Mrs. Banting arranged for a maid to bring a drink for her, Saffron summoned a nearby footman and whispered a word. When her lemonade arrived, she accepted it with thanks, then begged off with assurances that she would wait in her room for news. Then she set off for Leo's office, taking the servants' halls to avoid being seen.

She slipped inside the room, shivering at the chill. Unfortunately, she could not light a fire without risking someone finding out what she was doing. She would have to hope the footman would deliver the message she had imparted.

To take her mind off the cold, she walked a square route around the bulky furniture until her shins ached.

"Saffron!"

The doors thumped open, and Leo rushed inside, his hair mussed. He charged forward, grabbed her in his arms, and crushed her against his chest.

In those few seconds before she could reassemble her scrambled wits enough to react, she was overwhelmed by the hard planes of his chest beneath his waistcoat, the tang of cigar smoke that clung to his hair, the even thud of his heart beneath her cheek. Then he pushed her away.

"For God's sake, don't scare me like that!"

She staggered back, one hand falling on the desk, the other hovering at her breast. "How have I scared you?"

Leo ran a hand through his golden hair. "The footman told me a woman was in trouble. I thought it was you."

"Oh," she said, still shaken by the ferocity of his embrace. "He must have misunderstood. I told him I needed to talk to you, that is all. My sister has gone missing."

"You checked the retiring room?" Leo asked.

"Of course." She paced the room. "When was the last time you saw Mr. Mayweather? Was he in the room before you left?"

"No. He wasn't. And before you ask, yes. He would be capable of what you are thinking." He scowled. "If he has ruined her, I will convince him to do the honorable thing."

Saffron resisted the urge to retort that Leo had done his own share of ruining quite recently and had so far shown no intention of doing the "honorable thing."

A soft knock at the door made them both jump.

"Hide!" Leo hissed as the doorknob turned.

She ducked beneath the desk. A whispered exchange occurred, too quiet for her to follow. She carefully peeked around the side of the desk to see a footman slipping back out the door.

She scrambled to her feet. "Well?"

Leo's look of relief salved her panicked heart before he even responded. "There are no carriages or horses missing. Wherever your sister is, she must still be on the grounds."

Saffron slumped forward and splayed her hands on the desk. "I feel like a governess with a wayward charge. Perhaps I should check the nursery next."

"Or the gardens," he said, tugging at his cravat, which was significantly longer on one side than the other.

Stepping up to him, she pushed his hands away from his throat. "Stop that. You're only making it worse." She unwound the soft fabric and then looped it around his neck. "We need to think about this logically. If you were the duke, where would you take Angelica?"

He crossed his arms. "Bed."

She jabbed him in the throat with a pinky. "Do not even joke." She shuddered at the possibility. The only thing keeping her from a complete loss of control was the fact that Mr. Mayweather had expressed a fondness for Angelica. She had to believe that meant he would not do anything that would risk her reputation.

She stepped back to examine her work. The folds in the neckcloth were not even. She undid her work, then formed a knot with the ends of the cravat, tucking the extra fabric beneath his vest. "You know this property. Where would he take her?"

Leo touched his fingers to his neck, pulling the fabric to the side. "Have you tried the library?"

She sighed. "Of course I checked the library. Mr. Mayweather is smarter than that. He would have taken her somewhere they would not be interrupted." She returned to her pacing. "Discussion is pointless. Return to the ballroom and tell everyone who asks that Angelica accompanied my aunt to her room. I will find a maid and begin searching the servants' quarters."

Leo took her hand and kissed her fingers before she pulled them away. "I will do as you ask, fair maiden."

SAFFRON'S HEART THUNDERED in her ears like a stampeding racehorse as she flitted from one cold, dark room to the next, hissing her sister's name.

Where the devil could she be?

The Briarwood estate was vast, but she was certain she had searched at least half of it in the hour since leaving Leo's side. Her thighs ached, and there was a burning in her heel that was the precursor of a blister.

Finally, she struck some luck when she overheard a trio of servants gossiping in a stairwell.

"The poor dear was prostrate," a maid whispered. "I was doing dishes in the kitchen and heard her crying."

A boy wearing the livery of a stablehand shook his head. "A right shame."

Saffron grabbed the maid by the arm, causing the girl to shriek.

"Where did you see the girl?" Saffron demanded.

"N-Near the kitchen," the maid stammered.

Saffron raced for the room, shoving past a shocked Mr. Sinclair. Nothing mattered in that moment but ensuring her sister was safe.

At last, she found the door the maid had mentioned and threw it open, fully expecting to see Angelica sprawled on the floor, or wrapped in Mr. Mayweather's embrace, but she was confronted with nothingness. A dark, empty room.

No. Not empty.

Although the sounds of the kitchen filtered in through the wall, soft murmuring and pots and pans clattering together, there was a faint sniffing. She searched the dark corners and found her sister sitting on a cloth-covered couch in the corner, her head in her hands. Saffron rushed across the room and grabbed her sister in a tight embrace.

"I thought I was doing the right thing," Angelica whispered. "If I hadn't, I never would have... Oh, Saffron. I've ruined everything. How do I fix this?"

A fierce protectiveness welled up in her chest, and she vowed to knock some sense into Mr. Mayweather the next time she saw him.

"I forgive you," she said, hugging her sister closer. "It doesn't matter what you've done. I will always forgive you."

Angelica sighed. "It's all my fault. I just wanted to be like you."

Each word sliced at her heart. "What do you mean?"

Her sister grasped at her gown. "You and Lord Briarwood. I've seen the looks he gives you. I wanted what you have." She shook her head. "I should have known it would not work. Simon is not like the viscount."

She clutched her sister closer.

"I'll explain everything to Aunt Rosemary. Mr. Mayweather won't get away with this. I'm sure Lord Briarwood will help us."

Angelica gave a hiccupping laugh. "What? No, sister. That's not why..." She sniffed. "Well, I suppose this is Simon's fault. He asked for my hand. I refused."

Saffron stared at her sister, not understanding. "Why?" Mr. Mayweather wasn't a duke, but neither did he seem to have the cruel streak that Canterbury possessed. "I thought you liked him."

Angelica closed her eyes. "I did. I do. But he has spent each night since he arrived gambling, to earn enough of a fortune to support us. He nearly came to blows with Mr. Morgan over his winnings last night. I can't let him continue risking everything for me." She huffed, then opened her eyes. "I will marry His Grace, and I will make the best of it."

"But if Basil is still alive, you might not need to marry."

"Sister, there is no *proof*. You must end this obsession." She turned a glare on Saffron. "Do not try to stop me, sister. I've made up my mind."

Saffron's throat was too choked with tears to respond. She settled for nodding, although she had no intention of allowing Angelica to sacrifice herself. If she could find proof that Basil lived, Angelica would realize that she did not need to marry for money. *BOOM*.

The door flew open, and a scowling Leo rushed inside, dragging his cousin by the arm. Mr. Mayweather's hair was tousled and there were bags beneath his eyes. It was as if the man had tumbled out of bed moments ago.

"Mr. Mayweather is prepared to marry your sister," Leo said loudly. He released his cousin and shoved him forward. "I found him in the garden with a bottle of my best brandy."

Mr. Mayweather met Saffron's gaze and winced. "I-I tried to tell him, Miss Summersby, but he would not listen. Angelica—"

"I will be marrying the Duke of Canterbury," Angelica said. She shot to her feet. "Please excuse me. I must tell Aunt Rosemary the good news."

Chapter Nineteen

S AFFRON LIT A match and held it to the wick of a candle until it flickered to life. Then she placed it in a tarnished pewter candle-holder she'd found in the kitchen and held it close to her face, inhaling the scent of beeswax.

Rosemary had been thrilled over Angelica's decision, but Saffron was not yet willing to give up.

Somewhere in the house was a painting that was the star of the auction, and if her brother's face was in it, that might convince her sister not to marry Canterbury.

She wavered between her lightest chemise, for greater freedom of movement in case she had to make a quick retreat, and a dark gown that would better hide her in the shadows. In the end, she slipped on the chemise, tying up the silk ribbons on the bodice into tight bows. Then she rummaged through her trunk and pulled out an old, woolen cloak, wrapping it around herself. At a glance, she might appear to be a member of the staff making their nightly rounds. In the unlikely event she was recognized, she could claim she was fetching a warm glass of milk.

Cupping one hand around the flame, she creaked open the door to her room, glancing either way up and down the hall before stepping out. The hallway was dark and her shadow cast by the candle was a ghostly specter on the wall. She palmed a letter opener from her writing desk and pulled the scratchy, woolen cloak tighter around herself. She could not be too careful. There had, after all, been a thief prowling around the estate, and an unaccompanied woman was a target to men of all social classes, rich and poor alike.

Her stockinged feet were silent on the floor as she ascended the stairs and began a methodical room by room search, skipping the occupied ones. Half of the rooms were lushly appointed, Mrs. Banting's hand at work. The other half were filled with furniture covered in white sheets, like ghosts of the previous inhabitants.

What happened here?

She had never been inside a country house that was such a contradiction. It was as if, in his grief, the viscount had shuttered away the rooms that held memories he did not want to revisit.

She tugged open a heavy door and stepped inside. It was the last of the rooms on the wing. If the painting wasn't hidden within, she would have to return to her bed.

A large bed dominated the space, surrounded by wooden posts and topped with a canopy. She searched for signs of life. The bedspread was smooth, no shape beneath the sheets. The dresser drawers were closed, the writing desk bare.

Nothing.

She sighed, accidentally blowing out her candle and leaving her in complete darkness.

She was searching her pockets for a match when a flickering light around the edge of a door at the far side of the room caught her attention. She took a step forward, then another. Through a small crack in the door, she spotted the frame of a painting.

Triumph rushed through her.

She tiptoed across the plush carpeting until she reached the door. Inch by inch, she pulled it open, each slight movement emitting a low creak. She squeezed through, closing the door behind her as softly as possible. Inside, paintings surrounded her in a world of color. One after another, like an entire museum shoved into a closet.

"Well, this is a surprise."

Her head swiveled around.

Sitting on a low stool in the corner of the room, holding something long and thin in his hand, was Leo. His cheeks unshaven, his golden hair loose around his shoulders, he looked like his namesake, the king of the jungle, the top of the food chain.

"What are you doing here?" he asked.

She licked her dry lips. What could she tell him that he would believe?

He shook his head. "I should have expected this. You were searching for the Ravenmore. Well, as you can see, it is not here. These are all mine." He turned away from her, and the words that followed were softer, as if he were unsure of her reaction. "What do you think?"

She reached out and touched the frame of the nearest painting, admiring the bold colors and confident strokes. It was a scene of a forest with a woman lying on the grass in a clearing, wearing a diaphanous gown. Her cheeks heated as she could make out the nipples of the woman in the grass.

Most certainly not a Ravenmore.

She checked another, and with mounting embarrassment, found it was as explicit as the last. Three women were twined together on a bedspread surrounded by cherubs, and what the women were doing to each other…

"T-The colors are lovely," she said.

Leo's eyes crinkled at the corners. "Thank you."

That was the precise moment she realized he was not wearing a robe, or any kind of proper garment, but rather a kind of gray smock splattered with thin streaks of color—and nothing else. Her eyes flitted down over his torso to his bare legs and then back to his face.

He turned around and kneeled over, revealing the firm lines of his back, tapering down to narrow hips and a firm behind. He placed the lids on the various pots of paint on the floor.

"So," she said, keeping her eyes firmly above Leo's waist. Her traitorous mind urged her to drift lower, but she refused. "You paint in the nude?"

Leo laughed. "I prefer the freedom. Clothing is too restrictive. The paint comes off skin easily enough."

"Oh," she said. That seemed reasonable.

He grabbed a handful of sand from a bucket and rubbed his hands together. Then he turned around, reached over his head, and pulled off his apron, throwing it to the side.

Saffron's gaze traveled down his stomach, covered in a fine dusting of blond hair, to the darker curls that surrounded the jutting erection staring up at her. She'd never seen a naked man in the flesh.

He desires me.

A powerful ache shot through her, and all thought of her mission faded.

"You understand that I will not marry you," he said. "I... I simply cannot."

It should have mattered, but it didn't. She wouldn't deny herself any part of him he'd offer. "I know."

"Then touch me, Saffron," he growled.

The use of her name made her mouth dry. Her fingers sought the small buds of his nipples and he groaned.

Strong arms enclosed around her shoulders, and his lips crushed against her own. His tongue thrust forward, and she met it with her own, tangling together until she gasped away, breathing hard.

His hand crept beneath her skirts and squeezed her thigh, making her gasp. His fingers inched closer, pressing into her flesh with soft, crawling motions. She squirmed, wanting to feel him inside her, and he obligingly drew his fingers down and dipped them between her legs. He slid his fingertips back and forth along her slit before gently pressing inside. She arched her back and hissed in pleasure.

"More," she cried. "Faster."

"If I had known this is what I would have found when I bed you, I would have done it the moment I met you," he said, pressing her against the wall.

She wrapped her legs around his hips and ground her pelvis against his. "If you'd have troubled to ask, I would have told you."

She pressed her breasts against him and buried her nose in his neck. The rumbling in his chest reverberated through her body. He dragged his nails along her thighs and she shuddered in pleasure. The sharp pain melted into her liquid center. His teeth grazed along the space where her shoulder met her neck. He bit lightly, then ran his tongue along the spot. The sensation curled her toes, and she tilted her head to the side to give him better access.

"Oh, oh, yes. Right there. Keep doing that." Heat gathered between her thighs as his fingers moved. He rasped his tongue up her neck, nipping and sucking as she moaned against him. His hand left her skin, and she was about to complain when he brought the hand back in a spank that sent a shock of electricity through her and startled a gasp from her lips.

He chuckled deep in his throat as he rubbed and kneaded her sore bottom. "Like that, did you?" He took her earlobe into his mouth and bit down. "Do you want more?"

She was too breathless to respond, but she squeezed her legs around him.

A deep moan rumbled through his chest, and she fell backward through the open door, supported by his arms. They dropped onto the bed, and he thrust her legs apart. Something hot and hard pressed against her inner thigh.

"Are you sure you want this?" he asked, panting. "If you say *no*, I will walk away."

"What will you do? Tell me."

"I will press my cock deep inside you," he said. "There may be pain, but then there will be pleasure."

"Yes," she breathed.

Inch by careful inch, he pressed into her. It was glorious, like the empty part inside of her was finally being filled. He pushed deeper, anchoring her with a hand on her hip. She remained tense, but the pain never came.

He pressed until he was speared as deeply as he could go. Then, with a guttural growl, he surged forward, and she felt it in her core, burning her from the inside. He was alive inside her. Throbbing and pushing into her so deep, she thought he would touch her heart. Yet somehow, he still went deeper.

He didn't pause long, and soon, he was thrusting. She reached down and touched the bud of her pleasure at the apex of her thighs. She twitched it and the tension grew, getting closer and closer until she could feel it, a piercing sensation that crested into an explosion of fireworks.

When she became aware of her surroundings again, Leo had slipped out of her and pulled the thick coverlet from the bottom of the bed up and over them. She curled against his chest with a soft sigh, and he juggled her until she lay half over him, her hand curled over his heart.

"Wake me before morning," she breathed, her leg curling around his. "I must return to my room before anyone finds me missing."

He kissed the top of her head. "I will."

LEO CRADLED THE sleeping bundle of woman against his chest as he struggled to contain the whirlwind of emotions in his chest.

What have I done?

He hadn't intended to let their attraction go so far. He'd counted on his experience and control to guide her through the initial strings of the chorus of their amorous congress, without ever reaching the crescendo. He'd failed to account for how irresistible she was.

He buried his nose in her soft hair and breathed in her unique smell, committing it to memory. She was all soft, warm curves, a perfect complement to the lean, hardness of his own body.

It's more than that, though.

There were plenty of curvy, experienced women who would have leaped into his bed at the crook of his finger. Women who would have bedded him then walked away that same night, sated with their conquest. But he didn't want any of them—ever again. He only wanted Saffron.

He wrapped his arms more securely around the faintly snoring woman in his arms.

What the hell am I going to do?

Chapter Twenty

L EO DREAMED, AS he always did, of the day Sabrina had died.

It began with his father punching him squarely in the jaw. Leo staggered back, hitting the back of his shin against an old trunk, and falling to the ground. Blood filled his mouth.

His father's teeth were bared beneath his wiry, black mustache, and his dark-brown eyes were bloodshot. "I regret ever siring you," his father said. "I could overlook your drinking and gambling, but this is inexcusable."

What had he done to earn his father's censure? Memories flickered past, too fast to catch. His legs ached as if he'd run a mile the previous day. Had he gotten into a fight? Knocked out some young lord at the gambling hall? His father nudged an empty bottle on the floor with his foot. "Pathetic. You have no idea what has happened, do you?" He tossed a crumpled paper onto Leo's chest. "Read that and see."

Leo smoothed out the paper, which appeared to be a telegram. His tired eyes struggled to focus on the small script. Finally, he puzzled it out. "An accident?"

He had a vague recollection of being woken up at the crack of dawn by his sister's pleading voice. He had thrown her aside, having no desire to wake up after getting so deep into his cups the night before. Sabrina had been insistent, ranting and raving at him, then sobbing when he'd refused to move.

He checked the telegram again. The name of the ship was familiar.

Why? The fog in his brain parted, and he remembered that he'd promised his sister he would accompany her on a trip to visit a young man she had met in London. That was it—the tickets she had shown him had been for the same ship.

He tore the paper into small pieces. "No. I don't believe it."

"Get out of my house," his father said. "Don't come back unless Sabrina is with you."

Leo pushed past his parents. His sister wasn't dead. She couldn't be. His father couldn't see it. He would have to go to the scene and find Sabrina himself. Somewhere, she was laughing at him, certain she had punished him for not coming with her on the trip down the river. He was sure of that; he simply had to find her and end the game.

He hitched up a horse and set off. The light of the rising sun was insufferably bright, pounding into his head. He paid a fisherman to take him across the river. There was still no reliable transportation other than taking a boat. It was a long crossing, but once he finally arrived, he started hearing the whispers.

"Those poor people," one woman said.

"There were mostly women and children on board," a man replied. "Such a tragedy."

As he journeyed closer to the city, he pieced together the gossip to learn what had happened. Two boats had collided on the river, a cargo ship destined for London and a small river cruiser laden with tourists returning from a day exploring the pleasure gardens.

"Please, brother. It will be cold soon, and I might not get another chance to meet with him."

Sabrina's wheedling voice echoed in his mind. They'd been on their way back from a shopping trip, laden with boxes, when she'd bumped into a young man. Leo had been so preoccupied with keeping them from missing their ferry that he remembered little about the man except that he was skinny, wore a striped, yellow suit, and had sputtered his apologies for so long that Sabrina had giggled. To keep them from being late, Leo had finally agreed to chaperone Sabrina on an outing with the man the next day.

It was worth it to see her smile.

She couldn't be dead.

Finally, the coach could take him no farther and dropped him at the edge of the city, near the river and the foul stench that came with it.

The scene was chaos.

The bodies dragged out of the water were white, clammy things covered in a sick layer of mud.

"Sabrina!" he called.

She's around here somewhere.

Even if she had been on the boat, she certainly would have survived. She had been a strong swimmer all her life.

He could only just make out the remains of the transport ship, lilting to one side in the river. The pleasure cruiser was gone, but dozens of other boats bobbed in the gentle waves. Their operators held long sticks with barbed ends that they used to pull up hulking shapes and haul them onto the boats.

He accepted a perfumed rag from a woman holding a basket and staggered between one row of bodies to the next.

"If you have not found your loved one here," a man shouted from a few feet away, "search on the other side of the river."

The dream skipped forward, and he was standing beside a body, trembling with exhaustion and fear. He flipped the corpse over with the toe of his boot.

It was Sabrina, her curls plastered to her swollen face.

He fell to his knees, ignoring the wet squelch of the mud that seeped through his trousers, icy daggers cutting into his flesh.

Then the dream twisted from reality, and his sister's eyes flew open.

"You were supposed to protect me," she whispered. "You promised you would come with me, brother."

He reached for her, but a heavy-set man wearing a long, black coat shoved a cudgel in front of his face. "Take 'e number," the man said, gesturing to the strip of leather tied to his sister's legs. The number seventy-five was scratched on the surface. "Them at the big tent will give 'e a form. Bring the form back to take the gel."

He tried to push the cudgel away, but two others grabbed his arms and pulled him back, then dropped him and crossed their arms.

"Fine," he said. He carefully untied the scrap of fabric then stumbled away, past others who were sobbing into each other's arms or shouting and fighting. He reported to the main retrieving area and was given a letter of permission, which he accepted and returned to give to the undertaker. With no cart, he simply picked up his sister's limp body in his arms and walked through the crowds.

WHEN SAFFRON AWOKE, it was to find Leo snoring beside her. His hair was splayed over his pillow, and every few seconds, he thrashed his head from side to side. She reached for his temple but then pulled back. She wanted to comfort him, but she couldn't stay. She carefully slipped out of his bed and crept through the halls until she returned to her room.

She had only enough time after to change into sleeping garments and muss up her bedsheets before Lily arrived to help her dress for the day.

As Lily prepared her gown, she wondered if Leo was still asleep, and what he would say the next time he saw her. She supposed she was his mistress, a role she'd never expected to fill. The very idea filled her with a shivering kind of excitement. All her life, she had been trained in the duties of a wife, but being a mistress was something new.

She shook her head. There were more important issues at hand and convincing Angelica not to marry the Duke of Canterbury was paramount. That meant speaking to Ravenmore as soon as she could.

A knock interrupted her thoughts, and when Lily opened the door, Rosemary entered.

"Not dressed yet?" her aunt asked archly.

Saffron was certain her aunt could read her guilty conscience all over her face, but she forced a smile. "I did not want to get out of bed this morning."

Rosemary raised one eyebrow but otherwise did not comment. Then she strode forward and sat on the bed. "I came to speak to you about Angelica. I believe we should encourage a short engagement. She could be married by month's end."

Saffron thumped down on the bed beside her aunt. Although a fire roared in the room, she felt as cold as if she were neck-deep in a snow drift. She imagined Angelica walking down a church aisle, a chain around her ankle. "Give me a chance to change her mind," she said. "Lady Allen has offered me a position as a companion—"

Rosemary silenced her with a slice of her hand. "That's enough. You can pursue employment if you choose, but I won't allow you to interfere with your sister's future." She paused, then added, "Angelica will be a duchess. Is that truly so bad?"

Saffron closed her eyes, and a tear slipped down her cheek. "He will crush her spirit."

Rosemary sighed. "You underestimate your sister."

She wanted to scream, but what good would it do? Angelica shared her stubbornness. In her view, marrying a cold, heartless man was the lesser of two evils. The other being a life of poverty for them all.

"I'll leave you to consider things," Rosemary said. As the older woman left the room, Saffron dashed away her tears. Her aunt had given in, but she would not surrender.

There was still one skirmish remaining before the war was decided. She paced the room three times before settling by the window. She felt restless, like she was on the cusp of an important discovery that was just out of reach.

As she stared at the grounds, two figures walked into view. The first was Mr. Morgan, easily identifiable by his size and the handkerchief clutched in one hand. The second was a nervous-looking man in a shabby, green suit.

Who is that?

She'd seen the man before, but she couldn't remember where. His wardrobe occupied that awkward gap that was neither plain or consistent enough to mark him as a servant, nor elaborate enough to indicate his status as a guest.

She peered closer, until her nose was pressed against the glass. The two men were talking, but the glass was too thick to make out the words. Mr. Morgan was gesturing wildly with his hands, including the one that held the handkerchief. The other man pulled a sheaf of papers from his pocket and thrust them at Mr. Morgan.

Mr. Percy.

Leo's solicitor, who had given up his own invitation so Saffron and her family could attend.

What's he doing here?

She rushed for the door, intent on sneaking down to listen to their conversation, but by the time she reached where they had been, both men were already gone.

Chapter Twenty-One

S AFFRON RUSHED UP the stairs and then down the hall until she found Leo in his office.

"Did you know your solicitor is here?" she asked.

Leo put the pen he was holding down. "Are you certain?"

She gestured to the window. "I just saw him talking to Mr. Morgan. They must be working together."

Leo pushed his chair back. "You think Mr. Morgan is trying to steal the Ravenmore? Why would he need a solicitor's help?"

She had to clench her hands to keep from shoving them in her hair. So much was happening. She had to stop Angelica. She had to keep the auction moving. She…had to…

Leo grasped her upper arms. She hadn't even noticed him moving.

"Breathe," he said. "We'll figure this out."

Tears dripped down her cheeks. "I-I can't do this, Leo. It's too much."

He wiped her tears away with his thumbs. "How can I help?"

"Tell me who Ravenmore is. If I talk to him, I can fix this situation with Angelica and then I can focus on helping you."

He dropped his hands and turned his back to her. "Why are you so determined to find Ravenmore?" he asked.

She sniffed. It was time to tell him everything and hope he would not react as Rosemary had. "The last time I saw my brother was when we closed his casket at his funeral three years ago. That is, until I saw the Ravenmore painting at Lady Jarvis's party. He was in it. That's when I realized we must've been mistaken. My brother lives, and once Ravenmore confirms it, Angelica will call off her engagement."

Leo's shoulders drooped. "You are speaking of the painting you saw the night we met."

"Yes, that's the one."

As Saffron watched Leo's face, clues she had previously disregarded pieced together in her mind. The humor in his eyes when she'd demanded to know who the painter was. His late-night painting. The location of the auction.

She felt the desperate need to punch something. It was so obvious, and yet she'd missed it. She put her hands on her knees. "You are Ravenmore."

The fragile hope in her breast bloomed. After so many days, she finally had him. It wasn't too late, after all. He could tell Angelica where he'd seen their brother and then Angelica would not feel duty bound to—

He gave her a rueful smile. "No. The painting you speak of was not painted by me."

Her thoughts stuttered to a halt. "But if you aren't the painter, then who—"

He placed his head in his hands. "My sister."

His dead sister. She bit the inside of her cheek. That was not the news she had hoped for, but all was not yet lost. The lead was cool but not frozen cold. There was still a chance.

"Do you know when she painted it?"

"No. She did not date her paintings. I'm sorry. I should have told you last night. My sister died three years ago. I've been distributing her old paintings as new."

She stared at the back of her hands through a haze of tears. After everything she'd done, all the effort spent getting to the auction, speaking to each of the guests, and it was a dead end. There was no proof Basil was still alive. Her heart felt like it was tearing in two. She didn't have leverage to stop the Duke of Canterbury's suit, after all.

A sudden surge of anger coursed through her, and she kicked the paneling under the desk with a strangled scream.

CLUNK.

"What was that?" Leo asked.

She kneeled to where a chunk of the paneling had come away, revealing a small door. She moved it away, and a puff of stale air filtered out, making them cough.

"Paintings," she said. "They're paintings." She ran a hand along the bumpy gilt frames, all stacked together. They were coated with a thin layer of dust. She reached in and pulled out the first one. A plume of dust rose, and she sneezed.

Leo took the painting and set it against the wall. Although dusty, Saffron recognized the bold, distinctive style of Ravenmore.

"Why were they in here? Did you put them in here?" she asked.

"I've never seen these before. Sabrina must have hidden them. She sometimes used this room as her studio." He ran his hands along the frame. "The wood is soft. She commissioned an artist to carve a batch from fir three years ago. Most painters prefer tougher wood, for durability." He studied the painting. "If my sister painted your brother once, perhaps she painted others. There may be more clues yet, even if they are years old."

It was the flimsiest scrap of a chance, and it would likely lead to nothing, but Saffron pulled out a sheet of paper and a pen from the writing desk, buzzing with renewed excitement. "How many are there?"

"Over a hundred, at least." He peered into the space beneath the desk. "I thought I'd found all her paintings. I should have guessed she would not have made it easy for me."

"Let's begin, then." If she could find more evidence of Basil in Sabrina's paintings, maybe that would be enough to shake Angelica's determination.

Working together, they uncovered and inspected each painting.

"This would have been much easier in my old studio," he said as he lifted yet another piece from the hidden alcove.

"It is amazing how I can see the progression as her art evolved," Saffron said. "She was quite talented, but it is more than that. She was determined."

"Nothing would stop her from achieving what she desired. I loved that about her."

Saffron examined the latest painting he'd grabbed. As disappointed as she was that none of them had included an image of Basil, she marveled at the beautiful scene of horses in a meadow. She felt like she could reach out and touch them.

"What are you going to do with them? Add them to the auction?"

Leo rubbed some dust from a frame. "No. They belong in museums."

She touched his hand. "She would not have wanted you cooped up here with them, like ghosts."

He crumpled under her touch. "If it hadn't been for me, she might have survived."

There was no point in telling him it wasn't his fault. She didn't know the circumstances of her death, and it felt uncomfortable to ask. If he wanted her to know, he would have offered the information. "Sometimes we have to let them go. We are only hurting ourselves by hanging on."

"Enough of the past," Leo said. "Come with me. There's somewhere I'd like to take you. The estate will survive for a few hours without us."

Chapter Twenty-Two

S AFFRON CLUTCHED LEO'S arm as they navigated the ruts in the road.

"Are we not taking the carriage?" she asked.

Leo smiled. "I thought perhaps you would approve if we chose the scenic route. Although…" He gestured to the trio of muttering maids who followed them, picking their way through the muck. Saffron had enlisted them as impromptu chaperones, as they had been heading into town anyway. "They might not appreciate it as much."

As they got closer to what Saffron thought was a town, she spied a bramble of flowers. She walked closer, taking in their varied perfumes.

"This town is known for its gardens," Leo said. Then he took her hand and pulled her into the maze, leaving behind the giggles of the maids. They stopped in a small clearing, surrounded by clinging vines braided into patterns. She reached out and touched a petal, and a drop of water splattered in a puddle. The path led straight ahead, then branched to the left and right with tall hedges forming walls around them.

"It is so beautiful here," she said.

A dozen starlings settled onto a cherry tree nearby and chittered at them.

They must be used to being fed.

She pulled a bow of the tree down and released it, spraying small cherries to the ground. The birds fluttered away, then returned, falling on the fruit, and pecking them to pieces.

"Come," Leo said, taking her hand and placing it on his arm. "We're nearly there."

"The town?" she asked.

He nodded. "I thought this was a good opportunity for us to see if the injured man is awake."

"Oh," she said. "Yes. Of course."

They exited the maze and rejoined the maids to walk into town. There, he drew her through the crowd of merchants along the road and directly toward a particular vendor. An old woman sat in front of steaming buns, smiling a gap-toothed smile at them. He handed her a coin, and the woman passed over two white, steaming buns.

Saffron accepted one and held it in her cupped hands. It had a pillowy texture and a yeasty smell. She laughed in delight. "Saffron buns. How did you know I was named after these? My mother loved them."

"I didn't." Taking a bite out of his own bun, he gestured for her to continue walking through the streets. "But when I remembered that this town had a market, I thought you might enjoy it."

As she walked, the steady wash of waves hit the embankment, along with the crunch of wheels on gravel and the muted chatter of voices. She knew he was giving her a chance to change her mind, to avoid talking to the man who might be their thief.

"What are you going to do after the auction?" Leo asked suddenly.

She swallowed the last of her bun, which turned sour in her stomach at his question. "I was considering employment with Lady Allen as a lady's companion."

"There are better options."

She pulled her hand away from his arm and took a few steps in front of him, distancing herself from him and his impertinent questions.

"Let's walk by the shore," she said.

They walked arm and arm toward the bluffs. The seagulls squalled and dove as children threw bits of bread for them, white flashes against the blue sky. She stood behind a gaggle of children and watched them indulgently.

She could easily imagine they were her own, with her husband at her side.

But he didn't want her as his wife.

She could understand why. Society called her odd. What viscount would want a wife who barely tolerated crowds, who had attacks that rendered her unable to speak? She was, quite simply, unmarriageable.

"Are you ready?" Leo asked.

She swallowed heavily. "Yes."

❦

THE SMELL WAS the first thing to hit Saffron when they stopped at the closed door at the back of the church. Sour and astringent at the same time, with the foul undertone of rot. It made her gasp and clutch Leo's arm.

"You don't have to do this," Leo said, in a low voice. "I can question him."

Saffron blew out a breath. "No. I want to hear what he has to say myself."

The odor of decay was strong, but she had been through worse. The Thames itself was so rancid that passing over bridges was an exercise in self-control. Many of the city's poorer citizens had to wear cloth across their faces during the hottest days of the year.

That gave her an idea. "May I have your cravat?"

He frowned, touched his neck, then removed the long cloth and pressed it into her hands. She wrapped it around her nose and mouth, and the difference was immediate. The smell was still there, but duller, and drowned out by the rich scent of Leo's cologne.

"Better?" he asked, with a smile. The collar of his vest gaped without the cloth, making him look even more the rogue.

Rather than respond, she placed her hand on the doorknob and turned.

The door creaked open, shining light into the dark, cramped room that held a single bed, chair, and table. A white-garbed older woman was slumped in the chair, but as the light hit her face, she startled and rose to her feet.

"We wish to speak to the man," Leo said.

"I am his nurse," the woman said, stepping between them and the narrow bed. "He's back with fever. You might not get any sense out of him."

Such bravery.

Even with Leo's rumpled appearance, he was recognizable as a lord, if not as the viscount himself. Yet the woman still stood in their way, protective of her charge.

"We will not stay long," Saffron said.

The nurse twisted her hands together, then stepped away, giving them their first look at their suspect. She recognized him as the driver of their carriage, even though his skin was as pale as the grimy sheets beneath him, and his brown hair was plastered to his head. His eyes were closed, but as Leo stepped closer, they flew open.

"What d'ye want?" he croaked.

"You broke into Briarwood," Leo said. From his tone, it was clear he wasn't asking.

"Aye." The man coughed, spraying his sheets with a fine mist of red. "Shouldn't have taken that job. Skittish horse in a storm."

"Foolish, indeed," Leo said. "Who paid you?"

The man thrashed on the bed, his eyes rolling around in his head. "Scrawny, rough voice, looking loike a ha'penny from a fountain. Should've spat in his ale. Wasnae worth the boat."

Fountain? Boat?

"That's enough, my lord," the woman in white said. Her cheeks were flaming red, and she held a dripping rag in her hand.

Saffron felt the tension in Leo's arm and knew he was going to argue. She also saw the lines of worry on the nurse's face.

"We should return," Saffron said.

Leo patted her hand, all tension in his arm gone. "Of course."

They left the church and followed the road the way they had come, skipping the gardens and the market. They were walking past some trees when Leo threw up his arm in front of her. "Do you see those tracks?"

He leaned closer to the trees at the side of the road and moved some greenery aside with his hand. There was a clear imprint of horse hooves in the mud. He pushed his head through a tangle of branches to reveal the prints trailed away through a small path.

"What does it mean?" she asked.

They gingerly stepped through the mud, following the tracks until they reached the side of a river. He looked up and down the riverbed. "There was a boat docked here recently."

Just like the sick man said.

"Whoever it was, they are long gone," Leo said. "Let's return to the house. I'll send out volunteers to search for more clues, but I suspect our thief is still one step ahead of us."

Chapter Twenty-Three

S AFFRON CROUCHED IN front of a steamer trunk and flipped open
the lid. She bent over the edge, up to her elbows in slippery fabric,
and pushed the material around, tugging a section free to inspect it
before moving on.

She knew she was procrastinating, throwing herself into activity to
avoid thinking about how she had failed. Her sister and aunt were
right. The painting was a coincidence. Now she had to decide her own
future and if it would include Leo.

"Where are you?" she muttered, tapping her closed fists against the
rim of the trunk. She reached all the way to the bottom on one side,
then the other before giving up and hefting the contents into her arms
and onto the floor.

Leo had communicated his intentions clearly, and on several occa-
sions, but she still wanted more. She had no one to blame but herself.

She dug through the mountain of fabric until she found one of the
evening gowns Lily had repaired. She shook out the fabric, then laid
the dress on the bed, smoothing out a wrinkle.

There was no longer a reason to help Leo, but she'd given her
word. She remembered the man, thrashing about in his bed, spittle
flying from his lips. Had they waited too long, and the fever had
damaged his mind?

She found a pair of slippers and placed them at the foot of the bed,
then picked up a needle and thread from her drawer and set to work

repairing a new hole in Angelica's last pair of white gloves, one of the few items they had not ordered replacements for. Her stitches were small and precise, borne of long practice.

A ha'penny from a fountain. That's what the man had said.

What does a ha'penny look like, after it's been sitting at the bottom of a fountain for a few years?

"You know, there are maids here who could do this," Angelica said, interrupting her thoughts.

Saffron smiled at her sister. "I don't mind. And anyway, soon, I won't get to do this anymore and I will miss selecting your evening wear."

Angelica tugged off the skirt and bodice of her gown and dropped them into a pile. "Everyone treats you like a servant."

She collected her sister's discarded clothing, folded it, and set it aside. "I chose this life, sister. No one forced me to do anything."

"It's just not right. Neither of us has a dowry, and yet you are treated differently. It makes me so mad." Angelica kicked off her slippers with such force, they flew across the room and hit the wall.

Saffron put her hands on her sister's shoulders. "The world is not always fair. I've accepted my lot in this life."

Angelica crossed her arms and pouted, but Saffron continued to style her hair and put her together for the night's festivities. She could have asked Lily or another of the maids, but she enjoyed doing it, on occasion. When she finished, she helped her sister into her gown as Angelica smoothed her hands over her bodice, her face full of wonder. Saffron couldn't blame her. The dress was radiant.

The sapphire-hued gown had puffed sleeves and a low neckline. The pale-blue silk underdress was of the finest material she had ever felt, and beneath were a full three layers of petticoats. The skirt was gathered in pleats around the waist and fell to the floor in alternating flounces such that made her look like she was standing in a spray of seafoam.

"It needs one more thing," Saffron said, reaching into her pocket to withdraw a small box. When she opened it, Angelica gasped.

"Mother's brooch?" Angelica said, a note of awe in her voice. "Are you sure? You are the eldest. You should be the one to wear it."

"Nonsense." She affixed the delicate ornament to her sister's dress, marveling at how the quivering brooch reflected the candlelight. It was made of diamonds and sapphires formed with silver wire into a bouquet, set on delicate springs so with every breath, the jewels quivered, catching the light and sparkling.

"All eyes will be on you tonight," she said, placing the last pin. Their father had bought the brooch at great expense during his courtship of his future wife. Angelica had coveted it for years, but Saffron had insisted they save it for a special occasion.

Tonight is that occasion.

"They won't know what to do with you." She pulled the ribbons of her sister's bodice tight enough to support the weight of the gown, but not so tight she would have difficulty breathing.

"It should be you in the spotlight, not me," Angelica whispered. Saffron pulled the ribbons tighter, and her sister fell silent, aside from an occasional muttered curse.

"Keep your distance from the gaslights," she said. She selected an ivory comb carved into the shape of a butterfly from the vanity and slotted it into her sister's hair until it sat like a tiara.

Angelica wrinkled her nose. "I have no wish to light up like a candle." She rose and stood in front of the full-length mirror beside the vanity. She made a small twirl, sending the brooch on her bodice into movement. "Oh, sister. I feel like a princess."

Saffron pulled her sister into her arms, mindful of the care she'd put into her garb, and kissed the top of her head. "You *are* a princess." She paused. "Mr. Mayweather will be in awe."

Angelica's expression shuttered. "His opinion is of no consequence. I am betrothed."

"You don't have to do this," Saffron said. "Lady Allen has offered me a position. Mr. Mayweather might not be wealthy, but I know you care for him."

Angelica sighed. "You don't understand. I'm doing this for *all* of us. We will never have to worry about money again."

"But Lord Canterbury will—"

Angelica twisted out of her grip. "I will hear nothing more about His Grace."

As Angelica left, Saffron looked out the window at the dark-red sky. A storm was brewing.

"Deep thoughts?" Rosemary asked, entering the room and settling onto the bed. "Tell me what worries you. I have some experience in matters of the heart."

Saffron stared at her reflection in the mirror. Rosemary was right. Her skin was washed out and there were large bags around her eyes that even Lily had not been able to hide.

"I'm in love with Lord Briarwood," she said. Saying the words clicked something into place in her heart, as if by saying them, she confirmed the reality of her situation. "I love how much he cares. I love how sensitive he is beneath the gruff exterior. I love how safe I feel in his arms." She dashed away her tears. "But he won't marry me."

Rosemary touched a finger to her cheek. "You've always been sensitive, ever since you were a girl." Rosemary's expression softened. "Marriage was not at all what I expected. I loved my first husband, in my own way. I'd never felt that way for a man before. He wanted a little wife he could stash away in the country and raise a brood of children to ensure his legacy. When time passed and I did not become with child, we were both devastated. But I do not regret my choice, no matter what heartbreak it has brought me."

Saffron ached for her aunt, who had suffered so much. She wanted to offer comfort, but before she could, Rosemary returned to her normal, icy demeanor. "What is your plan, then? You have a plan for everything."

She flushed. "Lady Allen showed me there's another way."

Rosemary chuckled. "I can see why you are torn. Lady Allen is a beautiful woman. I knew her husband. He was not a man I would have chosen for either you or your sister." She breathed a long sigh. "I know you do not approve of His Grace. But I believe in your sister. If anyone can bring the man to heel, it is Angelica." Her aunt wrapped her in a hug. "You are not my daughter, but some days I wish you were. I see the pain in you, and I wish I could take it away. Follow your heart, my dear."

Saffron sniffed. "Thank you." She pulled back and inspected her aunt's expression, seeing a mixture of sadness and guilt. The latter made her pause. "There's something else, isn't there, aunt?"

Rosemary stood. "It is time for you to know the truth. I pray God will forgive me for how long I've kept this from you." She withdrew through the adjoining room and returned holding a red, varnished box with the outline of a silver fox inlaid in the lid.

Basil's old letterbox.

Saffron accepted the small box and placed it in her lap. "Where did you find it?"

"I've had it all along. Please understand, I only wanted to protect you."

Saffron tilted open the lid and took out a stack of letters wrapped in a golden ribbon. Swallowing her apprehension, she unwound the ribbon and opened the first of the letters.

Sister,

It is difficult to find the space to write in my small compartment on the train, but I know you would wish to hear from me, so I borrowed a traveling writing desk from a fellow Englishman. My winnings are small, but I hope they are enough to help.

I will be home for Christmas. I cannot wait to see you and Angelica.

Basil

The date was only a few weeks after his departure. She flipped to the last letter in the stack, tearing it open with trembling fingers.

Sister,

I have been a fool.

I should never have left you, even though I feared the responsibilities of my title. I've returned to London but cannot bear the shame of facing you all. Please allow me a few days to compose myself, and then I will again take up the mantle of our family title.

There is a small bit of good news. I have met the most amazing woman. She is a painter, and a talented one. When I have summoned my strength, I will bring her to meet you.

Basil

She sobbed, holding the letter to her chest.

"Where is he?" she demanded of her aunt.

"He's dead," Rosemary said, dabbing her cheeks with a handkerchief. "The letters stopped after his body was found."

Saffron placed the letters back in the box and replaced the lid. "You lied to me." She held back the brimming anger that threatened to boil over and consume her.

Rosemary twisted her handkerchief. "Yes."

"Why would you hide this from us?"

"I am well familiar with the kind of man who cannot keep his promises," Rosemary said, standing. "Basil would never have returned. If you believe otherwise, you're still a child."

"Get out," Saffron said, dashing her tears away. "Leave me alone."

She had been betrayed after all, and not only by Basil.

Chapter Twenty-Four

S AFFRON STOOD IN the shadows of the ballroom, watching her sister stand stiffly beside the Duke of Canterbury. She had considered and rejected the idea of telling her sister about the letters. It would only hurt her, and she needed all her strength to survive marriage to Canterbury.

Assuming Mr. Mayweather doesn't call him out.

Simon lurked at the fringe of Angelica's entourage, casting baleful glances at the duke. He had made several attempts to engage Angelica in conversation, but she expertly deflected him each time.

In a corner, Lady Allen stood with a drink in her hand, surveying the room. Saffron made her careful way toward the woman, sticking close to the walls, nearly bumping a maid carrying empty glasses back to the kitchen.

"Quite the crush," Lady Allen said. "It's as if the whole of London descended upon us." She wore an elegant gown in olive, watered silk. Large emeralds dripped from her ears and her hair was done up with an oil that smelled of violet.

"The estate has been closed off for so long," Saffron said with a sigh. "We could not turn them away, not when there are no other inns for miles."

The parade of guests had started after they'd returned from the village, and had not let up, keeping them busy for hours. Almost all the guest rooms were occupied, after a herculean effort by Mrs. Banting.

Lady Allen inclined her head, her lips twitching. "Do you intend to purchase anything?"

"I do not have the funds. And you, my lady?"

"I have set my eye on a few," Lady Allen said, although her gaze passed over the paintings and settled on the guests. As her eyes came to rest on Leo, Saffron's shoulders tensed. That would be just her luck if the lovely woman desired an arrangement with the man who had captured her heart.

"You feel something for him, don't you?" Lady Allen asked.

Saffron startled. "You did that on purpose. You were trying to provoke a reaction out of me."

"Well, it worked, didn't it?" Lady Allen laughed, hiding her mouth behind an ornate, ivory fan inlaid with mother-of-pearl gems and fledged with chartreuse lace.

What would it be like to be a companion to such a lady?

"So, you aren't interested in him?" Saffron asked, trying to sound as if she didn't care.

"I do not steal what belongs to others," Lady Allen replied. "I don't need to. However, if he wishes to return to me, I might consider the idea."

Saffron leaned closer, forcing Lady Allen to retreat. "That's enough."

Lady Allen's eyes were wide above the curve of her fan. "Pardon?"

Saffron flicked her hand in a dismissing gesture. "I know what you're doing. Trying to force me into action. It won't work."

She turned and strode away, leaving the older woman standing alone. It took three rotations of the room before she regained control of her emotions.

I can't believe I just did that.

Lady Allen had deserved the rebuke, of course. The woman was an incessant meddler. Given free rein, her interference would only have worsened.

I stood up for myself, that's what I did.

A curious lightness filled Saffron's chest, chasing away the fear and anxiety she'd felt only moments before. She used the moment to peruse the paintings. In each of the smudged faces, she imagined her brother. A hand grazed her hip as Leo came to stand beside her.

"I see Sabrina's face in all of them," he said, in a disturbing echo of her own thoughts. He took her hand and escorted her around, earning gasps from several of the older ladies, who gathered and muttered behind their fans, shooting dark looks their way.

What did they think, seeing her on his arm?

Curiously, she didn't care.

LEO STRUCK THE match against the top of the small, wooden table set at the front of the ballroom. The room was silent, all eyes on him. Wind rattled the shutters and whooshed down the fireplaces to make the flames dance.

"Quit the dramatics," Mr. Morgan called out before being shushed by his wife.

Leo lowered the match to the wick of a four-inch white candle set on a burnished silver stand. The wick flickered and caught flame. When the candle burned out, the auction would end.

As the guests dispersed, he wondered if the thief was present. Detective Jansen had reported nothing, and neither had his sources in the village. But he knew better than to let his guard down. He searched out Saffron, who had taken a position by the exit, artfully laughing with one of his guests. She caught his eyes and winked.

"Capital idea, this auction."

He turned to find Simon standing with a cigar in one hand.

"Ravenmore is quite popular," Leo said.

Each of the pieces of art was presented at a singular platform, with a special moderator to start the bidding on each purchase. With each sale, a footman ran into the room and took one painting and ferried it into the auction room. He stood and watched as painting after painting was removed and the crowd thinned. He was not interested in learning the prices each piece had fetched. He was only interested in the star piece.

The final Ravenmore.

As far as the art society is concerned, anyway.

He expected a pang of loss, but there was none. Seeing how his staff had suffered without his oversight had made him realize he'd been stuck in his own selfish guilt, obsessed with furthering his sister's legacy. He would still paint, of course, but in his own time. The needs of his people had to come first.

It was Saffron who had opened his eyes. Without her caustic tongue and no-nonsense manner, he would have remained mired in darkness.

It's time.

A trusted footman carried the sheet-covered Ravenmore up the stairs and placed it on an easel. Leo waited for the crowd to settle down before pulling the sheet off the painting.

There was a collection of *"ooh"*s and *"aah"*s.

It was an oil painting, like all his sister's other works, with rich colors and bold brushstrokes. In the distance, a woman collected plants from a garden, a straw hat on her head. She was in the upper right of the painting, looking away from the viewer. Looking at it gave Leo a sense of homesickness, as if the woman were waiting for him. That was what made Sabrina's paintings so popular—not the technique, or the setting, but the emotion her artwork elicited.

Leo tore his gaze away from the canvas and watched the faces of his guests, but he could discern nothing from them, other than generalized excitement.

The auction attendant cleared his throat and took his place behind a podium. "The next piece in tonight's auction is the last piece by the celebrated, anonymous painter Ravenmore. An oil painting on canvas.

A pastoral landscape scene in vivid hues. Let us begin the auction at a hundred pounds."

The bids started slowly, which was not at all surprising. The early participants were Simon, to Leo's surprise, and Mr. Morgan. The bidding increased until almost everyone present had bid, aside from Leo, Saffron, and Saffron's sister and aunt.

Eventually, tensions escalated to the point even the auctioneer could not keep the peace. Mr. Morgan struggled in his wife's grip. His face reddened as he screamed bids at the top of his lungs.

"Enough!" Leo glared at Mr. Morgan. "If you do not act like a gentleman, I will have you removed."

Mrs. Morgan clutched at her husband's arm, and the man coughed into his handkerchief.

The bidding then continued until the only remaining bidders were Lady Allen, whom Leo suspected only wanted to tweak the other participant, and Mr. Morgan. The flush on the man's face brightened with each increase in price. Lady Allen giggled behind her fan. But eventually, she stopped bidding and laid back in her chair with a defeated sigh.

"Are there any other bids?" the auction attendant asked. When no hands were raised, he continued. "In that case, our winner is Mr. Morgan, at fifteen hundred pounds."

The crowd mumbled appreciatively. Even Leo was pleased.

With the auction over, he congratulated each of the winners, starting with Mr. Morgan. The man patted his face with a napkin, sweating profusely. "That wretched woman almost bid me out of house and home." He glared at Lady Allen, who was giggling.

"Had I not expected this, she might have won," Mr. Morgan said.

"What do you mean?" Leo asked.

The man gave a smug grin. "I had my solicitor, Mr. Percy, sell several antiques to ensure I had sufficient funds."

So that was why Saffron had seen the two men outside.

"What will you do with it?" Leo asked.

The man puffed out his chest. "Show it off, of course. Now I can say that I own a piece of art from the famous Ravenmore."

Leo sighed.

I should have guessed.

He no longer suspected Mr. Morgan. If the man were his thief, it would not make sense to keep the painting.

At least the auction had brought Saffron into his life. She was already busy coordinating the activities for the next day, and he thought he could hear her asking about the breakfast buffet.

"Rashers of bacon, and poached eggs for breakfast," she said. "With the cool weather, the guests will need to warm themselves up before departing."

The words sent a chill through Leo's heart. She was going to leave. A few days earlier, the thought of having his studio back would have filled him with joy, but all he felt was emptiness. She had returned his estate to what it had once been before time and tragedy had worn away the joy that had once penetrated every stone of the walls.

She was still talking, but Leo didn't hear a word. All he could think was he was out of time.

Chapter Twenty-Five

S AFFRON HELD HER fist up, preparing to knock on the door to Lady Allen's room, while resisting the urge to run. In the hours since the auction had ended, she had changed her mind a dozen times about approaching the woman.

Angelica has settled to her fate. Now it is my turn.

Rosemary was right about putting away her fantasies. If Lady Allen's offer of employment was still open, she would accept it. She would become whatever Lady Allen required, even if it meant being the subject of gossip and derision.

As she debated, a jumble of nerves, a gray blob bounded across the hall, dragging a white string.

Cinder!

Eager to have any excuse to delay her decision, she darted after the waddling shape, but the kitten moved with surprising swiftness, using her claws to propel her along the carpet runner. Then she veered right through a half-open door and vanished.

Saffron hesitated at the threshold. She did not want to barrel into an occupied room or be spotted and questioned as to why she was wandering the halls at night alone. A quick recall of the floor plan confirmed she was outside the viscountess's rooms.

Where Leo's future wife will sleep.

She grasped the door handle and hesitated. She couldn't enter. Visions of the room would haunt her dreams.

She averted her eyes and pulled the door slightly so that Cinder would not get trapped inside, then spun on her heel and marched back the way she'd come. She was halfway back to Lady Allen's door when a hissing came from behind her, then a yowl and a muffled curse.

A shiver of unease rippled down her back. She tiptoed back to the entrance to the room and clung to the wall, listening intently.

Claws clicking against wood. Shuffling. Another, louder, curse. Then Cinder galloped out of the room, her fur on end.

Saffron pressed herself against the wall as the door creaked open and a man in a black suit exited, carrying a white-shrouded canvas in his arms. She held her breath, but the painting blocked his view of her.

It might be nothing, she thought. Several of the guests were leaving early, and they might have arranged for their paintings to be brought to their carriages.

But it might also be the thief.

She couldn't see the painting the man carried beneath the shroud, so she didn't know if it was the Ravenmore or one of the other paintings from the auction.

The man walked quietly away from her, and she followed, staying far enough behind that if the man noticed her, she had time to run.

He crept through the house, down the stairs and into the servants' hallways, where it was harder to keep up. After three twisting turns, she lost sight of him and recklessly increased her pace until she rounded a corner at a fast speed and ran face-first into a muscular chest.

"Whoa, there," Leo said, clasping his hands around her upper arms.

She craned her neck. "Did you see him?"

He quirked an eyebrow. "Who?"

"The thief!"

He released his grip on her arms. "There's no one the way I came. What, precisely, did you see?"

As she filled him in, his lips thinned.

"Wait here," he said. "I'll summon Sinclair to search."

He strode purposefully away from her, and she followed. A few chaotic moments later, a storm of sleepy-eyed servants were up and scouring the estate. Then he took her arm and insisted on accompanying her back to her room, which she accepted.

"What were you doing?" he asked softly as they ascended the main staircase. "It's not safe for you to be walking around so late, unchaperoned."

She sniffed. "I was going to tell Lady Allen that I accept her offer."

His arm stiffened beneath her fingers. "You're leaving."

The flat finality in his words stabbed at her heart. "I have to."

As they reached the top of the stairs, he abruptly turned in the opposite direction of her room, steering her with him. Her heart fluttered in her breast, but she didn't comment. If it was their last night together, she wanted it to be one to remember. Consequences be damned. Neither her family nor her future employer needed to know.

Leo led her to his room, then stopped. "Are sure you want this?"

She swallowed reflexively. "Yes."

He opened the door for her, then locked it behind them.

The room was as she remembered, with a towering bed against one wall, and the blinds drawn tight. The only light came from the smoldering remains of a fireplace.

Arms closed around her from behind. She relaxed into the comfort of his embrace.

He feathered kisses down her neck and her pulse hammered with anticipation, dampness gathering between her thighs. She was powerless to resist him.

He pulled away and tugged off his waistcoat and shirt, tossing them into the corner. His finely sculpted chest was beaded with perspiration, and she watched a droplet of sweat slide from his navel down to the waistband of his trousers. Her mouth watered as she remembered what lay beneath the layers of fabric.

He stepped closer and she met him in a searing kiss, their tongues tangling in a slow dance. He tasted like caramel and apples, and the coarse stubble that rubbed her cheek sent heat pulsing to her core.

He slipped his hands under her skirts, then up her sides, until the fabric of her gown was splayed around her hips. Then he dropped to his knees and trailed a line of hot, open-mouthed kisses from her ankle up to her quim.

"This is unfair," she said, pointing to the prominent tenting of his trousers. "It's your turn now."

"As you wish." He placed his hands on his stomach then slid them down until his fingers pushed beneath his waistband. "You want me to remove this?"

At her halting nod, he unbuttoned his trousers, then stepped out of them one leg at a time. His erection tented his drawers, and she reached out a hand, but he danced out of her reach.

"Remove the rest," she said impatiently.

Leo unbuttoned his fall, and his cock sprang free. He stroked it twice before releasing it and removing his drawers, leaving him standing nude before her but for his socks. He put his hands on his hips and waited, as if daring her to comment.

Remembering how he'd responded before, she fell to her knees and grasped his cock in both hands, then slid her mouth over him. He tasted salty and the skin her tongue caressed was so soft.

He gave a strangled moan and dug his fingers into her hair, guiding her movement with his strong hands, until he grew even larger and hotter in her mouth.

"Enough," Leo said. "It's my turn." He stepped back, pulling his cock out of her mouth, then took her hands and drew her up to stand, facing away from him. "Put your hands on the bed."

She did so, her cheeks pulsing with heat at the impropriety of it. His touch warmed her skin and made her tingle all over.

"I want to see all of you," Leo whispered, rubbing her thigh. "May I undress you?"

Her response was more gasp than words, but she followed up with an audible, "Yes."

His fingers left her skin, making her want to cry out. But it was only a few moments of soft shuffling before her gown gaped open at the back, and his hands returned to caress her shoulders. He continued in that manner, removing layer after layer of fabric until she stood in a heap of it.

He turned her around and captured her lips once again. She wantonly pressed her naked flesh to his, cradling his still-erect cock with her stomach.

"What do you want?" he asked between kisses. "Tell me, Saffron. Say the words."

"I want pleasure," she said. "I want you inside me."

"As you wish," he whispered. Then he took her hands and guided her to the bed. He crawled up the bed, and she wrapped her arms around his neck, meeting his lips as he speared her, then rocked gently up and down. The burst of pleasure was different, gently fluttering up from the space where their bodies joined and warming her all the way to the tip of her head.

"That's it," Leo said. "It feels—ah!" He withdrew from her before finishing on the top sheet of the bed. He then balled it up and threw it in the corner. The act seemed wrong, somehow, although she could not put her finger on why that was.

Then he lifted the covers, and she snuggled up to his chest, putting his earlier actions out of her mind. They were together, and nothing else mattered.

"I cannot stay long," he whispered. He pressed a kiss to her temple. "When you awake, I will be gone."

"I understand," she said, but secretly, she was imagining what it might be like to wake up with him at her side. How she would crawl onto his chest and twirl his glorious hair between her fingers until his eyes fluttered open.

That can never happen.

The realization that they might never sleep in the same bed again settled over her and made her shiver.

"Cold?" Leo whispered.

She nodded, unable to trust that her words would be free of tears. She didn't want him to know what she was thinking, as it would ruin the moment. Their last moment.

Leo splayed an arm over her and gently rubbed her hip until she drifted into a restless slumber.

Chapter Twenty-Six

S AFFRON STOOD OUTSIDE the small, two-roomed cottage at the edge of the forest, at the far edge of the Briarwood lands, preparing herself for what would be an unpleasant conversation. She looked down at the sheet of thick vellum in her hands, the words "Come at your earliest convenience" written on it in large, dark ink. A footman had delivered it to her shortly after she'd snuck out of Leo's bedroom. She'd been tempted to tell him, but her heart was too conflicted where he was concerned.

She shifted. The woman she was about to meet had once been a paragon of society, unmatched in influence, but she hadn't been seen in years. Saffron knew what it was like to grieve, had done so for her parents and brother.

She pushed open the door and stepped into a relic of a lost time. A table was set with cutlery and small cakes. She took a cautious sniff, but there was no rot in the air, only a stale smell, like laundry left out in a wet pile to dry instead of being hung up.

A shuffling noise had her turning her gaze to the chair near the fireplace. The small woman sitting there was dressed in a black gown with long sleeves, black shoes, and a black veil over her face.

"You've come," a thin voice said. "I was not sure you would."

The woman pulled the veil from over her face, and Saffron curtseyed. "It is my honor, Lady Briarwood."

The Dowager Viscountess Briarwood waved her hand. "Please, sit, and call me 'Clara.'"

Saffron sat in a matching chair in front of the fireplace and waited as the dowager summoned a maid and ordered tea. They sat in awkward silence as the maid left and then returned and served them.

Finally, the dowager broke the silence by leaning forward, making her chair creak. "So, you are the woman who has ensnared my son. Mrs. Banting has told me much about you."

Saffron paused in the action of reaching for a cup, torn between feeling insulted by the bold claim and pleased by the dowager's approving tone.

"You do not deny it, then," the dowager said, with a smile. "Well done, girl." She shuffled in her seat. "Has he asked for your hand yet?"

Saffron gaped. How had she so completely lost hold of the conversation? The dowager truly was a formidable woman.

"Answer the question, girl, and close your mouth."

"N-No. Lady Briarwood, I—"

"A summer wedding is out of the question, but we might consider next spring. Assuming you are not already with child."

"He will not marry me!" Saffron shouted. Then she winced, expecting the dowager to reprimand her impoliteness. "And I would not bully him into it against his wishes."

Instead, Clara burst into wheezing laughter. After several long moments, during which Saffron was too puzzled to speak, the dowager slapped her thigh with her palm. "Excellent. You have spirit. Please excuse my teasing. I had to see for myself."

Saffron squared her shoulders. "It was a test. Lady Br—Clara. That is why you asked to see me."

The dowager sipped her own tea, then set the cup down. When the porcelain bottom of the cup hit the saucer, it made several clinking sounds, as if the hand holding it were unsteady.

"There are rumors about you, my dear. I am glad to see they are incorrect."

Saffron almost laughed. "The rumors are true. I cannot abide many things. A crowded room. Disruptions to my carefully laid plans. Many in society call me odd."

Clara raised one thin eyebrow. "What does that matter?"

Saffron felt her cheeks flushing. "I did not come here to be toyed with, my lady."

"Why did you come, then?" The dowager picked up a small cake and nibbled on it. "You might as well get out with it. I'm not getting any younger."

Saffron bit the inside of her cheek. How could she ask the woman about her brother, when the dowager had already lost so much? Although part of her hoped that the dowager would have answers, another part of her feared those answers would be ones she did not want.

"I have... *had* a brother," Saffron started.

"Yes, I heard about the incident."

Saffron's stomach twisted in knots. "The incident?"

The dowager raised her eyebrows. "The dissolution of your family."

She flushed. "Yes. Well, then I saw my brother's face in one of Miss Mayweather's paintings. I asked Lord Briarwood, but he does not know when she painted it." She pulled the portrait of her brother from her pocket and handed it to the dowager. "That is why I am here to ask you if you know when your daughter could have painted him."

"I remember him," the dowager said slowly. "Sabrina said there was something about his face that inspired her. She painted him the night before she died." The dowager's face filled with pity. "I'm sorry, my dear, but your brother is dead."

Her hands twisted the fabric of her gown in her lap. "How can you be sure?"

The dowager sighed. "Because I was there when they boarded that ship together. Sabrina could not wake Leopold, so I took her instead.

But I've never been able to abide boats, so I sent one of my maids with her. It is a decision I will regret as long as I live. They both died that day when the ship crashed on the Thames. Your brother died the same day as my daughter."

Chapter Twenty-Seven

WHERE THE DEVIL *is she?*

By the time Leo completed his third rotation of the estate, he was certain something was wrong. Saffron had worked so hard to arrange the event. It was unlike her not to be bustling about. He'd even had to unsnarl two minor emergencies on his own, which further spiked his concerns.

Finally, he set out for her room again, taking the steps two at a time. When he arrived, the door was open, and Mrs. Banting was inside, talking to a fiery-haired maid.

"Where is she?" he barked, storming into the room.

"We aren't sure," Mrs. Banting replied. "I was just speaking to the maid assigned to assist her. Lily—"

"She would'nae let me see the note!" Lily cried. "I tried to tell her it was a bad idea, but she—" She broke off, lower lip trembling. Mrs. Banting patted her on the shoulder. "It is not your fault. A more stubborn girl I've never met. I doubt even I—"

Leo held up a hand. "Stop. Fill me in from the beginning. What note?"

The story tumbled out of the maid in pieces, with Mrs. Banting filling in when Lily broke into sobs.

"The footman came early, and then she called me. I tried to convince her, but she wouldn't budge."

Mrs. Banting squeezed the girl's shoulder. "Lily outfitted her with riding gear and a cloak, then came straight to me when she finished. I spoke to the footman, but he'd never seen the person who delivered it before. She took a gray mare and headed out. That's all we know."

Leo restrained himself from throttling the woman. It wasn't her fault that the situation was eerily familiar to the morning he'd woken up to learn Sabrina had gone on the cursed boat without him.

Not this time. I won't fail her the way I failed Sabrina.

He'd grown, changed. He wouldn't rush out on a horse, thick in denial, determined to solve the problem on his own. There were other people who cared about Saffron, and he would leverage every single one of them.

"Find Miss Summersby's sister and aunt," he said to Lily. "Maybe she told one of them where she was going." Then he faced Mrs. Banting. "Assemble as many servants as you can to climb to the top floor and look out the windows. If she's within eyesight, someone might see her."

SAFFRON WALKED ALONG the shore, arms limp at her sides. She thought about going through the garden, trailing her fingers over the delicate buds. Instead, she made for the river where the small boats floated, the soft swish of water hitting their halls, the chains and bells jangling.

Thoughts flickered through her mind, too fast for her to track. Everything she'd feared had come true. Basil was dead. Angelica would marry the duke. Rosemary was content to rent a small room, supported by the small pension left by her late husband.

Where does that leave me?

She could stay the path. Put the thought of her brother and her sister behind her, and join Lady Allen as a companion, free to pursue her own interests, including being Leo's mistress.

Is that really what you want?

For the first time in longer than she could remember, Saffron considered herself as others saw her.

Strange. Fidgety. Unmarriageable.

But that wasn't right. She'd facilitated an important event despite a near stream of disruptions. She'd earned the trust of Leo's household staff. She'd explored her passions with a willing man and fallen in love.

With so many successes under her belt, why should she care what society thought of her?

A heavy weight seemed to slip from her shoulders, and she spun around, ready to return to the auction. She would remain at Leo's side, married or not.

That was when she saw the ship.

It sat in the bay, a silver chain draped over the edge, anchoring it. There was something about it that was so familiar, and as she rose and approached, her brows rose.

It was black, with a line of white near the top and a hint of red beneath the waves. Her heart stuttered. The figurehead was a man with a curling beard holding a round shield in one arm and a sword in the other, facing forward as if charging into battle.

It was the boat from the painting.

She picked up her pace, her heart pounding in her ears. Was it possible that the dowager was wrong, that Basil had survived the wreck?

She halted at the edge of the waterfront before she accidentally tumbled in and drowned. She had to be sure it was the same boat. She searched for a dinghy that she could use, while thinking she was mad for even considering such a thing. She didn't know whose boat it was. She had no proof that it had anything to do with her brother. But something inside her insisted she needed to get on the boat.

She followed the waterline, her eyes scouting the rocky shore, looking for a dinghy someone had left behind. Instead, she found a fisherman loading his tools into a small boat close to shore.

"Sir!" Saffron cried.

The man turned toward her, tilting his hat back from his head. "Aye, lady?"

Before she could answer, arms closed around her from behind, crushing her back against a heaving chest.

"There you are," Leo said, breathlessly. "Thank God."

Her earlier concerns forgotten, Saffron struggled out of his arms, then pointed to the boat. "Look! It's the same as the painting. How is that possible? Your mother said it crashed."

"It's just a ship, Saffron. Many of them look similar."

Why couldn't he understand? Even if it wasn't the same boat, she had to know. If she didn't find out, it would haunt her dreams, the possibility that Basil had been there, and she'd dismissed it.

Leo cupped her cheeks in his hands, then touched their foreheads together. "This is important to you?"

"Yes." Her voice sounded small and far away.

"Then it's important to me."

He released her, handed over a handful of heavy golden coins to the fisherman, then swooped down and picked her up in one smooth motion.

She squirmed in his grip. "W-What are you doing?"

Leo shuffled her in his arms then began walking toward the boat. His boots sank deep in the sludge with a loud, sucking sound.

Saffron's cheeks heated. She flexed her feet in her thin slippers. "Oh."

"You would never have made it," Leo said as he struggled through the deep mud. "Not without ruining that dress."

She crossed her arms. "I don't care about the dress."

"Nevertheless, gather it up before it gets wet. I don't want you to get sick."

She clutched the heavy fabric to her chest, but by the time he deposited her on the boat, she was filthy, with leaves sticking to her hair and dress, her hem completely soaked. She took a moment to rip off the bottom of her gown, muttering an apology for Lily for her treatment of the fine material, and then put it at the bottom of the boat.

As Leo took up the oars, she kept her eyes on the ship. It loomed over her like the Tower of London, casting a shadow on everything beneath it. The birds chirped, the waves lapped against the shore, and the trees creaked in the wind. She could smell the damp, rotten wood, and the salty sea air.

"I admit the resemblance is uncanny," Leo said as the small craft thumped against the side of the hull. "What is it doing here?"

"Let's board and see." Saffron knew she was being impulsive, but the excitement of their find simmered in her blood, making her jittery.

Leo tried to dissuade her, but she could tell from the way his eyes kept darting to the side that he was as curious as her.

"Help me up." She turned to the boat and placed her hands on the cold hull. There was no rope or ladder, but a life raft hung over the side above her head. With Leo's hands supporting her hips, she grabbed on to a trailing rope and hauled herself onto the deck, falling into it, her hands burning from the strain.

She didn't wait for Leo and ducked around beams holding the sails, walking to below decks, hoping to find some proof that it was the same one she had seen in Ravenmore's painting.

The boat rocked gently as she walked, and she had to clutch at ropes to keep from falling. Leo called her name, but she couldn't stop. Not when she was so close.

"Basil! Basil, are you here?"

She checked the first door in the hall but found nothing other than crew quarters strung up with hammocks and smelling like they needed desperately to be cleaned. Waving her hand in front of her face, she firmly closed the doors and continued. The largest door at the end of the hall was a wooden affair intricately carved with sailing imagery of waves and mermaids. She opened it and found mounds of white cloth that smelled strongly of oil.

She grasped the edge of one of the slick clothes and tugged it off.

There was no doubt. It was a Ravenmore. As she wiped the oil from her hand, she recognized Ravenmore's distinctive style. She sorted through the paintings. All were Ravenmore's.

Her heart sank. The ship had nothing to do with her brother. She pushed away her disappointment and focused on the significance of her discovery.

How did they get here?

She pressed her thumb into the scalloped edge of a frame. The wood was soft.

These are the originals.

Was the thief going from museum to museum, stealing artwork? If that were true, she would have heard about it in the paper. Unless, of course, the paintings had been replaced with forgeries.

She returned abovedeck and saw for the first time that black clouds loomed on the horizon.

Leo was beside the life raft, his head swiveling around, his hair loose and flying in the wind. When he spotted her, he grasped her upper arms in a gentle grip. "God, Saffron! Don't do that again." He made to pull her close, but she held out her arms to stop him.

"They're all here, Leo. All the Ravenmore paintings. Come see." She took his hand and drew him back to the room, then stood back as he inspected the canvases. Finally, he stood, his lips thin.

"I think we've discovered how our thief intends to escape."

"What do we do?" Saffron asked. They couldn't bring all the paintings back to land, not on the dinghy, and the ship was too big to bring to shore. How long did they have before the thief returned?

We can't do this alone.

"We need help," Leo said, in an uncanny echo of her thoughts. He slicked back his wet hair. "The constable. The village is a short row away. We can be across and back before the thief returns, God willing."

They returned to the deck and peered over the edge, where the dinghy floated. There was no ladder or other way to shimmy down.

"There must be a rope on this ship somewhere," Leo said. Then he glared at her. "Promise me you will not move from this spot until I return."

She promised, and she was still waiting, leaning against the railing, the howling wind drowning out the sound of the waves, when a clunk of heavy boots on the deck made her turn.

A tall man walked toward her, dressed in a green suit with bronze buttons and smiling with malice.

"You!" Saffron exclaimed, incredulous.

Mr. Percy, Leo's solicitor, made an exaggerated bow, then pulled a pistol out from behind his back and held it at his side.

A ha'penny from a fountain. Tarnished bronze. The exact color of Percy's suit. That's what the sick man meant.

"Well, what are you waiting for?" Percy gestured toward the side of the boat with his pistol. He had closed the distance between them so that there was nowhere for her to escape.

Leo, where are you?

She hoped he was close by, waiting for a chance to attack Percy. "Why are you doing this?" she asked, casting her eyes carefully over her surroundings, searching for a weapon, or a glimpse of Leo.

"Searching for your lover?" Percy laughed, a nasty sound. "Don't bother."

"What have you done with him?" Saffron asked.

Percy whistled, then mimed a splash.

Oh, God, no.

She lunged forward, hands reaching for the pistol, but Percy was too quick. He struck her across the cheek with the weapon, sending her staggering to the deck. A hot rush of blood streamed out of her nose, and she clamped her hand to the tender side of her face.

"Don't do this!" she cried.

"Get up," Percy commanded.

Saffron struggled to her feet, one hand on the railing, the other on her nose. When she glanced up, Percy had backed away and lowered the pistol to his side.

"Damn woman," Percy said with a snarl. "If it weren't for you and your dogged interest in the Ravenmores, I could have convinced Briarwood to give up this auction nonsense. This is all your fault."

It wasn't true, of course, because Leo had caught on to the swapped paintings before she had met him. Perhaps Percy had settled on her as the source of his problems because he'd wanted a way to re-assert control over his failing plan. Regardless, she wasn't about to argue with a man holding a pistol.

"You should've died in that carriage," Percy said.

The accident.

"You gave me your invitation," she said, wiping blood from her cheek. The clues were piecing together in her mind to form a disturbing whole. There was only one road to Briarwood Manor. The perfect place for a trap.

"Enough talking," he said, gesturing with his other hand to the railing. "Over the side. I insist."

Saffron blindly reached for the rope holding the lifeboat while keeping her assailant in her field of vision. It took a few tries, but eventually, she caught hold.

She looked over the side of the boat and had only a second to se-cure herself before an ashy smell alerted her to the smoke trickling out of the entrance to the lower deck.

Fire. The ship is on fire.

"Damn you, woman, get off this ship," Percy said angrily. Then he sniffed, and his face paled. "Smoke. The paintings!" He whipped around and dashed for the doorway. Before he could reach it, Leo dove out of the shadows and tackled him.

A shot rang out, and Saffron screamed.

Chapter Twenty-Eight

L EO AND PERCY struggled on the ground, both bloodied. Saffron couldn't tell which had been shot. The smoke choked the air from her lungs and burned her eyes.

The boat lurched hard to one side and she had a flash of how her brother and Leo's sister, Sabrina, must have felt knowing that the ship they were on was going down, wondering if they would survive, listening to the screams of everyone around them.

She mentally shook herself. There was no one else, no huge group of innocents who would be taken down with the ship when it sank.

She grabbed the edge of the railing and returned shakily to her feet. The pistol was only a few feet away. She didn't know how to use the weapon, but she could remove it from Percy's reach. She dove for the chunk of metal and tossed it as far away from the struggling men as she could.

She fell against a wooden crate and clung. It would not be long before the boat slipped beneath the waves. She put her hands on her waist, digging her fingers into the thick fabric of her corset beneath her dress. The ruffles and layers of fabric were like a cage. Once she hit the water, it would soak into the layers and send her down into the deep like an anchor. Gooseflesh puckered down her arms as the boat lurched again.

She stripped off her clothing until she wore only her shift, stockings, and slippers. Then she gathered up the rest of her clothes in a ball and searched for something that would float. The nearest box was cracked open. She shoved her clothing inside and peered over the edge of the boat into the writhing ocean beneath.

"Saffron, get off this boat!" Leo shouted. "I am right behind you."

Stop waiting, and just do it.

She tossed the box overboard and followed it. When her feet hit the water, the shock of intense cold made her stiffen, biting into her like a thousand little knives. She paddled toward the dinghy as quickly as she could, but it drifted stubbornly away. A loud bang sounded, and she whipped around to see Percy's pistol pointed toward the boat.

She swam, knowing that if she stopped, the water would drag her down. But with every stroke of her arms, the lethargy set in. She wasn't cold, but hot.

Darkness crowded in the side of her vision, and it was harder and harder to move her limbs. The sea tugged at her, sucking her down into its dark depths. She wanted nothing more than to stop and rest, but if she did, that would be the end of her until they dragged her bloated body from the ocean.

Cold, salty water rushed into her nose and mouth. She gasped out a breath. Beside her, the ship continued to sway. Seconds later, there was a splash.

"Leo!"

She turned around and kicked as hard as she could until she could kick no more.

LEO'S MIND SPLIT from his body as he stared down at the frothing waves below. Saffron was gone, swept beneath the seafoam. His leg pulsed blood, and his head swam from Percy's blow. He coughed as the smoke curled around him, a reminder of the fire he'd set.

I'm sorry, sister.

The paintings, covered in oils, had erupted into flames even faster than he'd expected. But the distraction had worked, and his solicitor was no longer a threat. Shortly after Saffron had jumped, a heavy crate had tumbled onto Percy, crushing him. They were lucky that Percy was a terrible shot and had missed them.

Leo felt as if he were floating above his body as he lifted one leg over the railing then fell into the waves and sank.

A rush of cold water threw him back into his senses and he gasped a harsh breath. Wave after wave broke over his head, pulling him down into the depths of the harbor. Even so close to shore, it was fifteen, twenty feet or more to the bottom, and the sea was angry.

He listened for the sound of Saffron's voice, hoping against hope he would see a pale hand sticking up, or hear her yell his name. But as he spun around, kicking his legs against the strong current, there was nothing but cresting waves around him, battering him against the side of the ship.

The water rushed over his head and filled his nose with salty brine. His chest burned as it dripped down his throat, and he coughed.

As he floated there, unsure of what he was even doing, he heard his sister's voice crying out.

"Leo!"

The waves around him darkened. Countless voices around him called out for help.

But whom to help first?

Women and children scrambled in the muck, drowning each other in their attempts to get to freedom. There was crying and splashing all around as the ship moaned as it sunk beneath the water.

His sister was there, inches in front of him, struggling to pull herself out of her layers of clothing that pulled her down. He saw her face, heard her call out his name, and then she was gone, her hand disappearing in a flash.

"No!"

He dove, following the specter of his sister as she sank, her ghost-white face staring up at him, mouthing words he couldn't hear.

Then he was being pulled back to the surface. His head broke the water, and he coughed, the water burning his lungs. Something sharp pricked below his knee and he realized too late there was a jagged piece of metal sticking up from the side of the boat that had sliced him open.

"Leo!"

Saffron's voice.

He rubbed the salt from his face. She had stripped down to her shift, her hair a wet mass on top of her head. She hung from the side of an unfamiliar boat, her hands tangled in his coat. Simon and Miss Angelica stood behind her, clutching her coat to keep her from falling overboard.

"Remove your jacket!" she said, and he did, shrugging it off and grabbing her hands as wave after wave hammered them.

"We're almost out, Leo, hold on." Her face was twisted with worry, and she clutched his hands tighter.

A fiery sensation licked his toes, but his mind was far, far away, still diving deeper, his sister forever just out of reach.

Chapter Twenty-Nine

L EO WAS SURROUNDED by a suffocating warmth.

It's so damn hot.

A series of coughs racked him as he thrashed, desperate to feel the cool air on his skin.

"More cool water. Open those windows. Where is the doctor?" Saffron's fear-ridden voice carried as she barked commands.

He closed his eyes. His face was so hot, and his right leg throbbed. He kicked the blankets away, but someone held him and wrapped him up again. He moaned, then coughed until his throat was raw.

"Rest, Leo. It's not over yet."

A small hand slipped into his and squeezed. He pulled all the comfort he could from the gesture and did his best to avoid fighting the people who were trying to save his life.

A cool cloth touched his temple. It felt so good against his skin that he moaned.

"I'm here," Saffron said. She swept his hair away from his forehead. He leaned into her touch, a distraction from pain. As if sensing his need, she ran her fingers through his hair, again and again. At the same time, she kept talking to him, soft words that he clung to without any real understanding.

"You might not have made it if it weren't for Angelica and Mr. Mayweather following you. My sister was so angry with me."

"Angelica is still determined to marry the Duke of Canterbury, against my advice." A deep sigh. "She won't listen to me. I told Mr. Mayweather to show her how he feels. Maybe he will be able to get through to her."

Silence, then, for a long time, although Saffron's hand continued to caress his head.

Later, the embers burning around him transformed into a cold so intense that his teeth chattered, and his fingers prickled. He curled his legs to his body and burrowed deeper into the nest of blankets.

"Leo?"

Footfalls approached, then the bed dipped.

"How are you?" Warm fingers touched his cheek, then she gasped. "You're freezing!"

She tugged at the blankets. "Leo, please, let me check your leg."

Grudgingly, he relaxed his grip and let her peel the blankets away from his lower body. When she was done poking and prodding him, she covered him up and then vanished. He strained to hear her voice, wished he could shout for her to come back. She could do whatever she wanted to his leg, if only she stayed. Her touch, her voice, chased away some of the pain.

After what seemed like hours, she returned. This time, he didn't wait for her to make up her mind. He shot his arm through the blankets and grabbed her hand.

"Stay," he croaked.

More sniffling. Then he felt her lie beside him on the bed, above the covers. He wanted more, longed to have her sweet warmth pressed against his frozen flesh.

"Leo?" she whispered.

He forced away the fog of pain to focus on her voice. "Yes?"

She peeled away the blankets around his head. He was glad to see her, even if her eyes were puffy, her cheeks flushed. She touched their noses together once, gently. The tenderness in her eyes made his heart throb.

He inched his head close enough to press a gentle kiss to her lips, then pulled back. "If I don't survive this, know that I love you."

She smiled, even as tears dripped down her nose to dampen the sheets. "I love you too. And you will survive. I won't let you die."

"Get under the covers."

She blinked twice, then laughed. "When you recover."

"Stay until I fall asleep, then," he said.

She sniffed again. "Of course."

With that promise, he let his fatigued body drag him into slumber.

WHEN LEO WOKE next, the world was clearer. Aside from the gray haze and pinch in his chest, he felt almost normal. As he made to stand, his head spun, and he fell back. The door creaked open, and someone stepped inside. It was a young maid who approached him cautiously.

He groaned, getting up from the bed. Every muscle in his body ached. "Where am I?"

"The home of Mr. Simon Mayweather, milord," the maid said. She scurried forward, set a tray containing a large breakfast on the table beside the bed, then left, almost catching her skirt in the closing door in her rush to depart.

Odd.

How long had it been since the crash? Simon's home was miles away from the Briarwood lands, in the middle of the countryside. How had they transported him so far without him realizing it?

More importantly, where is Saffron?

He remembered her calling to him in the water, her pale arm sinking beneath the waves. A moment later, new memories slid into focus, hazy snippets of conversation as he thrashed beneath covers that were too hot. Her voice calming him, her soft hands touching his cheek. Their declarations of love.

His heart soared. She loved him. He hadn't dreamed that part. Wherever she was, he was certain she was safe. She could not remain by his side throughout all hours of the day, nor would he have wanted her to.

The savory smell of the tray beside the bed made his stomach growl. He tried to remember the last time he had eaten but couldn't. Pulling his legs out from beneath the blanket, he reached for the tray.

Then he realized that below his knee there was nothing but a rounded stump marred by an angry, raised scar.

He could still feel his foot, could still flex, and sense the motion of his toes, but there was nothing there. He reached for the air where his foot would have been, and the sensation was eerily familiar, as if the bottom part of his leg were invisible.

I'm seeing things, he thought, waving his hand back and forth beneath his knee. *I'm still delirious in bed.*

He grabbed a pitcher of water from the tray and peered into it. The face that stared back was pale and thin, with heavy bags under the eyes. It was a face that spoke of a long convalescence.

He threw the pitcher against the wall and fell onto his back on the bed. Anger swirled inside him, at the doctors who could not save his limb, and at himself for making the mistake that had led to the amputation.

What will Saffron think of me now?

He tucked his mangled leg beneath the blanket, unable to look at it.

His stomach rumbled, and he grudgingly rose. When he'd finished sopping up the last of the eggs with a rich slice of bread, he went to itch his foot, but there was no foot there to scratch. His fingers curled into a fist. He put the tray aside and attempted to rise. His remaining leg nearly buckled beneath him, but he forced his way to stand, stretching out each muscle until it screamed.

He found a crutch by the door and slipped his arm over the padded leather fabric. The world spun around him before settling again. He pulled open the nearest trunk and found, to his relief, a pile of clothes. The trousers were tight around the waist, and he had to tie the bottom of one leg beneath the knee, but it was better than waiting to be tended upon like an invalid.

As he struggled to close the small buttons on the cuffs of the white linen shirt he'd found in the trunk, the door opened, and Leo turned to see Saffron clutching at the door frame. She was dressed in a gold-embroidered bodice without the matching skirt, her petticoats clinging to her legs. A maid followed her, hauling a mass of gold fabric in her arms.

"Madam, you ought not—" The maid spotted Leo, and twin circles of red appeared on her cheeks. "Christ, m'lord, you're awake!"

Saffron flung herself into his chest, and it took all his strength to keep her from bowling him over. He staggered back to fall on his rear on the bed, with Saffron kneeling in front of him, her arms around his shoulders.

"I'll leave you two to get reacquainted," the maid said, closing the door.

"I thought I would lose you," Saffron whispered. "Thank God. Thank God."

He pulled her close, breathing in the clean smell of her hair. "You are with me now. That is all that matters." He kissed the top of her head. "Would you mind explaining why we are at my cousin's home?"

"You floated so far down the river. When we got you out, we were afraid to move you. This was the closest house." She pressed her lips to his collarbone and his body reminded him urgently that it had been a long time since he'd last indulged himself. At the same time, he was painfully aware of his own limitations.

"Saffron, I might not be able to... complete the act," he said between gasping breaths. She was doing miraculous things with her tongue that made his toes curl.

"I want to take care of you," she said, continuing her path down his chest. She rasped her tongue over his nipple, and the sensation made his cock throb. He grasped her hips and fell on his back. She remained atop him, her hair unbound and falling around her face.

He'd never seen anything more beautiful in his entire life.

SAFFRON PLACED HER legs on either side of Leo's hips and felt the solid length of him beneath his trousers. She couldn't believe she was acting in such a wanton fashion. Seeing Leo standing had lit a fire inside her that would not be extinguished.

She unbuttoned his shirt, then kissed the inch of skin that was revealed, until there were no buttons left, and her lips had reached a thatch of crinkly hair.

"Should I continue?" she asked, running one finger along the visible bulge in his trousers.

Leo threaded his fingers through her hair. "God, woman. You will make me come undone."

His words fueled her desire, and she could no longer stand the games. With frantic movements, she tore the remaining clothes from his body, and her own, until they were both naked and panting. His scarred leg gave her pause, but not because it disgusted her. It was a wound Leo had received while trying to save her life.

He looks bigger, she thought as she touched the head of his cock. It twitched and a bead of milky liquid appeared at the slit. She wrapped her fingers around the shaft and pumped twice. The bead of liquid dripped onto her knuckle. She rubbed it between her fingers, fascinated by the stickiness of it.

"I can't take much more," Leo said thickly.

She tucked a stray strand of hair behind her ear, nervous despite their earlier coupling. How did it work, with him on his back?

"Tell me what to do," she said.

Leo guided her to crawl up until her quim was positioned above him, although she was careful not to bump his wound. Then he took his cock in his hand and guided it to her entrance. As he slipped inside, he uttered a deep moan and closed his eyes.

"What now?" she whispered.

He squeezed her hips, then guided her down, until the curls outside her sex touched his own, and he was seated fully inside her. The feel of him, so hot and deep, sent her skin skittering with pleasurable electric tingles.

More. I want more.

She lifted herself up until he was at risk of falling out, then fell again in one quick motion.

"Ah!" She threw her head back, then repeated the act. It was similar to their previous joining and yet different. She enjoyed him this way, able to pierce her deeper.

She languished in the heady sensation until she could sense the familiar spark of pleasure hovering nearby. It frustrated her, knowing it was close but out of reach. She increased her speed, her thighs burning, but the spark refused to budge.

"Let me help," Leo said. He cupped her breasts, then bent his body up and touched his mouth to her nipple. His ministrations brought her closer, but still, it was not enough. Finally, when she was exhausted from exertion, Leo reached between their joined bodies and touched her.

She exploded in a burst of fireworks that stole the last of her strength. She felt Leo throb within her, and then they were both lying on the bed, staring into each other's eyes.

"You continue to surprise me." Leo dipped his head to give her a long, languishing kiss that brought her tantalizingly close to the spark for a second time, then pulled back.

"Will it always be this way?" she asked.

How did married women ever get out of bed?

Leo chuckled, and the sound reverberated in his chest. "Between us? Perhaps."

The smoldering embers of the fire inside her gave her the courage to be wicked. "Then we must invest in a sturdier bed."

"I agree. I will buy you one as a wedding present."

Her eyes burned with tears, and her throat felt like she'd swallowed a handkerchief. "Does that mean…"

Leo smoothed her hair behind her ear. "I foolishly believed I was protecting myself by not marrying you, that I would not grow to love you if I knew that our time together would eventually end. Instead, I discovered that you are the piece that fills the hole in my heart. Marry me."

There was only one answer to that question, and in the hours that followed, he encouraged her to repeat her answer several times.

Chapter Thirty

T HE SUN HAD sunk below the horizon, and Saffron had re-donned her dress—much to Leo's disappointment—when there was a knock at the door.

"Come in," he said.

The door creaked open, and Simon stepped in. "Do you feel up to getting around?" his cousin asked. "My wife is eager to hear from you."

"Your *wife*? You, Simon Mayweather, are married?" Leo shook his head. "I must still be dreaming. How long was I in that sickbed?"

"Not so long that you will not be forgiven."

Saffron, still clinging to Leo's side, giggled. "You should have seen it. Lord Canterbury drank rather more than he should have and lost a small fortune to Simon at the card table. He accused Simon of cheating and demanded he give back everything he had won. When Simon refused, the duke challenged him to a duel. A duel! Can you believe it? Angelica was furious."

Leo scanned his cousin from head to toe. "I assume you won this duel?"

Simon snorted. "*His Grace* didn't show. He sent his second with a note saying he wished me..." Simon coughed. "I will not repeat the words with a lady present."

"My sister *still* almost refused to marry Simon," Saffron said. "After the duke fled, it took both me and Rosemary to convince her to seize her chance at true happiness."

Simon looked acutely uncomfortable. "Yes, well, I am no duke, but I've given up gambling and taken up a post as an assistant to a barrister. What I won from the duke is not enough to last us a lifetime, after all."

Leo suppressed the urge to laugh. His cousin, a working man. A true miracle.

"I'll gift you some funds, as a wedding present," Leo said. "Enough to rent a small house in London for a year or two."

Simon's cheeks reddened, but he didn't refuse the offer. He made a slight bow and murmured his thanks.

He really has changed.

"Well, let's not keep Angelica waiting," Saffron said, breaking the silence. She stuck close to Leo's side as they followed Simon down a grand set of stairs and into a warm, inviting dining room.

There, Angelica sat at a table, breaking her fast. She was dressed in a soft muslin gown of striped lavender. When they entered, her full lips turned down in a frown. "Sit, Lord Briarwood. My husband forgets his manners. You do not want to strain your leg."

Simon pulled out a chair, and Leo slumped into it.

"Well, now that the reunion is over," Simon said with a small cough. "Perhaps we should tell you what happened after we pulled you from the water."

"I would appreciate that," Leo said, linking his fingers with Saffron as she pulled up a seat beside him. "I feel I may have missed some important details. What happened to Percy? Is he dead?"

"Yes," Saffron said. "His body washed up this morning."

Simon put a hand on Angelica's shoulder. "We don't know exactly how he did it, but as far as we can tell from your records, that boat held dozens of Ravenmore paintings. I am sorry, cousin, but we could not recover them in time."

He felt a pang of loss. His sister had spent so many hours working on those paintings. But in the end, that was all they had been. Fragments of a sister he had once loved. They could not fill the hole in his heart.

"Do we know why he had all the paintings in the boat?"

Simon tapped his fingers on the table. "Scotland Yard searched Percy's office in London and found a ticket to the continent."

Leo whistled. "Clever man."

"How so?" Angelica asked. "That's what I don't understand. Someone would have figured it out, eventually. As soon as the museum appraisers checked any of their paintings, I would imagine "

"Ah," Saffron said. "But if Percy had replaced every Ravenmore supplied to him with a forgery…"

Angelica laughed. "Oh, I see. Without an original for comparison, the forgeries would have passed authentication, assuming the same forger painted all of them. That is clever."

"The auction," Saffron said, suddenly. "If that boat held every known genuine Ravenmore painting except one, he had to have it."

"Why?" Simon asked, helping himself to a piece of bread on Angelica's plate and getting his hand swatted. "What harm could one genuine painting have done? Why not simply leave and cut his losses?"

"Greed," Angelica said. When all eyes turned to her, she shrugged. "What purer motive is there?"

"More than that," Saffron said. "Mr. Morgan was determined to purchase that painting. He brought a purse large enough to buy a small country. Percy would have researched the prospective buyers and known that. And Mr. Morgan would not have been content to let such a piece sit in his home. He would bring the painting to an appraiser. The appraiser would compare the painting to the known samples in museums and since the painting was genuine, it would appear aberrant, and therefore would be declared a forgery."

"And where would Mr. Morgan go next, but Lord Briarwood, where he had purchased the piece," Angelica said, crossing her arms over her chest. "To demand a return of his money."

"From there, the entire plot would have unraveled," Leo contin-ued. "Percy's plan depended on my remaining out of society and unaware. The moment I saw one of the forgeries in a museum, I would have known at once. Percy must have decided, because of greed or fear, that it was worth the risk."

"We should be glad he did not simply choose to kill you and avoid the whole mess," Simon said. "There are ways to kill a man that would seem like an accident."

"Like a carriage accident?" Saffron asked.

The room fell silent for a moment, then Angelica put down her silverware. "I believe I have lost my appetite."

Chapter Thirty-One

Seven Years Later

A HIGH SCREAM pierced the air, followed by gurgling laughter.

"Be careful, dear," Saffron called without taking her eyes off her work. Her hands were deep in the earth, massaging the tender roots of a rosebush free from its neighbor. If left to grow so closely together, the lack of airflow would cause the plants to not dry properly, and the roots would rot.

Six months prior, she would not have known and would have allowed the bushes to grow and strangle each other. But soon after she'd taken up her new hobby, the groundskeeper had put his foot down. Although he did not approve of her pastime, he was smart enough to realize that without training, she would do more harm than good.

A soft brush against her leg made her turn and hold out her hand for Cinder. The slinky cat butted her head against Saffron's elbow, then flopped onto her side and aggressively groomed her chest.

"Faster, Daddy!"

Saffron dusted the dirt from her hands and stepped carefully back onto the grass. Some distance away, Leo frolicked with their daughter, spinning her around in the air.

"Faster, faster, faster!" Daisy cried, kicking her small legs beneath her muddied pinafore.

"Don't let her bully you," Saffron called, eyeing her husband's wooden leg with concern.

Years had passed since he'd lost his foot, and Leo had spent much of that time in recovery, with Saffron refusing to leave his side. She thought she would never get the smell of poultice out of her hands. It had been a long and difficult recovery, but Leo's determination had won out in the end.

Every member of their staff was paid enough to see to their comfort. It was an incredible expense, but one she had insisted upon. She'd seen what life was like for them, and she would have no one in her employ living in squalor. They could afford the increase in wages, now that Ravenmore had been revealed to be Sabrina. The story that accompanied the paintings, and the tragic, short-lived romance she'd had with Sir Basil Summersby, baronet, had created such a demand that she had convinced Leo to sell the paintings they'd found hidden in the wall.

"Higher, higher!"

She walked over to the nearest bench, waving at Leo as she sat.

Her husband was older, of course, as was she, with more silver in his hair, and more lines on his face, but he was still the man she fell in love with. Still as caring as he had always been.

He threw Daisy in the air, and the girl raised her arms and legs, squealing with joy. At six years old, she was still light enough to hold. Saffron's heart squeezed as Daisy ran toward her. Soon she would be too big to carry.

"My little one, you've made a mess of yourself," she said, wiping a smudge of dirt from her daughter's face. "What will your governess say when she sees you?"

Daisy shook out her skirts and made a perfect curtsey. "She will say I am becoming a young lady."

Saffron burst into laughter. Already, their daughter was wreaking havoc upon the estate. Her cerulean-blue eyes, dimples, and raven-black hair gave her a doll-like appearance.

She pulled her daughter into her arms and squeezed her close, wishing she would stay small and innocent forever.

"May I go visit with Great-Aunt Rosemary, Mother?" Daisy whispered, patting Saffron's hair with her small hands.

They had converted the small cottage by the river into a cozy home, and Rosemary had taken up residence. Saffron had tried to convince her aunt to stay in the manor, but the older woman preferred her independence. Leo had suggested Rosemary move in with his mother, but the dowager had not yet agreed.

"As long as you bring at least two maids with you," Saffron said to her daughter. "But please, try to keep your pinafore in order."

Daisy gave an angelic smile and then raced off through the mud, spattering her dress with brown flecks. Saffron doubted the girl would come back with an inch of her skin or clothing free of dirt.

Leo reached out and took her hands, a gentle smile on his face. "She reminds me of you. She never stops moving."

"She needs a playmate," Saffron said. "What do you think: a sister or a brother?"

Leo touched her stomach and smiled from ear to ear.

She found herself hoisted in her husband's arms and spun around as Leo had done with Daisy.

"Careful of your leg!" she urged.

"Damn the leg," he whispered into her hair. "I'd give the other up if it meant staying with you."

She squeezed her arms around Leo's neck. "I was right. I make a great companion."

Leo pulled back and looked at her. "A companion to whom?"

Saffron pressed a kiss to her husband's cheek. "A companion to a count, of course."

THE END

About the Author

Melissa lives in Regina, Saskatchewan; the capital city that feels like a small town. A passionate public speaker, board game enthusiast, and lover of all things Halloween, she spends her free time writing and spoiling her two cats.

Website –
melissakendall.ca

Amazon –
amazon.ca/stores/author/B0B8JVQKMC

Facebook –
facebook.com/MAKendallAuthor

Instagram –
instagram.com/makendallauthor

X (Twitter) –
twitter.com/MAKendallAuthor

TikTok –
tiktok.com/@makendallauthor

Made in United States
North Haven, CT
19 November 2024

60579717R00134